This Bed Thy Centre

Also published by Hodder

An Impossible Marriage

The Unspeakable Skipton

The Holiday Friend

The Last Resort

PAMELA HANSFORD JOHNSON

This Bed Thy Centre

HODDER

First published in Great Britain by Chapman and Hall in 1935

This paperback edition published in 2018 by Hodder & Stoughton
An Hachette UK company

1

A CIP catalogue record for this title is available from the British Library

Paperback ISBN 978 1 473 67985 6
eBook ISBN 978 1 473 67986 3

Typeset in Plantin Light by Hewer Text UK Ltd, Edinburgh
Printed and bound CPI Group (UK) Ltd, Croydon, CR0 4YY

Hodder & Stoughton policy is to use papers that are natural, renewable
and recyclable products and made from wood grown in sustainable
for‌‌‌   ‌cted to
co‌   origin.

Preface

I was twenty-two when I finished this novel, and I do not know its genesis. The whole idea and structure came to me in one day, and the writing took me a little over two months. I had, I think, realising that I was no poet and that the short story form constrained me, wanted to write a novel; if you want to do something deeply enough, you are likely to do it. But I had not consciously thought the book through before I began to write.

It sprang out of the ambience I knew best, but, luckily for me, not at all out of my own direct experience. Young writers have a tendency to use *themselves* up at a first try, and then be faced with a long and horrible pause while they struggle to learn about something different. It was not until nearly twenty years later that I wrote a novel of which the early section was more or less autobiographical.

All literature is a continuum, and I must have had my influencers. But I don't know who they were. Self-educated after the age of sixteen, my reading had been almost entirely classical and totally random. A few modern writers had excited me: Dreiser, Thomas Wolfe, perhaps Joyce, though Joyce was so much the fashion among the young people I knew then that I have never been certain how far my admiration was real and how much induced. I read poetry more than anything else; Shakespeare and all the Elizabethans, Donne, George Herbert, Chaucer, Skelton. I had read Dickens with fascinated distaste (love came ten years later),

Jane Austen with uneasy politeness. Some of Lawrence. A great flurry of Conrad, to whom I cannot now return. The short stories of Chehov and Maupassant. *The Scarlet Letter* – which seems to me as wonderful and as misinterpreted now as it did then.

Yet I was far and away outside of the academic world, or the working literary world. While I was writing *This Bed Thy Centre*, I had made one literary friend, Dylan Thomas, who supplied the title. The original title was *Nursery Rhyme* – not good, but better, I think, than Thomas's suggestion, which gave the book an immediate shine of lubricity very far from my intention.

For I had thought of the novel simply as an attempt to tell the truth about a group of people in a London suburb, whose lives were arbitrarily linked. I began it with the entrance of the sun upon the new day; and when I jumped at Thomas's idea, I had the unruly sun, rather than the unruly bed, upon my mind.

When the book appeared, it was uncommonly successful. Times have changed since, and it would be quite a feat, today, to provoke such a *succes de scandale* as I did, without trying, in 1935. Words like 'outspoken,' 'fearless,' 'frank' (dirty words, the lot of them), flashed out of my headlines. I was shocked and terrified. That wasn't what I had meant, at all. Living in isolation from literary people, I shrank beneath the reactions of some of my kin, and some older acquaintances less than kind. I was given to understand that I had disgraced myself and the entire area of Clapham Common. It was as though a huge white finger had prodded through the clouds to point out, for ever, an indelible pool on the carpet. I was absolutely miserable. My dreams were black with fear of the Public Prosecutor. The happier my publishers, the unhappier I. I did not want another single copy sold.

I was not experienced enough to understand that, among serious critics, the book was commanding a certain degree of attention, that it was being talked about, as *Lucky Jim* was to be eighteen years later, as a 'seminal work.' (For myself, I don't think it was seminal at all. In any case, just as I don't see its forerunners, neither do I see its successors.) Only one thing hauled me out of the first traumatic shock: a generous review by Mr Cyril Connolly, who did not appear to regard me in any diabolic light whatsoever.

It has taken me over twenty-five years to look at this first novel at all objectively. Letting it appear again, I have had to resist the temptation to tamper with it. How much less sentimentally I should cope with Mrs Macginnis (my earth goddess, prototype of Helena, in *An Avenue of Stone*) nowadays! How much less flat-footedly with the schoolmistress's poetic lover! Yet I doubt if I could improve on Elsie, dank as she is.

Today I should reject so absurdly tidy a form, so close, so circular; but I think that form did much to compensate for my lack of psychological experience, and my green insights. Today I should not look down the slope of Battersea Rise and see the whole neighbourhood bathed in the glow of the Arabian Nights; but that is because the glow would be there for me no more. It was there, when I was twenty-two; and in that, as in other things, I told the truth as I saw it – which is not the seeing I have learned since, but was then the best I could do.

PHJ

3

Locality

The morning, drawing within itself, moved in sun and shadow over the common and through the pond till it came to the houses. In Haig Crescent, Mrs Godshill angrily opened her Bible in search of solace for the coming day. Glancing through the windows of her back room at the stairwayed walls of the Lying-in Hospital, she thought what a poor trade that institution would do were the girls on the cindertrack to attend her more carefully on Sunday afternoons. She looked at the clock. Ten minutes before she need get up. She lay back again in the bed, trying to imagine that her bones were greasing into sleep once more. She heard the rattling of the cups in the kitchen. Soon Ada Mary would bring her a cup of tea, and the day would start properly after all. A stream of sunlight poured through the windows into her eyes, reminding her unpleasantly of Mrs Maginnis, who had golden hair and no God. At this very hour, Mrs Godshill thought, she is sleeping with a man. Closing her eyes to the light, she added aloud, 'Dirty beast.'

Five minutes' walk away, in Lincoln Street, Mrs Maginnis, sliding from her nightgown into a cotton kimono, shouted to her new lover. He flung his arm out of the sheets across his face and settled down again to another slumber. Mrs Maginnis put a match to the stove. 'Nice hot tea before you can say knife,' she called to nobody, as she filled the kettle.

Then she sat down before the mirror to comb out her hair. Lucky I see him before he sees me, she thought. I used not to get greasy like this in the morning. She lifted her hands to her face, smoothing the lines of age away. That was you, my girl, ten years ago. Very cautiously, so as not to disturb her lover, she lay down on the floor and noiselessly went through the ritual of her morning exercises. One, up; two, down; one, up; two, down! That's the way to get the fat off. Maisie could do with a bit of this. She's putting on weight lately.

The kettle boiled over. Jumping up, Mrs Maginnis turned off the gas and swished out the teapot.

Daylight came earlier to The Admiral Drake than to anywhere else in the neighbourhood. By seven Maisie was washed, dressed, and as bright as a button. She went briskly round the bar, peering for signs of wear in the paintwork, or holes in the carpet. She touched the stool in the corner with loving fingers, for that was where Mr Wilkinson sat, he who was so glum to the others and so jolly to herself alone. There he is, she thought regretfully, and here am I. He with his good job, going around all by himself. What he wants is a wife.

Wilkinson, as he walked down Morley Road to the candle factory, pondered upon his bad luck with the dogs, and upon the ten shillings he owed to Parsons. Snuffle-nosed Parsons, as he arranged his apples, thought of the ten shillings Wilkinson owed to him.

In her small bedroom at the back of the end house in Stanley Street, Elsie Cotton dabbed the cold flannel in her armpits. Ten minutes to breakfast, and she was still in her knickers.

She scrambled into her blouse, only to find that she had it on back to front.

I ought to get someone to change it for me; it's bad luck if I do it myself.

But it was too late now, and she had to wrench her arms out again and pull it round the right way. Dragging her gym-tunic over her head, she sat down before the mirror to do her hair, wondering, as she did every morning, at the strangeness of her own face. She gazed without understanding at her fine, colourless eyes, her long nose, and her small, patient chin. I wish I could have my eyebrows shaped.

Mrs Cotton called up the stairs.

'All right, I'm coming,' Elsie answered, fixing a couple of grips in her hair. As she left the bedroom she stopped to look at a watercolour sketch given her by Miss Chavasse.

Drawing lesson today. That's why I woke up happy. I'll please her terribly, so much that she'll pick me out of all the others for praise. I love you, Leda. You have the loveliest face in the world. I love you. Leda, Leda.

She curled the name over her tongue as she went into breakfast.

Miss Chavasse was thinking of Elsie. You have definite abnormal tendencies in that direction, my darling Leda, she said. She always used love words to herself, for it was such a long time since anyone else had done so. She craned her neck out of the window, to see, at the end of Belvedere Row, the bright sun flashing upon the river. Mutable as the weathers, the stream changed its appearance every day for the exclusive delight of Miss Chavasse, who was the only person who ever noticed it. Now the light, striking the windows of the factory on the far side, flashed into her eyes. A boat with red sails went by.

She withdrew her head and, tying a scarf over her hair, started to make up her face. I'd like to kiss Elsie, she thought. I'd like to paint her, too. That is, if I could paint.

Her mind went back to her fourteenth birthday, that glorious occasion when one of her sketches had been accepted by a real magazine that paid its contributors. I used to think I'd be a second Angelica Kauffmann. Mother thought so too, but she was the only one who did. They laughed at me in London. Just art school tripe, Leda, my sweet, just art school tripe. Never mind. A lot of worse artists than you would be glad of a chance even to teach children to draw, and be paid four pounds a week for it. With her lipstick, she drew a fine red line around her jawbone, and smoothed it into the flesh. You were a beautiful girl, once, my dear. I must try and teach Elsie the rudiments of design today. If only the little swine would goggle a bit less at me and a bit more at her work, she wouldn't be too bad.

And Miss Chavasse, pulling down her nightdress, gazed critically at her breastless body.

Elsie, as she boggled as usual over her breakfast, resented the maternal blindness that forced eggs upon her at such an early hour. 'Eggs,' she had recently remarked, in a flash of inspiration, 'make you constipated, and I'm rather constipated lately. That's why,' But all she got was an ugly dose of something unnecessarily horrible, and the eggs continued as usual. Now she pushed the plate away from her and got up. 'You haven't had enough to eat,' Mrs Cotton said. 'Young bodies need feeding up.'

Suddenly resentful at the stigma of youth, Elsie slammed out of the room, catching her dress in the lock as she did so. This entailed the humiliation of opening the door again to release herself, and her eyes filled with tears. Snatching up her hat, she ran out of the house. Leda, she whispered to the sun, Leda.

The school gave on to the back of her own house; she generally got up from breakfast at the sound of First Bell so that she could get to her form room before Second Bell was rung. This morning, however, as she was a full twenty minutes early, she started off for a walk down to the edge of the common, up the road of The Stalls, along the High Road, and finally down Mornington Street and round the corner to school. As she stood on the path bordering the cinder track, she saw Mr Parsons hurrying along just a little in front of her, wheeling his barrow. She knew him slightly, because he was one of the men with whom her father had always stopped to joke. She ran to catch up with him.

'Hullo.'

'Hullo, Elsie.'

This made her angry. If I were only a bit older, he'd call me Miss. She walked by his side in silence for a while. Parsons snuffled awkwardly.

'Off to school?'

'Yes.'

'Like an apple to take with you?'

Elsie said, 'No, thank you,' and was sorry immediately afterwards, for the fruit was a lovely, fair green and as bright as china.

'How is your wife, Mr Parsons?'

He gave her a sidelong glance, sniffing up the hairs in his nose. Sidey little runt, he thought.

'Pretty all right,' he said aloud, 'but she always gets the 'ay fever in July.'

'Oh, I'm so sorry to hear that. Has she seen a doctor?'

Elsie, the Lady of the Manor, the District Visitor, was properly concerned.

'No time. No money, either. Them panel swines are no good.'

8

He sighted Wilkinson coming out of a tobacconist's. 'Well, Elsie, I must love you and leave you. Remember me to your mum.'

'I'm going this way.'

'Oh,' said Parsons, adding something under his breath, as Wilkinson, bearing his ten shillings with him, faded like a beautiful dream into a side road.

Miss Chavasse, as she turned into The Stalls, caught sight of Elsie. Self conscious little democrat, she said to herself. Tickle her, Leda dear, make her hop.

Elsie saw Miss Chavasse.

'Well, goodbye; I think I'm rather late,' she gabbled to Parsons, and left him before he could reply. She walked back a few yards down the road.

'Good morning, Miss Chavasse.'

'Good morning, Elsie. What are you doing round here? I thought you always scrambled into school at the last minute.'

'Got up too early. Can I walk with you?'

'The pavement, my child, is as much yours as mine.'

'Can I carry your bag?'

'Why should you? I'm not a hundred. I always dread the day when some small girl will give up her seat in the bus to me.'

Elsie looked blank.

You're too subtle for her, Leda darling. Tone it down.

'I mean, it makes me feel so old when you offer suggestions like that.'

'You're not old!' Elsie cried, indignantly.

'A good bit older than you, infant.' Leda, softened and appeased, smiled into the sky.

'You're not so very much older than I am,' Elsie whispered, very daringly.

'We won't argue about that. Look!' Leda flung out her arm suddenly, to where a young man with a green tie was

9

standing, looking into a shop window, beneath a green sunblind. 'There's a painting for you. Look at those colours, just thrown together by accident! Look at the lighting on that boy's face.'

' "A green thought in a green shade," ' Elsie said, feeling, directly she had done so, inexplicably childish and silly. I wish I hadn't said that, she thought. I wish she wasn't here. I wish I wasn't here.

'Is that terribly witty, or terribly intellectual? Do tell me.'

'It's a poem. Miss James read it to us in English lesson yesterday. I don't know why I said it. He would make a lovely picture, wouldn't he?' she went on, eagerly. 'He's nice looking, too.'

Leda shaded her eyes. 'Think so? You shouldn't be able to distinguish one man from another at your age.' She was suddenly angry, both with Elsie and with herself. A shadow fell over the morning, and the sickly draining of a forgotten hope left her naked. She said, strangely, 'Do you think about boys, much?'

'Boys? Of course not. I can't stand them.' Elsie flushed.

They walked on in silence, till they turned the corner of Mornington Street. Then she blurted out: 'Miss Chavasse.'

'Yes?'

She had started now, so she had to go on. The houses swelled and flattened before her eyes, until the whole row was as unreal as a nightmare.

'What do men and women – do?'

'Do? I don't understand.'

Leda saw the houses as Elsie saw them.

'What do you mean?'

'I mean – oh, you know! I can't explain. I shouldn't have asked you.'

'Go on at once.'

'When they're married.'

When at last Leda answered, her voice was as cold as a flute, and as brisk as death.

'My child, you'd better ask your mother. She's the proper one to tell you, so for Heaven's sake, don't ask me. There's plenty of time for you to worry about that sort of thing. Let's see, how old are you?'

'Nearly sixteen.'

Sixteen. Leda looked back down the years. Just about then I met John. I didn't have to be told anything.

She remembered his hands, closing like weeds upon her breast, and the searching of his small, dark mouth. I used to pretend I understood his rotten poems. The sick feeling it gave me when I picked his rejected manuscripts off the mat and told him not to worry, as people had no taste. 'You'll be recognised, one of these days,' I told him, 'and then you can make them crawl in the muck to you.' But no-one save a slug and herself would ever have crawled in anything to John.

And I wouldn't do it again. By God, I wouldn't.

First Bell rang out as they reached the school. 'You'd better hurry,' Leda said.

Elsie did not go.

'What are you waiting for?'

'I'm sorry I asked you that, Miss Chavasse.'

'Doesn't matter. Come on, you'll be late, and so shall I.'

They went into school together.

Mr Parsons, who lived his life by rote, regarded the shop as open when he heard First Bell clanging over the houses. He would give the final pat to his oranges, shuffling a few indifferent ones from the front to the back, quieten with a touch of his finger the swinging bunches of grapes, and step to the front of his stall with his battle-cry: 'Lemons, lovely, lovely!

Three for two, keep away the flu!' This morning, however, his customary cheerfulness was offset by an inward melancholy. Even Ma Ditch, who kept the cat's meat stall next to his own, noticed and made a comment.

Parsons looked at her with disfavour, noting the string of beads around her neck, and her new blue earrings. 'Hullo, Ma,' he said shortly, turning away from her to straighten a recalcitrant bunch of bananas. 'All dressed up and nowhere to go?' he muttered, trusting that she would not hear, half hoping that she would. That's what she does with the money Joe sends her, he thought. Bloody little the kid gets. If Minnie played games like that with my earnings, she could have things chunking round her ears, too.

His eyes filled with pity at the thought of his wife, all by herself in the back room, running with cold and fretting at her own indisposition. Minnie was only happy at work by his side, exchanging back answers with Ma Ditch and rearranging the fruit to her own individual taste. If I can screw that ten bob out of Wilkinson, Parsons said to himself, I'll buy her a necklace and earrings and a bracelet too, and then will that old bitch laugh!

The old bitch slapped down a randy cat who was attempting to climb the front of her stall, where the meats hung, red and appetising, for the taking.

'Seen Wilkinson lately?' she asked, '' 'e owes me seven-and-a-kick.'

'You're lucky,' Parsons answered her fiercely. '' 'E must owe a packet to the 'ole neighbourhood. It's the dogs. Why doesn't 'e stop mucking about?'

Why don't I stop it? Wilkinson asked himself, as he hung up his cap. He was tired and worried. For the last month he had suffered losses, and his future salary was so heavily mortgaged for the next month or so that he scarcely thought it worth while to draw his pay envelopes. I'd ask Maisie out, if I weren't so broke. I know she thinks I'm rolling in it, just because I'm in The Admiral every night, pushing the boat out for a lot of the boys. I know what she thinks, all right, all right. Why don't I stop it? He searched anxiously down the back pages of the morning paper.

Maisie gave the glasses a final polish. 'Morning,' she said to Harry, the potman, who had just come in.

'Morning,' he answered.

'Nice bright day, isn't it? Not a cloud in the sky. Like my new frock?' She pirouetted before him.

'Oke. All that for Wilkinson?'

'You get along with your work,' she retorted, flouncing off into the back parlour. Here she lay down at full length upon the sofa, and lit a cigarette.

I'll try to get him up to scratch tonight, she thought, choking a little as the smoke went down the wrong way. Maisie did not really like nicotine. I'll keep his stool for him till he comes in, even if I have to put the cat on it.

For some reason or other, the customers of The Admiral Drake respected the rights of the cat, leaving him, regal in his selfishness, entirely undisturbed, even if every other seat in the bar were occupied.

'I'll try being mysterious with him,' Maisie said aloud, 'Try and make him feel there's something different about me.' She got up, and looked into the overmantel mirror. Drawing the lids of her eyes halfway down, she attempted to achieve the right expression. After a little while, she gave it up. I shouldn't think he'd care what a girl's type was, if she happened to please him. Not that he likes them noisy, though. I've never noticed him taking much interest in Ma Maginnis. 'Now there's a cow for you, if you like!' she remarked to the cat, who had loafed into the room. 'Wonder who she's going with now?'

At the moment she spoke, First Bell was arousing Mrs Maginnis's lover far more effectively than Mrs Maginnis herself could have done. Loudly imputing all sorts and conditions of vice to his God, he sat bolt upright in bed, to knuckle the sleep from his eyes.

'Awake, are you, ducks?' commented Mrs Maginnis, 'I've been keeping the kettle boiling for you. Sleep well?'

She sat down on the edge of the bed, drawing the kimono decently across her breasts.

'All right,' he answered. As the sleep wore away, he began to take in the details of her large pink face and her golden hair. Stretching out his hand, he laid it on her throat. She smiled at him. He jerked her down and kissed her.

'Here, none of that, my lad,' she said, pushing him into the pillows. 'You ought to be ashamed of yourself, you ought, and at this time in the morning, too.' She gave him a fond shove in the face before she arose.

'What are you doing with yourself today, Patty?' he asked her, lazily.

'Oh, nothing much. Few bits and pieces of shopping this morning and the pictures this afternoon. You know where you'll find me this evening, don't you?'

'I'll be there,' he said.

'And if I see old 'Oly-Oly Godshill when I'm out, I'll give her a bit of my mind,' added Mrs Maginnis, vengefully. 'I went over to look in at her funny meeting last Sunday, and no sooner did I get there than she started talking about "scarlet women."'

He sniggered. 'Gave the boys a laugh, I bet.'

'Well,' she said, fairly, 'It was her turn, really, because I was having a bit of a lark there the Sunday before. She was starting the gang off on that hymn, you know, her favourite, "La tumty tiddlety turn, the Lord is on our side." Well, I started to dance a bit – like this – and the boys all joined in. It was like the Palais by the time we'd done.

'Here you are, bacon and eggs, and good enough for you, my lad.'

He accepted the tray.

'That girl of hers is a funny bit of work,' he remarked. 'Ada Mary. Not bad looking, if she'd use some of the stuff you use on your face.'

'Mister Observant!' she said. For a while she was silent, for the thought of Ada Mary was enough to silence anyone.

'Looks ill, doesn't she?' he went on. 'She and that brother of hers always look as if they'd been eaten and brought up again. Good change at the sea is what they want and everyone but that old devil knows it, yet, wet or fine, she drags them up on the common with that hammonium. God knows what she gets out of it, anyway. They don't take a collection, and she can't just like it.'

The sight of Mrs Maginnis, discreetly slipping on her vest and knickers beneath the tent of her kimono, distracted his mind, for a moment, from the bacon and eggs.

'Come here,' he said.

Prettily, she came.

Morning – conscious of the neighbourhood's aversion to herself, ill tempered with lying too long in bed and thwarted even by her Bible, which refused, when opened at random, to yield constructive answers to her most vital problems, Mrs Godshill was taking it out of her daughter.

'That's Second Bell,' she said, putting her arms around the

girl's neck to cross them on the thin throat. 'Wouldn't you just like to be back at school, my dearie?'

Ada Mary shuddered. 'No.'

'No? And yet they say that our schooldays are the happiest of our lives. Look at young Elsie Cotton, now. I often see her coming out of school, looking so pleased with herself. Wasn't she in your form?'

'She was in the third when I was in the fifth.'

'Well, she likes her school, anyway. And you ought to have liked it too, considering all it cost me to keep you there. Your scholarship grant didn't go far, let me tell you.'

'It was the girls.' Ada Mary trembled a little as she thought of them.

'They gave you a life, didn't they?' Arthur said suddenly, across the table.

'Nice girls, I thought they were,' Mrs Godshill reproved him. In reality, that was not her opinion of them, for they had formed a band of mockers on their own, every Sunday afternoon, to jeer at Ada Mary and herself,

'You shouldn't have made me help at the meetings while I was there,' Ada Mary cried, her nerves raw with the recollection of her misery.

'You care more about your God than about a lot of cackling schoolgirls, don't you?' Mrs Godshill withdrew her arms from Ada Mary's shoulders and walked round to the other side of the room, where she could confront her properly.

The girl was silent.

'Don't you? Answer me.'

'Of course.'

'No, you don't. You wanted to run around with them on Sundays, showing off before boys, and talking about babies and other nastinesses.'

Ada Mary tried to wash down the lump in her throat with a gulp of tea.

'Honestly, Mother—'

'Honestly, Mother!' Mrs Godshill mimicked. 'You make me tired. No better than the other little tarts around here, that's what you are.'

'Oh, for the Lord's sake, leave her alone!' Arthur muttered, fumbling with his matches.

'Both of you against me now, is it? And just you leave the Lord out of it, my son. And put out that cigarette. I won't 'ave smoking in this 'ouse.'

Mrs Godshil's aitches always went to the four winds in moments of emotional stress.

Ada Mary began to cry, very slowly and quietly. A tear dropped on to her plate.

'Stop that!' Mrs Godshill roared, swinging her large body around. 'This place is getting on my nerves.'

Nobody spoke. Arthur sneaked his cigarette back into the packet. It occurred to Mrs Godshill that it was strange for Ada Mary to be sitting there at all.

'Why aren't you at work? It's half past nine.'

'I'm not going this morning. I'm not well.'

'What's the matter with you?'

'I feel ill. My head aches.'

'Have you had an aspirin?'

'No. They do me no good.'

'You'll take one now. Here you are. Swallow this down in a drop of milk, and then get along to the shop and tell Mr Hawkins that you were sick when you woke, but you're better now.'

'She does look rotten,' Arthur pleaded. 'They wouldn't mind if she stayed home just for today, would they, Ada?'

'She'll go. If she loses her job, how do you suppose I'm going to keep her going? Come on, dearie. Swallow it down. Look, I've crushed it up for you nicely. It acts quicker that way.'

Ada Mary took the aspirin. Then she got up and put her hat on.

'Feel better now? Well, you will later on. Goodbye, dearie. Kiss mother, and then run along as hard as you can go.'

The girl offered a teary cheek.

'We'll practise that new harmony when you get in tonight, so don't be late.'

The hall door shut behind Ada Mary.

'And you,' Mrs Godshill said, rounding on Arthur, 'Why don't you get a job?'

'I'm doing my best.'

'Well, do a bit better, then. Try at the Labour Exchange again today, and don't let me find you here when I get back from shopping.'

Setting her velvet toque defiantly on her head, she picked up the basket. 'Remember what I said,' she called as she went down the passage, adding – 'and remember, too, the Lord is fighting for you.'

When she had gone, Arthur lit his cigarette. Getting up from the table he roamed around the room, touching the walls, the furniture, and the ornaments. Terrified by the swiftness of his own heartbeats and the dampness of his palms, he lay down for a few minutes on the camp bed in the corner.

'I'm ill,' he whispered, 'I'm ill.' Then, pressing his forehead against the coolness of the varnished wallpaper, 'I want a drink. Oh, God, I want a drink.'

Mrs Godshill braved Abaddon at The Stalls.

Mrs Maginnis, hiding her disarray behind the door, thrust out an arm to wave goodbye to her man.

Maisie dreamed the old dreams, and some new ones too.

Wilkinson, in the candle factory, refused to laugh at his mate's best story.

And Elsie, with a knocking in her throat, climbed the stairs to the art room to face her love again.

18

'You Can Paint Leaves Blue'

Agnes, double chinned and classically minded, leaned over the drawing board to screw her pencil point into the back of Elsie's neck. 'Who's Leda's cygnet? I saw you two come in together.'

Elsie bent forward out of reach, making no answer. She looked at her roughly sketched design – 'For the Cover of a Book, to be tooled in leather,' and found it good. Out of the corner of her eye, she could see Leda working her way down the row of girls, making a comment here, scribbling in one illuminating line there. She ought to get round to me in about ten minutes, Elsie thought. I'll try to paint a corner by then. Pink and yellow flowers, I think, with bright green leaves, and the lettering to be done in brown.

'Who's Leda's cygnet?' Agnes's hoarse whisper came to her ears again. 'You shut up,' Elsie wrote on a scrap of paper, and screwing it into a pellet, tossed it neatly over her shoulder.

Elsie's neighbour, fat Joan, prodded her elbow. 'Duck your head,' she whispered, 'I've got some news. Great news. Listen: you know Winnie Striker, who left suddenly during last term? Well, my sister's husband works with Winnie's cousin – he's a clerk in the office – the cousin, I mean, and he says Winnie had to leave because she was going to have a baby!'

Elsie felt sick. Quite suddenly, she recalled Winnie Striker's thin, haunted face.

'I never knew her,' she answered.

'But you heard about her when she was here, didn't you? She used to play around with all those boys on the Parade, in the evenings. Agnes saw her once, talking to a fellow when she was wearing her school hat.'

Elsie coloured a flower and a leaf. 'Beastly yellow in these boxes,' she said.

'They don't know whose baby it was, either,' Joan went on, bending over Elsie's painting.

'Did she marry someone on the quiet when she was here, then?'

'Marry?' Joan giggled. 'Don't be silly. Of course not. That's the point.'

'Then how . . .?'

'How? Don't tell me you don't know!'

Elsie conquered her sickness. I've got to be told. Joan will tell me, if Leda won't. It will be dreadful for the moment, but then I shall know, and I shan't have to worry again.

'I don't. Tell me.'

'You mean to say . . . Well, I shan't tell you. Yes, I will. No, I won't. It's too awful.'

'Please, Joan, please. Only don't let the others know I don't know.'

Leda, make me strong. I love you, Leda, and there's nothing horrible to hide about that.

'You can count on me. Well, you know a man isn't, well, quite the same as a girl, don't you? Made differently.'

'Yes, I know that.'

'Well, then. No, I can't, really. You ask someone else.'

'You've got to go on. Hurry up. Quickly.'

'Well, you see, it's quite easy to understand. If he – no, I can't say it.'

'Elsie and Joan!' Leda came to them suddenly. 'I won't have this gabbling. You can finish your conversation in Break. I don't doubt for one moment that it was clever and very important, but, strange as it may seem to you, my time is more important still. Get on with your work, both of you.'

She walked away.

Dirt talk, I bet, she said to herself. Elsie in search of the Tree of Knowledge.

Elsie painted away furiously. Those leaves are all wrong. The green's wrong.

'Joan,' she murmured, 'lend me your paintbox. My brown's run out.'

'Stay behind at Break,' Leda called. 'If you won't stop talking, Elsie, we shall have to find a means of making you.'

'I was only asking Joan for a loan of her box.'

'You heard what I said. Stay behind.'

'Leda doesn't love her any more,' Agnes blues sang, just loudly enough for her friend to hear.

Elsie knew she was going to cry. She lifted her finger, very furtively, to draw off the string of water beneath her lashes. She dabbed at a flower, splashing the colour over the pencilled lines, so that she had to draw a new bulge on to a petal to cover the mistake. Ten minutes to Break, then an awful ten minutes with Leda, and then it will all be over. Twenty dreadful minutes. I can live through that; can't I? Don't be a fool, Elsie, tomorrow's got to come and before you can count five it will be next week, and you'll have forgotten all about it. Perhaps she'll like your painting so much that she won't be very angry. Now I'll think about something else. Perhaps when I leave school, I could be an artist, do designs for wallpapers and things like that. Not a real, academy artist. I might do tiles, as well, like William Morris. And I won't marry, ever, so that I need never find out beastly things. Why has the world got to be so horrible, so full of things people don't talk about? I wish everyone talked about everything, and then, and then ... Don't be too terribly cruel, Leda. Or perhaps I shan't mind if you are.

Break bell rang.

'Put the boxes back in the cupboard, empty your waterpots and put the sponges back inside them. Pencils in the left drawer, rubbers in the right. Unpin your designs, and if you leave them on the boards, I'll collect them myself. Look sharp, now, all of you, except our voluble Elsie. I shall want her for a few minutes.'

'Nasty beak the swan's got when she's roused, hasn't she?' whispered Agnes, who always laboured a point.

The girls joined in a general scuffle round the cupboards. 'Aren't you glad you're too big to spank?' said Celia the sarcastic, as Elsie pushed past her.

'Done your algebra for this afternoon?' asked a surer sadist, knowing full well that whatever Elsie had done, it was not her homework.

Leda stood looking out of the window, where the sun could shine on her fair hair. Elsie, seeing the set of her shoulders, fought against terror. There's no reason why, at my age, I should get a stomach ache just because a woman not so much older than I am is going to row me. I'm a woman myself, really.

But she knew that she would never be a woman until she understood.

'Shut the door behind you,' Leda, without turning her head, called to the last departing girl. 'Sit down at your desk, Elsie.'

For fully three minutes she stood without speaking, drumming her fingers on the sill. The clock ticked so noisily that Elsie could not distinguish it from the clock beating in her own breast. Then Leda walked slowly over to her.

'What a rotten design,' she said naturally.

Elsie burst out crying. She sat there, helplessly, with the tears pouring down her face.

'Elsie. . . my dear.' Leda, taking the chair beside her, put her arms around the jerking shoulders.

Suffocating with the pain in her heart, Elsie turned herself about and laid her head on Leda's thin throat.

'Silly girl, silly girl, stop crying. What's the matter? Look, I'm not angry. Look at me, Elsie! Come on, sit up.'

She bent her head, and kissed the girl's mouth. Even the lips were salted with tears. She kissed her again in the wet hollows beneath her eyes, until the violence of Elsie's response frightened her.

'Now then,' she said, briskly, 'let's have a look at your design.'

She scraped her chair away a little, drawing Elsie's arms from her neck as she did so.

'It is rotten, now, isn't it? And you can do so well. I only wanted to speak to you about your work, really, and you can tell the girls so, if you like. Why pink and yellow together, and why, in the name of everything hideous, that frightful green?'

'Well, what can you do with leaves? They've got to be green, and that means you've got to choose your other colours to go with them.'

Make me brave. I must stop crying.

'Look here,' Leda said forcibly, 'get this well into your head: you can paint leaves blue, if you like. There's no limitation at all, and anything's permissible in design. Suppose you had the flowers in two shades of green, and the leaves blue. Wouldn't that have looked better?'

'I see.'

'Take shadows, now. Look at that one the tree outside is throwing on the floor. What colour should you say that was?'

'Grey, I suppose.'

'Grey! Grey! Grey! Can't you see anything else? Take a good look.'

'Well . . . purple.'

'Better. Don't you see, every shadow alters with circumstances, more or less – though that's a bad explanation. Take the shadows on a sea, or on a lawn. You can get every colour under the sun from them.'

'I could paint leaves pink, if I wanted to?'

'Any old shade.'

23

'I see. That's funny, really. It means that you can look at all sorts of things different ways.'

'A thought, my dear, definitely a great thought. Now then, when you come to art lesson again on Friday, I want you to draw out that design again, because it's quite good and original, and then try a different colouring. Will you?'

'Of course. Couldn't I take it home and draw it there, and then I could start painting right away on Friday?'

'Energetic child. Yes, if you like. Now go downstairs and see if there are any buns left. I'm afraid I've spoiled your lunch.'

'There will be digestive biscuits,' Elsie answered, smiling weakly, 'they are always left till last, because everyone hates them. The macaroons go first.'

'You might find a stray one lurking in a corner, if you hurry. Goodbye.'

'Goodbye, Miss Chavasse, and thank you.'

She ran downstairs, two at a time, whistling 'Jerusalem,' which Agnes had once described as her Resident Hosanna. She was still whistling when she left school at half past three, despite the discomfort of the algebra lesson which had occupied the early part of the afternoon. She hung about for a little while outside the gates, waiting for Leda to come out. When at last the staff door opened and a corner of an unmistakable green attaché case appeared, Elsie set off slowly down the road, as if returning from a walk.

Leda, sensitive to these manoeuvres, pleased by them, and a little scared, quickened her pace to catch up with the girl.

'Hullo. Who kept you in?'

'No-one. I went home and came out again for another walk. Can I carry – oh, I'm sorry. I forgot.'

'You can if you like.' Leda handed over the case.

'Isn't it a lovely evening, Miss Chavasse?'

'Lovely. I'm going to do some painting by the river tonight. It's a business that calls for considerable courage, because all

24

the dirty little boys from Dawes Street hang over the bridge and give you their opinions on your work. One of them spat on a beautiful sunset, once.'

Elsie laughed. Everything was well with the world again. There was a new intimacy in the air, for Leda had mentioned spitting.

'You should try a little sketching some day, Elsie.' She paused for a minute, then said: 'Would you like to come down and sit with me tonight, while I'm painting? I could tell you a few things about the job as I went along.'

'I will! I'd love to. Thank you.'

'Or perhaps it would interrupt your homework. I mustn't do that, you know.'

'I've done it. I finished my Lamb essay in Prep, this afternoon.'

'All right, then. I shall be down on the shore, just under the bridge, at seven. I'll see you there then.'

But she did not see Elsie that night, for as they turned into Mornington Street, Leda noticed a small crowd collected around Mrs Godshill and a young man.

'Here,' she said quickly to Elsie, 'you've come far enough with me. Go along home now and have your tea, and I'll see you later.'

She took her attaché case from the girl's hand. 'Goodbye. Thank you for carrying this huge load.'

As Elsie reluctantly left her, Leda concealed herself in the shadow of a doorway, so that she could watch the drama unperceived.

'Yes, you may talk, you may blaspheme,' Mrs Godshill was shouting, threshing the air with her umbrella, 'but 'E 'ears you. There's too many of you young men careering over the country where 'Is bleeding feet 'ave trod, taking 'Is Name in vain!'

'Firstly,' said the man, tidying his hair, which had been disarranged by the downward sweep of the umbrella, 'you are thinking of Palestine. Secondly, madam, I do not like your language.'

Several people laughed. Settling his tie with slow and deliberate daintiness, he started to move away. Mrs Godshill followed him, like a fat terrier at his heels. 'Come to Jesus!' she shrieked, at a loss for more constructive repartée, 'Come to Jesus!'

'Maybe I will,' he said, 'when I have a little more time on my hands. At the moment, however, goodbye, and thank you for the invitation.' He held out his hand. Mrs Godshill banged it down.

'Assault,' he said plaintively, to the crowd. 'Bear witness, all of you. Common assault. Not criminal assault, however, so we'll let it go. Good day.'

This time he went off down the street unmolested. Most of the spectators, satisfied that the curtain had fallen on the last act, drifted away. Mrs Godshill, remembering her publicity sense with her aitches, called out to the few remaining: 'That's the kind of man Christ doesn't want! I'll preach on him next Sunday, that's what I'll do, and there will be a warm welcome to any who like to attend.'

Leda left the doorway and ran home by another route, as fast as she could go. Hurrying upstairs, she changed her frock and plaited her hair around her head. He used to like it like that, she thought. As she spat on the cake of eyeblack that she dared not use at school, brushing a little on to her lashes, she was assailed by a fear that his presence in the neighbourhood was merely accidental. But then, why should it be? He wants to see me. I'm sure of that.

She sat down, restlessly to await his coming. Then she got up again and fidgeted about the room, hanging the least bad of her paintings in a better light, arranging her more finely bound books between the two china elephants and turning the novels out. Don't come yet, she said. I'm not ready.

Please don't come at all.

But when at last she opened the door to his knocking, to see him, thin and sleepy as ever, on the step, her heart quietened instantly, and the house was as cold as a stone.

'Hullo, Leda.'

He walked past her, down the hall and through the open door of her sitting room. 'Have you got a cigarette? I left mine behind on the bus, like a damn fool.'

'Here you are.' She lit it for him, and put it between his teeth.

'Rotten painting that, over there. Yours?'

'Mine.'

'Still rotten. What are you doing now? It seems years since I saw you.'

'It is years. About a hundred, I should think. How did you find your way here?'

'I know, and you know. I asked a mad woman for your address when I got off the bus, and somehow she involved me in a street argument. You saw me in the thick of it, darling. Don't attempt to lie. I saw you out of the tail of my eye.'

'I wasn't sure that it was you.'

'A nasty woman.'

'What did you do to her?'

'Me? I just asked her whether she knew where a Miss Chavasse lived, and, without a moment's pause for reflection she gave me full instructions for finding you. So I said to her, "Madam, you know everything. You must be God." And that started it all. I suggested a little later that she was the female Messiah.'

He lay back on Leda's divan, drawing his knees up to his chin. She looked at him for a while, wondering that his eyes were still so small and his brows so thick. She laughed suddenly.

'What's the matter?'

'You haven't changed. Why not?'

'Why should I? You haven't, either. Like me as much as ever?'

'I didn't like you at all, the last time I saw you.'

'Oh, no, I remember. You didn't. By the way, What did you say you were doing now?'

'Teaching drawing to children in a secondary school.'

'Fie on you. But then, you never could paint.'

'And you?'

'I've got some poems coming out in the spring. Lee and Sawyer.'

'At whose expense?'

'Mostly mine, of course. I think you'll like my new stuff. I'm calling the collection quite simply, *The Spire and Other Poems*. I shall dedicate them to you. Do give me another cigarette. I'm suffocating.'

She gave him the whole packet and a box of matches. They talked for a little while. He told her how he had married some three years ago, and separated in the next three months, his wife being pretty but a poor conversationalist. He had taken a variety of jobs since then, including selling vacuum cleaners from house to house and producing operettas for amateur societies. He had also found time to write a one act play and a monograph on James Joyce, neither of which had met with any success. 'The latter,' he said, 'is rather revolutionary, and the average publisher is terrified to touch it.' At the moment he was without a job of any kind, though there were one or two things in the air. 'I fancy my poems are going to make a slight ripple on the surface when they come out, but it's a question of waiting till then. By the way, Leda, could you put me up for a few days?'

The old game, she thought. Leda, my sweet, you know what he is, don't you? Turn him out. Throw him back into the water. Aloud she said: 'Yes, I suppose so. Where are your things?'

'I left my case at the pub on the corner. I said I'd call back for it.'

He knew I'd have him in again. He knew all right.

He stretched out his hand to catch at her skirt, tugging her gently to his side. 'Sit down near me.' He dragged at the vee of her dress and put his fingers to her breasts. 'Thin as ever, my sister, my spouse. Kiss me.'

Sick at the sight of his small, padded mouth, dark and dried at the corners, with a fleck of cigarette paper on the lower lip, she bent her head to his. As she did so, and the familiar smell of his flesh brought the sweetness of the wretched years very near to her, she said, almost without knowing she did so: 'I love you, John.'

'I know it,' he answered.

Elsie walked along the shore, kicking the pebbles into the water. The time by the church clock was fifteen minutes to eight. It's too dark to paint now, she thought. She won't come. As the sunset faded into the strong yellow of a late summer night, she climbed the steps to the embankment and walked away in the direction of her home. Crossing the common, she stared up into the still leaves and saw new colours there. A boy and girl, kissing under a tree, parted hurriedly as she passed them by. For a moment, she longed for something she could not understand. The knitting of her flesh, the strange dryness in her throat fretted her so violently that, all at once, she started to run, right past the pond, over the cindertrack and across the Parade into Mornington Street. Here, as she paused for breath, a boy in a mackintosh came to her side.

'Lovely evening, isn't it?'

She walked on. He followed her for a few yards, then went away. She looked back, covertly, over her shoulder to see if he were still there, and at the sight of the empty street she was filled with loneliness. One day I'll say 'Good evening' back, she thought, and then, I wonder what will happen?

Just as she reached her own gate, someone touched her shoulder.

'Hullo, Elsie.'

'Hullo.' She looked at the girl, wondering, for a second, who she could be. Then she said: 'Ada Godshill.'

'Yes. How are you? I haven't seen you for a long time.'

Ada Mary smoothed the curling lapels of her coat and tucked a string of hair under her hatbrim.

'It's so long,' she said, nervously, 'that I thought I'd just ask how you were getting on.'

'Quite nicely. I leave at the end of this term.'

'What are you going to do then?'

'Find a job, I suppose.'

'Will you like that?'

'I don't really know. It'll be a change.' Shall I ask her in? She looks as if she'd like to come, but I hardly know her.

'Goodnight, then,' said Ada Mary.

'Goodnight.' Still neither of them made a move to go.

'Have you got any new mistresses since I was at school, Elsie? I know there's one fair-haired one. A Miss Chavasse. Is she nice?'

'Awfully.'

'Well.'

'Well.'

'Goodnight. I really must be getting on.' Ada Mary walked off quickly down the street, one shoulder raised a little above the other, her loose shoes slopping on the pavement, heel – toe, heel – toe.

Elsie stood outside the house for a little while before she went in. The world was quite blank. There was no face in the sky, no colour in anything, no way to go. For a long time she heard the dying slip-slop of Ada Mary's feet along the road. Then at last, finding no answer, she resigned herself to the long waiting.

The Admiral

The bar of The Admiral Drake, blue with the evening smells, noisy with the chorus of evening backchat, led by the coloratura soprano of Mrs Maginnis, filled Maisie's heart with joy. Business was good, Wilkinson's temper was good, therefore life was good. Never before had she seen so many people so happy at the same time. Even little Mr Teep, darkly drunk in the corner, was indubitably happy in his own odd way. 'Blow the lot of 'em up,' he was muttering to Mr Parsons, who never listened. 'That's what I say. That's 'ow we shall win through. Blow 'em all dead.'

Wilkinson touched Maisie's hand as she gave him his change. Parsons, his ten shillings safe in his pocket again, for Wilkinson was now indebted to somebody else, back answered Mrs Maginnis with a gay heart.

Mrs Maginnis, keeping covert watch on the door, told new rhymes about entirely new old ladies in hitherto neglected localities.

Willy Sample thumped the piano. Nobody listened to him either, but there would have been a chorus of protest, nevertheless, had he stopped for one second.

'You are my Lily of Laguna,' Wilkinson whispered, sentimentally, to Maisie.

'Blow 'em all dead,' said little Teep, banging his glass on the counter.

'No more for you.' Maisie could be firm. 'You run along home. Mrs Teep will be waiting for you.'

'All right,' he answered pliantly, retiring to his corner empty-handed.

'There's a good show on at The Empire tomorrow night,' Wilkinson said, 'Like to come?' He had borrowed twenty shillings to repay Parsons's ten.

Maisie's heart leaped with joy.

'Could you get off?'

'I'd love to come, Mr Wilkinson,' she answered, charmingly, primly, as she nicked an imaginary fly from her hair.

'I'll come for you at eight, and we'll go to the second house. Ever seen the Three Chick Brothers? I don't quite know if I ought to take a nice girl like you to hear them.'

'I'm quite broad-minded, you know, Mr Wilkinson.' She blushed at the thought of the rude songs the Three Chick Brothers might possibly sing.

'Come and 'ave a game?' Parsons called from the skittles table. Mrs Maginnis was there with her lover, now. She whirled the ball nimbly, cocking her jolly pink leg backwards as she did so, and disposed of four pegs.

'She's bottled tonight,' remarked Wilkinson, scorning all women but Maisie, who murmured, generously, 'Oh, I don't know. She's a steady hand with those things. I'm sure I'm no good myself.'

'Who wants you to be?' He poured an Irish whiskey into his Guinness. 'I've no use for sporting women.'

'Sporting women! Get along with you. What do you know about them?'

'I look at the society papers in the library reading room, sometimes. You ought to see the pictures of them – big, beaky cows at hunt balls.'

'Ha! Ha! Ha!' pealed Mrs Maginnis, who had caught his last words. Fortunately, she failed to think of an appropriate pun.

'You keep out of it,' Wilkinson muttered under his breath, resentful of a boisterous serpent in his Eden. Milky with love, he stared at Maisie until she blushed again.

'Here, I've other customers besides you,' she said, attending to the wants of a gentleman who had been flagging his glass under her nose for some time.

'Bitter for you, isn't it?' Maisie never made a mistake.

Mrs Maginnis, emboldened by her customary success at things sporting and sexual, was leaning over Willy Sample's shoulder, singing a waltz song. Her lover, to whom women were things to be enjoyed in private and ignored in public, pretended to be absorbed in Parsons's new stories. Life, Maisie thought, staring out into the blue and golden air, is beautiful. She could just see Wilkinson's face, a little below her own, swimming like a white carp in a celestial sea.

Then the door opened, and Arthur Godshill walked in. For a moment all conversation came to a standstill. Willy boshed the bass notes. Mrs Maginnis's voice tailed away into a tactful hum.

'Blow 'em all dead,' said Mr Teep, loudly, seizing the still second.

The noise was tactfully resumed. Arthur came up to the bar and asked Maisie, rather shakily, for a whisky and soda.

'Good evening, Mr Godshill,' she said. 'We don't often see you here.'

Wilkinson was forgotten. She was all-curious.

'No,' he whispered, squirting the soda water into the glass, 'you've never seen me here before, as a matter of fact.' He glanced around him unhappily. Several people looked away. Maisie gave him her full attention.

'I'm not well,' he told her. 'I had a funny turn outside.'

'I can see you're not,' she answered, sympathetically. 'Lot of flu going around this year. Seems as though the fine weather don't do anything to help it.'

'It's not flu. I'm sick.' He gulped his drink quickly.

33

'Have another with me,' Maisie said. He thanked her. Wilkinson left the stool and prodded Arthur on to it. 'You sit there.'

He did sit there, for some time. After another whisky with Wilkinson and a fourth with himself, Arthur, unaccustomed to drinking, began to dread the moment when he should have to get up and walk to the door. There was a small table, bearing a plant and a Red Rail Guide, right in the middle of the room. I wonder whether I shall walk into that, or round it? he thought. His forehead, which he could just see between the bottles reflected in the mirror behind the bar, was red and bulging. He was aware of a dreadful sense of captivity. I shan't be able to get out of here. There isn't a space in all this wall of people and I daren't ask them to make way for me. The best route is round by the fireplace and under the window. I might try that.

He realised that someone had mentioned the meetings.

'I'm sick of them,' he said, noisily. 'I'm too ill.' Maisie was anxious. 'Is he all right?' she whispered to Wilkinson. 'I should think so,' he replied vaguely, his interest entirely absorbed by the sight of Hallelujah Arthur, thin as a rake and drunk as a lord, shivering on the familiar stool.

'Safe in the Bosom of the Lamb,
Safe in the Blessing of His smile,
Poor weak Sinner that I am,'

Mrs Maginnis chanted waggishly, to be instantly hushed by her friends, who deplored this breach of good taste. Maisie looked at the clock a little nervously. To her highly sensitive mind, the complexion of the evening had changed, suddenly, from a rosy pink to a drunken green. Willy had stopped playing. The others, with the exception of Teep, who was talking to himself, had given up any attempt at conversation and were concentrating on Arthur. Anything might happen any moment, she thought; I shall be glad to pack them all off home tonight.

'I'm sick,' Arthur was saying, 'feel.' He took Wilkinson's hand and thrust it inside his own shirt, right over his cropping heart. 'Now, am I sick?'

'You're sick,' Wilkinson agreed, disengaging himself. 'Well, I've got to be getting along now. I'll call in for you at a quarter to eight, shall I, Maisie?'

'That'll be lovely. Side door.'

He tipped his cap to her and walked across the room.

'Goodnight, Mr W,' Mrs Maginnis called to him, hoping to prove to her lover that she was everybody's friend. Wilkinson, however, did not answer her beyond a conventional twitching of one side of his mouth, and Maisie, for a moment, was happy once again.

'Now for Arthur,' she said to herself.

But things were not destined to come to a quiet conclusion in The Admiral Drake that night, for Wilkinson opened the door full in the face of Mrs Godshill. With the flags of the Church Militant in her eyes, she crossed to the bar, brushing Mrs Maginnis and her friends aside as though they had been curtains. Everyone watched and waited. Arthur did not move an inch. Clinging to his stool with both hands, he looked upon her coming as a man on a six foot island might regard the approach of a tidal wave, hopeless, interested. Muttering something about sinners and publicans, she laid her hand upon his arm, at the same time flicking her thumb towards the door.

Even then all might have been well, had not little Teep risen from the corner and made his way towards her, seeing, in her Juggernaut chestiness, the symbol of the whole social system he so deeply deplored.

'Blow 'em all dead!' he thundered into Mrs Godshill's face.

Enraged to boiling point by this final straw, she seized Arthur and jerked him from his perch far more violently than she had intended. He vomited over his clothes and on to the floor, trying unsuccessfully to stop a second gush with his hands.

'Dirty swine!' she shouted, hitting him across the head with all her strength.

'Here, you can't do that!' cried Wilkinson, striding through the uproar like a bad-tempered Galahad.

'And one for you!' Mrs Godshill, now thoroughly on her mettle, struck him hard on his chest, requesting him, at the same time, not to interfere in future between mother and son. Maisie banged down the counter flap and rushed to his aid.

'I won't have that sort of thing in this house! Get out, and take your Arthur with you!'

Mrs Godshill turned on her, revolving the umbrella like a machine gun. Wilkinson pinned her arms from behind. Parsons faintly called 'Police!' Mr Teep, a little ashamed of his outburst, secretly stole someone else's drink from the bar and retired to his corner. There was a long silence. Arthur stood in a sour smelling pool, weeping helplessly. Then Mrs Maginnis stepped forward to take command of the situation.

'You take one arm,' she said to Wilkinson, 'and I'll take the other. Mr Parsons, you bring her umbrella. Come along, Ma.'

And before she could protest, either verbally or physically, Mrs Godshill found herself on the pavement with a chattering Arthur at her side. The doors of The Admiral Drake were closed behind them, and there was silence within.

'I was taken ill, Mother. I just had to have one drink, and I'm not used to it.'

'You had to go in there, I suppose,' she answered, feeling, in her humiliation, as sick as he did. 'How do you suppose I shall be able to face them on Sunday?' Her eyes were wet in the dog mask of her face.

He staggered across the pavement. 'I can't go on. I can't walk home. I feel terrible. Mother, I think I'm going to die.'

She gripped his waist, forcing him on. She had done the same, many a time, for the late Mr Godshill. 'Steady,' she said, kindly, thinking of the things she would say without kindliness on the morrow. 'Two more blocks, one turning, and then bed.'

'Bed. Oh, God,' he gasped, forcing the retch back into his throat, 'bed is a thousand years from now.'

Within doors at Number Twelve, Mrs Godshill dragged Arthur's clothes off and put him into bed.

'Oh, Mother, oh Mother,' he moaned, groping along the floor for the chamber pot.

'I'm going to give you something to help that beastliness,' she said, mixing up mustard and water in the kitchen. 'Drink this down; come on, no nonsense.'

He swallowed it without tasting, and was sick again almost immediately. He lay back. 'The bed goes up and down,' he wailed childishly, tears running down his white face.

'You'll be better soon.' She turned out the gas and shut the door on him. He fell instantly into a black sleep. When he awoke it was as dark as pitch, and he could not guess the time. The door creaked open. He lay very still, locked in the pain of his head.

'Arthur,' Ada Mary whispered, sitting down on the edge of the bed, 'are you awake?'

He opened his eyes to see her, in the light from the passage, her hair in two lean plaits over her red dressing gown. She had been crying.

'Mother told me. Poor Arthur, is it very bad?' He stretched out his hand to find hers.

'Not so bad now, dear.'

'The room smells terrible. Shall I open a window?'

'No. Just sit here with me. She's going to be awful in the morning.'

'Never mind. I'll be there, and no matter what she says, you just think of me. I'll be with you. She can't hurt you, dear. You're a grown man now, aren't you?'

37

'A grown man.' He started weeping afresh, burying his face in the pillow. She bent, and kissed his head.

'Don't.'

'Dear Arthur.'

After a little while, she said to him, 'I've got to go. She'll make a row if she finds me in here. Don't you worry. Just go to sleep now, and tomorrow it may not be nearly so bad as you think.'

He raised himself on one elbow and nuzzled her neck with his lips. 'Ada Mary, Ada Mary. Goodnight.'

'It's nearly good morning, dear. Try to sleep.' He watched the narrowing of the bar of light beneath the door until it was nearly gone. Then he called her back, whistling beneath his breath to attract her attention.

'Tell me, how did she know where I was?'

'One of the men from the candle factory saw you go into The Admiral. She happened to meet him – she was very worried about you, dear, not finding you home, and all that – and he told her where to look. I suppose he thought it was very funny.'

'I bet he did. So she came in to make a scene, damn her eyes.'

'Oh, Arthur, oh, Arthur!'

He drew the sheets over his face. She passed her hand over the white mound on the pillow, resting her fingers for a moment on the breathing linen that covered his mouth. Then she went out, closing the door softly behind her.

It was a long time before he slept. Soon there was faint light in the room. The dawn rotted on the face of the hanging Christ above the mantelpiece. *Why don't you help me?* he asked. *Any old help would be welcome. You might let me die, or if that's too much to ask, give me a chance to get away from that bloody woman who calls herself my mother. Ada Mary and I could be happy in a couple of rooms, anywhere.*

38

Outside in the street, they were loading a lorry with garbage cans from the grocer's back yard. The wind, which had changed in the night, groaned along the aerial wires and flapped a loose end of rope from a clothes line across the window. Arthur stopped his ears against the rattle of the cans. He knew it must be nearly five, for the man next door, who worked in Covent Garden, had just left home and was slumping down the street whistling noisily, as if he resented the fact that the rest of the neighbourhood should still be in bed. Arthur swung his feet out on to the oilcloth and tried to stand up, but his head roared so strongly with pain that he had to lie down once more. He wanted a cigarette more than anything else on earth, and the cigarettes were on the mantelpiece.

How many miles across the room? Three score miles and ten, he thought. 'Stay where you are,' said the hanging Christ, 'stay where you are.'

After a while he no longer desired a cigarette but a drink of water. This, too, it was impossible to obtain. At last he tortured himself into a second dream.

In Belvedere Row John slept soundly, while Leda, sick with the horror that follows a manufactured love, lay long awake. Loathing the sight of his dark face on the pillow, of the lips, puffing and deflating with the contentment of satisfied slumber, she tried to think: I hate him because I'm still asleep. In the morning I shall love him, and be humble to him because I doubted.

She stared around the whitening room, counting the books along the shelves, the pictures on the walls. On the bedside table lay a sheaf of drawings, ready to be marked, Celia's, Joan's, Ruby's. I wonder what Elsie's will be like when it's finished? Poor Elsie. Keep your innocence and your schoolgirl loves, and you won't lie in bed with pigs like this one.

She slept no more that night. At half past seven she rose to get breakfast. A panic seized her. I've got to get him out, somehow. I don't want him here. To be alone, once more, quite alone, I and myself, Leda darling, our bodies unhandled.

Aroused by the noise of the boiling kettle as it clanked on the stove, he opened his eyes.

'Hullo, Leda love.'

As she turned to look at him, her heart was soft again. She came to him, drawing the bedclothes down from his throat. 'Hullo, darling.' She kissed him. 'Never leave me,' she said. 'Never leave me.'

'Perhaps I won't.' He laughed at her. 'Glad to have me back?'

'Glad, glad, glad. Now you stay there. I must be out of the house by a quarter to nine.'

'Lots of time, yet. Stay and talk to me.'

'I've got to make tea.'

'Give me a cigarette, then.'

'Here you are.'

'Leda, I've got to go into town today to see about my book. Can you lend me five bob?'

'I suppose so.' She reached for her bag, and tossed two half crowns on to the pillow.

'Thanks. Leda, my swan, you haven't soured much with the years, have you?'

As she got the breakfast and brought it on a tray to his side, she thought to herself: You love him, Leda dear. Of course you do. You can't expect to take up life with him just where you left it. There must be some readjustment. You love him. He needs you, and he's absolutely helpless. There's not another woman in the world who could make a go of him but you. After all, if you are unhappy, what does that matter? You're so unimportant, really. Think of all the millions of people in the world. What does it matter if your life goes wrong? Would anybody care? Give all of yourself to him, dear Leda. That's something to live and die for, something to jot down on your tombstone at the end.

She stared into his eyes, vaguely hoping that, just for one second in a thousand years, he would see the hate in her own.

He said: 'These eggs are a bit on the bullet side, my sweet. You must try to remember my small likes and dislikes, or I might open my wings and fly away.'

And she was filled with terror lest he should.

As she walked to school, she stopped once or twice to look at herself in the shop windows, that she might see if there were anything conspicuously different about her, something the children would notice, and be silent thereat. But she was still the same Leda, pale and over-tall, dressed like a school-mistress in a plain green dress, and hallmarked by an attaché case. She saw no signs of Elsie, and was glad. You can thank John for one thing, she thought. She strolled a few yards down Haig Crescent, half expectant of hearing some sort of noise from Number Twelve. Poor Arthur, poor Ada Mary. To have to live with that woman. However, there was silence in the house, as far as she could tell. Perhaps Mrs Godshill and her children were sleeping like Rip Van Winkle, to awake only when the neighbourhood was dust, and only the great grand-fathers remembered them.

Arthur, to tell the truth, had been wide awake for some time, but he gave no sign of it to his mother, who was stand-ing by the bed with a good opening sentence in the course of construction. Ada Mary had left for work early, sick with fear for her brother.

The light of the second morning sifted greyly over the roads.

Maisie, sitting with an aching head over the morning paper, had found a paragraph about a Cardiff man named Wilkinson who had cut his wife's throat with the neck of a broken bottle. She mused over the beauty of her lover's name in print. The murder meant nothing to her, nor the brusque, revealing details of the crime. She saw nothing but the magic letters wilkinson ('A.W., a greengrocer,') shining from the page. Tonight, she thought, ah, tonight! And took a Luminol tablet.

I will wear the black and my pearls.

I will have my hair trimmed and set. Perhaps I will ask Mr Dukes to cut me a curly fringe.

I will use a little blue on my lids and look at him, so – sideways.

I will buy a new lipstick. Men hate that painted look.

His first name is Harry.

Elsie searched for a design in the sky of the second morning, a pattern that she could trace in her head, with a bright star at the centre, but there was nothing there at all save a cloudiness, shapeless and shifting as her own thoughts.

There's no drawing lesson today. I needn't see her at all, unless I go upstairs.

And she knew that she would go upstairs, walking up and down the corridor, searching and pretending not to search. She would peep into the door of the art room hoping to be seen, not daring to see. Nothing would happen, nothing in all the world, because there was no more life to be lived. The old life, that. There was always a new one, and the dread of it was heavy at her footsteps. There was so much to learn, so much to be forgotten, such a lot of Bluebeard cupboards to be opened. A rhyme ran in her head. One, two, buckle my shoe. Three, four, open the door. That will be Monday. All new lives should start on Monday. For today and the next three days she would stay at the resting place, as though she were leaning on the handrail halfway up the river steps.

Three, four, open the door.

Elsie Incognita

Mrs Cotton, dragging upstairs with the breakfast tray, wondered if Elsie would be awake. She never aroused her until ten on Sundays. The child needs sleep, she thought, adding, vaguely, 'And, by God, she shall have it,' in reminiscence of a playlet seen long ago at a London theatre. Mrs Cotton rarely went to a play. 'Why bother,' she would say to her more rackety neighbours, 'to stand in a pit queue for hours and pay three-and-six when you can get into the pictures, if you go before one, for seven-pence?' But when, on her rare redletter days, she did go to the theatre, the glory of it remained with her for months, presenting, incidentally, an endless field for conversation.

As she reached the landing, she saw that the bedroom door was ajar. Queer, she thought. She pushed it a little wider and looked in. Elsie was lying on her back, wide awake, a sweet tin at her elbow, and a book on her knees. At this unusual sight, Mrs Cotton exclaimed loudly.

'Well, well, well! What's the matter with you?'

'I just woke early.'

Elsie put her arms behind her head, stretching herself strongly to the bedrail. Mrs Cotton set the tray down on the chair. Then a sight still stranger met her eyes. Beside the bed was the glass door stopper, and in the doorstopper was the butt end of a cigarette.

'What have you been doing, Elsie? Where did you get that?'

The girl straightened her mouth defensively.

'I bought a packet last night. I'm old enough to smoke.'

Mrs Cotton sat down by her side, perplexed and uneasy.

'But you've never done such a thing before.'

'I don't see why I shouldn't. I'm sixteen next week.'

'It's bad for you, dear. Do you know that I've never smoked in my life?'

'That's no reason why I shouldn't.'

'Wait just a little while. It will stunt your growth.'

Elsie laughed. 'I've no more to grow. I'm as tall as you are now.'

Her mother, temporarily flummoxed, changed the subject.

'How long have you been awake?'

'About an hour.'

'What gave you the idea?'

'Of waking up? I don't know. I just did.'

'You know what I mean. This.'

'Oh, that. Well, when I went to the pictures last night a lot of girls no older than me were smoking, so I thought I'd try, just to see if I liked it. I did.'

'Well, I don't like you doing it.' Mrs Cotton crossed the room and slashed the curtains open. 'I don't like this nonsense at all, so you just stop it till you're eighteen, and we'll see about it then.'

'I shall have a cigarette before that, now and then, if I want it. And mother – I'm not going to wear my gym dress to school any more. I'm too old. I'll change when I'm there, like Celia, or Agnes. Sometimes I feel quite ashamed of showing all my legs when I walk along the street.'

'Agnes might feel ashamed, with her great fat calves, but your pretty little legs won't hurt anybody.'

'I'm not going out in my slip, just the same.'

'Well, hurry up and eat your breakfast, anyhow. Your tea's getting cold.'

Mrs Cotton was very upset indeed. She was almost ashamed to look at Elsie with this new and terrible thought in

44

her mind: She is growing up. Every one of her daughter's belongings were suddenly inimical, from the sizeable shoes under the bed to the defiant powderbox on the dressing table.

'My darling,' she began, without knowing what to say next, when Elsie sprang another bombshell.

'Mother, do you think I could leave at the end of this term and go to work? I shall be over sixteen then, and I don't want to stay on for Matric. I couldn't pass it anyhow, with my awful mathematics. Let me leave, please do! I'm so tired of school.'

'Well see, we'll see,' said Mrs Cotton weakly, who, at that moment, could see no further than Elsie's deliberate eyes.

'I could learn shorthand and typewriting, or something, and get quite a good job. Matric.'s only a help to boys, anyway.'

'We'll see.'

'Yes, but do really see, won't you?'

'This is very sudden. I thought you were happy with all your friends. Would you like a bath, dearie?' she added, anxiously.

'Yes, in about an hour's time. Mother.'

'Yes, what is it?'

'There's something else.'

'Well, out with it.'

Elsie pushed her hand into her mother's. Mrs Cotton furtively groped for the pulse, at the same time eyeing her daughter for traces of a temperature.

'I've got to know, Mother. Tell me.'

'Anything you like, dearie.'

Elsie asked her. Mrs Cotton turned quite faint with the shock. Then, emboldened to tremendous bravery by the surprise of the moment, she gave a direct answer.

After that, she could feel the silence gripping her head like a tourniquet. She looked down at her lap, counting the many flowers upon her apron. My little girl. My little girl. All the bloom brushed off.

'I think,' Elsie said, 'that I will be a nun.'

45

Relieved at the uncomplicated normality of this remark, Mrs Cotton summoned up enough courage to say: 'Eat your nice toast.'

'I don't want any toast. I'll bath now. Would you turn the geyser on for me?'

'Not right away, dear. You must wait a little while after eating.'

'Now. This minute. Please.'

Mrs Cotton, coward at the last, hurried from the room just before Elsie began to cry.

Spurning, in the flush of her new independence, the hated egg, while making an irrevocable decision to spurn it for ever more, Elsie got out of bed and went to the wardrobe. Taking her work basket and her new brown skirt, she sat down in a chair by the window to let down the hem and take in the sides. This engaged her attention so completely that for the short time she was making these alterations she was happy again, her mind free from ugly thoughts.

Hearing a whistle in the street outside, she flung up the sash and looked out. Joan, who was standing in the street below, foreshortened to something grosser than her usual stoutness, lifted a flat face in welcome.

'Hullo. Are you coming for a walk?'

'I can't. I'm not dressed yet.'

'How are the facts of life, Elsie?' Joan hissed, keeping a watchful eye on the ground floor windows lest Mrs Cotton should be near.

'You shut up. I'll come out after dinner.'

'Shall we go to the meetings? I've got some awfully funny news to tell you about Mrs G.'s Arthur. Something that happened on Wednesday night.'

'I like your new clothes. They make you look about twenty.'

'Do they?' Joan was pleased. 'I think they're rather nice, too. I had the coat and skirt made for me. The skirt's to match.'

'I can't stop now.' Elsie felt a touch of vertigo. She wasn't well that morning anyway. Who would be, with life suddenly turned inside out, like an old coat? 'Call round for me at three, will you?'

'All right. What will you wear? I like to look nice on Sundays.'

'I'm lengthening my brown skirt. See you at three.'

'At three,' said Joan, standing two-dimensional on the pavement until the window was shut down.

The bath proved a new terror, for Elsie, as she lay in the steaming water, conceived a fear of her own body, rising above the surface into a white archipelago. There were the four small islands of her breasts and her knees, and the flat tableland of belly, all hostile and unfamiliar. When finally she came down to dinner, wearing the lengthened skirt and her only pair of highheeled shoes, Mrs Cotton found conversation difficult. She dared not even remark the fact that Elsie was wearing a pair of her own earrings. *I'll talk to her tomorrow. She'll be feeling different then, after she's been to school and had a nice time there. It's no good saying anything today.*

After lunch the cigarettes were again produced. Mrs Cotton accepted one for the first time in her life, hoping, in some misty amplification of the Helot idea, that she would show her daughter thereby how unbecoming was this habit in a woman. They turned on the wireless for an hour and complained about it in the usual way. At ten to three, Elsie got up to put on her outdoor things.

'I shouldn't wear those earrings, if I were you,' Mrs Cotton ventured. 'They're too ageing.'

'I like them.'

The doorbell rang. 'There's Joan. Go on, dearie, let her in.'

Mrs Cotton detested fat Joan. She felt that she wanted to open the windows after the girl had gone, or shake the carpets on which she had been standing. 'I don't trust that nasty, stuggy child,' she would say to Mrs Phillips, who lived next

47

door. 'I don't think she's a good influence for my Elsie. Puts ideas into her head.'

'Oh, I don't know,' Mrs Phillips, who never spoke ill of anyone, would answer.

'Good afternoon, Mrs Cotton. How are you?' Joan was always polite, being very often distrusted by parents for this trait alone.

'I'm all right, thank you, my dear.' Elsie's mother moved across Joan's line of sight, to blot out the telltale ashtray.

'I shan't be a tick, Jo. I'm just going to powder my nose.'

'All right, don't be long. I'll talk to your mother till you come down. Have you been to the pictures this week, Mrs Cotton?'

'Yes.' She hadn't, but they had to talk about something.

'I haven't,' Joan said brightly.

'Oh. . .' Deadlock. 'That's a pretty costume, dear. Did your mother make it?'

'Mother? Good Lord, no. She can't sew a button on without it coming off in five minutes.'

'I expect she's very clever in other ways, though.'

'No, she isn't. She can't even cook. You ought to feel her cakes! Dad says one needs a crane to lift them. We always buy shop pastries.'

'Elsie likes me to make ours. She likes my bread, too.'

'Elsie always was a pig. Aren't you, darling?' she asked, as her friend came into the room.

'Nuts to you. Come on.'

'Don't you look grown up! All haughty, like Leda. I'm coming now. Goodbye, Mrs Cotton.'

'Will you come back and have tea with us?' Elsie's mother smiled through her rage.

'Thanks, I'd love to.'

'You'll have to eat my cakes, I'm afraid.' This was the irresistible parting shot.

48

'Oh, I'm sure yours are lovely. Goodbye.'

As the two girls walked down Stanley Street towards the common, Joan told her the rumours she had heard regarding Arthur's night out. 'So there will be a great crowd up there today, you bet. We'll get a laugh.'

'Poor Arthur. I shouldn't be at all surprised if Mrs G. didn't hit him, when they were home.'

'With a rolling pin!' shrieked Joan, nearly falling over her feet. This thought cheered both of them for a long time, till at last Elsie said: 'Life is horrible, really, isn't it? People getting drunk, and all that.'

'Ah, life,' said Joan, 'that reminds me. Do you still want telling?'

'No, I don't. Not now.'

'You know then? Isn't it awful to think about? Our mothers and fathers, and even Mrs Godshill, once upon a time. . .'
She was helpless with laughter again.

'I don't want to talk about it,' Elsie said, fiercely.

'Oh, all right. Have it your own way. Look behind you! No, don't. We'll walk along a little way, and then you turn round as if you're looking at the traffic.'

'What is it?'

'Roly Dexter. You know. The son of the town councillor. He's terribly handsome and he knows all the girls around here.'

'Joan! Is he a friend of yours?'

'Well, not exactly a friend, but I've seen him looking at me.'
Elsie did not believe this for one moment.

'I'm not turning round for his benefit.'

'You are silly. He'd like you. He loves blondes.'

'I'm not interested in boys.'

All the same, she glanced over her shoulder. Bringing her head round sharply, she said: 'He's following us!'

'You're blushing!'

'I am not. I don't like him, anyway, and I daresay he isn't following at all. This is as much his road as ours, you know. I expect he's just going our way.'

'You can always tell when they're following,' Joan said, sagely, 'because they pretend they're not.' Out of the corner of her eye she could see young Roland Dexter, with his mackintosh and flannel trousers flapping in unison, drawing almost level with them from the shadow of the plane trees. 'Quick,' she said, 'Let's cut across the cinder track here.'

They hurried their steps, walking right across his path and over the grass towards the meetings, where the Salvation Army band was already in full blare and the patent medicine man was talking to nobody about a certain cure for corns.

'Mrs Godshill isn't here yet. Yes, there she comes. Arthur's pushing the harmonium truck with the platform thing on it, and Ada Mary's carrying the hymn books. Don't let's stand too near them, or we'll have a book foisted on to us.'

As the Godshills set up their rostrum, the Salvation Army audience rapidly decreased. The Communist agitator over by the pond remained in his lorry, knowing full well that he would speak in vain that afternoon. 'Come on,' said Joan, dragging Elsie into a gap on the edge of the crowd, 'we can see pretty well from here.'

Roland Dexter took up his position on the opposite side, where he could watch Elsie, who was trying hard not to look back at him. He turned up the collar of his coat and slanted his hat a little more over one eye. Conscious of his own excellence, he waited patiently for the moment of victory.

He had to wait for a long time. Still tingling with the morning shock, Elsie, at that moment, hated men more than anything else. She hid behind the thunderous shoulders of a policeman, leaving Roland to the admiration of the deluded Joan.

At that moment, however, the attention of all three of them was diverted by Mrs Godshill, who, in her new grey velvet toque and carrying an umbrella rather more menacing in design than usual, had mounted the rostrum. She glared round her, banging the bookrest for silence. Mrs Maginnis and her lover crept up to the edge of the crowd. Parsons and Wilkinson were hurrying down the path. Maisie was there with Willy Sample, Teep, and a sprinkling of The Admiral Drake's less notable clients.

Ada Mary, screwing up her courage, advanced to Mrs Maginnis to offer a hymn book. The Mocker, the golden-haired, looked at her for a moment as if she were going to burst out laughing. Then she patted the girl's arm and accepted the hymnal. The meeting proceeded for a little while without excitement of any kind, though Mrs Godshill's favourite hymn – 'A sinner coming home at eventide' – was accompanied by a little tap dancing from several of the young men who had collected behind the harmonium. Arthur, ghost-faced, stared rigidly at the keys, dreading the ordeal to come.

'He saved me, Yes He did,
And in His arms I hid,
A Sinner coming home at Eventide,'

rasped Mrs Godshill, at the same time clouting the head of a 'yob' who was attempting to snatch her umbrella. There was quietness while she offered up an extempore prayer. Then, as she climbed down from the stand, preparatory to ceding it to Arthur, the patent medicine man, hoping to attract some hearers to his side, roared out, with double strength:

'You put one of these little plasters on your feet, and the corns just fly out, pop, pop, all over the room, right into the old lady's lap.'

The Salvation Army crashed defiance at him.

'Look at this advert I got here,' yelled the medicineman. ' "Phitto!" You take a small spoonful every morning sprinkled on your bread and jam, and then you can jump right over the Albert Memorial, and they charge you ninepence a packet! Now, if you take a look at this little preparation of my own, for which I'm asking only fourpence, mark you . . .'

His voice faded. Arthur Godshill was on the rostrum now. Even the one small boy who had been interested, for a fleeting moment, in curatives, had joined the opposite camp.

Ada Mary, sitting down on the harmonium chair, clasped her hands in her lap. God will help him, she told herself, God will help him.

Arthur gazed fixedly at his own fingers. 'My friends,' he began.

Willy Sample pushed his way to the front of the crowd.

'A-a-a-a-h. Arthur!' he said with anticipatory pleasure, rubbing his hands together. 'Sh-h-h, all of you. Let's hear Arthur.'

'Ow jou take it, old mail,' came a voice from behind, 'watered or neat?' Everyone laughed tremendously.

'My friends, the text for today is one with which we are all familiar . . .'

' "Wine is a mocker, strong drink is raging," ' Willy Sample suggested. He had once attended Sunday school.

'You be quiet!' This, surprisingly, was Mrs Maginnis, who had seen the look on Ada Mary's face. Mrs Godshill mounted to Arthur's side, her cheeks crimson. 'May He punish you in your blasphemy!' she called to Willy and his supporters.

'You go down. Go down, Moses,' somebody said. 'We want Arthur.'

'We – want – Arthur!' The chant was rhythmically accepted by most of the young men. 'We – want – Arthur!'

But Arthur was no longer available. He had climbed down from the rostrum to stand behind Ada Mary, his hands on her shoulders, his head cast down. He was saying nothing more that day for all the mothers in the world.

Elsie felt unhappy. She had been talking to Ada only a few nights before, and this man was Ada's brother. The whole thing was cruel. For the first time in years she saw nothing at all funny about the Sunday baiting, and was somehow deadly ashamed that she should be there at all, looking on. She said to Joan: 'Let's go.'

'Don't be silly. This is going to be good.'

'I think it's beastly. I'm going if you're not.'

'Go, then.' Joan was standing on tiptoe, trying to see Arthur's face.

Elsie turned and pushed her way out, leaving her friend behind. As she walked away down the long path towards the railway station, Roland Dexter caught up with her.

'You walk fast.'

She quickened her pace. Her terrified heart had leaped right up into her throat.

'I say, haven't I met you somewhere? Don't you go to church at St. Peter's?'

'No.'

'Oh, but are you sure? Here, here, please slow up a bit. Your face is so familiar. Aren't you Elsie Cotton?'

She stopped, surprise conquering her fear.

'How did you know?'

'Quite honestly,' he said, eyeing her flatteringly as he spoke, 'I asked everyone I knew if they knew you, and one of the fellows happened to have a sister at your school. I spoke to you the other night, but you wouldn't answer.'

'Good evening,' someone had called to her, and she had looked round to see if he were still in pursuit.

Elsie smiled at him nervously. 'I didn't hear you.'

'Bad girl, you lie.'

As she started to walk on, he fell into step at her side. 'Do you know who I am?'

'Yes. You're Roland Dexter. Joan told me.'

'Joan? Is that the girl you go around with?'

'Yes.'

'I've wished many a time that she wasn't always with you on Sunday afternoons.'

'She's very nice. She's my best friend.'

'Oh, I expect she's fine, but she's just a bit large for my liking. Shall we go for a walk?'

'We're walking now, aren't we?'

'Yes, I suppose we are, come to think of it.' As he slipped his arm through hers, she shook him off indignantly.

'Oh, Elsie! What a prickly girl you are! And you've got such a kind face.'

She faced him. 'I've got to go home now.'

'Nonsense. You would have been up at the meetings until four if the Arthur baiting hadn't upset you.'

'I hated it.'

'It wasn't nice. I'm always sorry for that fellow, because he looks so rotten. Here, don't let's walk any more. Come and sit down.' He pointed to a couple of green chairs, cunningly placed beneath a group of dusty hawthorns. She nodded, and set herself on the extreme edge of one of the chairs, while he lolled in the other. At the sight of the approaching ticket collector, he stood up, raking in his pocket for coppers. 'They can spot you a mile off,' he said.

'Here, I'll pay for myself. No, please let me.'

'Don't be so silly. Two, please. Thank you. Oh, God, here come the kids.' He heaved a comical sigh of exasperation as two little boys bore down upon him.

'Hey! Hey! Roly Poly Gammon and Spinach!'

He pushed them away from him, smiling indulgently. 'These little blighters were in the second when I was in the sixth,' he explained. 'They can't leave the big fellows alone, even now.'

And it was a fine sight for Elsie, seeing him deal so firmly, yet so pleasantly, with his admirers.

'Roly Poly's got another girl!' shouted one of them.

His face became grim. 'Here, here, none of that. Be off with you.'

'Got any cigarette pictures, Roly?'

'Two cricketers and one film star. Catch.' He flicked the cards to them. 'Now run away, and disappear entirely from view.' Turning again to Elsie, he said: 'I like your hair.'

'It would be all right if I could have it waved.'

'It's curly enough as it is. I like blondes.'

'Joan said you did.'

'Oh, did she? What does she know about it, anyway? As a matter of fact, I haven't very much interest in girls, as a rule.'

He drew a face in the dust with the toe of his shiny brown shoe. 'I like you, though.' He stared boldly into Elsie's eyes. As she reddened, he laid his fingers on her wrist. 'You're not frightened of me?'

'Of course not.'

'Yes, you are. Don't be, please.'

'I've got to go and find Joan, now. Truly, I have. She's coming back to tea with me.' Elsie arose, very deliberately. 'Goodbye.'

He did not move from his chair. 'You can't run off like this. When are you going to see me again?'

The diving length of his body, monstrously shadowed on the grass, made her afraid. She didn't want to know him, ever, or any other man, for that matter. Shutting a single dreadful thought from her mind, she muttered: 'I don't know.'

'Tomorrow night, shall we say? I'll be near the pond, waiting for you, about seven.'

'Suppose I'm not there?'

'You will be.' Putting his hand beneath her chin – 'Won't you?'

'I'm going to be busy tomorrow.'

'I shall wait until you come.'

'I don't suppose I shall come.'

'You will, Elsie, you will.'

She slapped his hand down from her face. She was so unhappy that she could scarcely speak.

'What a naughty temper! Goodbye, then.'

'Goodbye.'

'See you tomorrow!' he called, as she ran off down the path towards the meetings. She did not look back until she was quite sure that he had gone. But there he was still, legs wide apart, hat on the side of his head, his bright tie flapping in the breeze; there he was still, laughing at her with his hard, confident eyes. So she did not turn around again.

Before she reached the cinder track, Joan ran slap into her, panting with excitement.

'Elsie! Elsie! Such fun! One of the boys made a remark about Ada Mary – I didn't hear what it was – and Arthur flew at him! They're fighting! Where ever did you get to? Come on, hurry, we'll miss it!'

But by the time they reached the meetings, however, the fracas was over. Willy Sample, the cause of the trouble, had seen a policeman in the distance, and was therefore making overtures of peace with the greatest possible celerity. Mrs Godshill, intimidated, for once in her life, by the moment's ugliness, had called the meeting off for that day, and Arthur and a sobbing Ada Mary were packing up. The crowd dispersed to listen to the other orators. The medicine man was offering an infallible cure for biliousness at a bespoke price.

'Let's go home to tea,' Elsie suggested, and the two girls cut across the common towards Stanley Street.

'Where have you been?' asked Joan.

'Oh, walking around.'

This was unsatisfactory. 'Doing what?'

'Nothing. I just strolled down the long path and back.'

'Did you see anything of Roly Dexter? He left the meetings before the row began, but I didn't see him go.'

'Oh, did he?'

'Yes. I thought he might have gone after you.'

'Don't be a fool.'

'He is good looking, isn't he? Have you seen him without his hat?' This was crafty. 'He's got such a lovely wave over the top of his head.'

'He looks just like any of the other boys to me.' Elsie could be crafty too. 'Buck up. I'm starving hungry, aren't you?' She forced her friend into a jog trot, for Joan always found it impossible to run and talk at the same time.

Just at the top of Mornington Street, Elsie caught sight of Leda. 'Look at that!' she said, 'Leda, walking with a man.'

'Do you care?'

'No. No, I don't. Not a tuppenny damn.'

Joan looked at her with respect, and some curiosity.

They did not go out again that evening, much to Mrs Cotton's annoyance, but sat in the window seat discussing the passers-by. Elsie was at peace once more. As she looked out into the dying sky, the shock and pain of the day fused into a space beyond her. She herself, remote, untouched, answered questions without hearing them, spoke of daily acquaintances as if she had never known them.

'Leda told me,' she said suddenly, 'that you could paint leaves blue, if you wanted to; they needn't always be green. That makes a difference to everything, somehow, doesn't it?'

'Of course,' Joan agreed fearfully, steeling herself against a sudden loneliness.

'Supper,' called poor Mrs Cotton.

Son of the Town Councillor

Passing, by normal stages, between the ages of seven and nineteen, from Plasticine to Meccano, from Meccano to wireless, and from wireless to love, Roly Dexter felt that, take it all in all, he excelled in the love. A mental rake and a temperamental virgin, his experiences had necessarily been limited on account of his fears. Once, at the age of sixteen, when he was strolling on Hampstead Heath, he had asked a pretty girl if she would walk and talk with him; finding, to his dismay, that her requirements exceeded these two entertainments, he had made the accepted excuse to leave her for a temporary period, and, when the bushes concealed him from her sight, had taken to his heels and left her for good. Since then he had restricted himself to milder conquests on the common or in the High Street picture house, and it might be said that these conquests surpassed his expectations. He had grown into what is termed 'a well set-up young man,' although he was, perhaps, a trifle too broad for Ms height. His hair, which waved pleasantly if he pressed it when it was wet, grew in a peak from his fore-head, and from the peak depended, as it were, his small, straight nose, and his small, round chin. His eyes, which were fine, dark, aqueous features, he used extremely well. He had a young aunt who called him 'Roly darling,' and he liked very much to take her for walks when she was in the neighbourhood.

This was Roly at nineteen years of age.

And now, on the morning of the day for which he had arranged his assignation with Elsie, here he was in the back garden, playing prettily with his dog for the delight of the adjacent houses.

As yet he had made no attempt to find a job; his father, who was well in the running for next year's mayor, had more than enough money to support an only son. 'And who'd work,' Roly said to the terrier, that fine summer day, 'who hadn't got to? Hup, boy, over master's hands. Good. We'll make a circus dog of you yet.'

How happy he was, how kindly life treated him! Roly took off his tie and put it in his pocket, baring his neck to the sunshine. A lazy morning and a good lunch. A lazy afternoon, that might include, perhaps, a call at the public library where the new girl was employed, and a good tea. After tea, a read on the lawn, a beer at The Admiral Drake, then off to the pond to meet Elsie. 'And she'll come' he growled into the dog's ear, 'we know she will, don't we, George?' A window in the house next door banged noisily. Millicent Young, who had engaged Roland's attention for the whole of the previous summer, was demonstrating how well she could get on without him.

Knowing that she watched him still from behind the curtains, he glanced up, slowly closing his lids and opening them. 'Bang as much as you like, my girl,' he said, addressing his dog, 'we've fresh fields to conquer.' And as he thought of Elsie, faint-haired, calf-eyed, he felt strangely excited.

After the lazy morning and the good lunch, Roland went round to the library. Here he saw Mrs Maginnis, asking the new girl for a nice book – 'something with lots of love in it.' Thinking of this bright-haired lady for the first time as 'the town's best unpaid whore,' a phrase used only last night by a friend of his (who was a traveller in the carpet trade) he was conscious of the gay suburb in which he lived. Here we do see life, he thought.

He wandered round the shelves for some time, playing unpremeditated hide-and-seek with Mrs Maginnis, who persisted in appearing like a genial demon king from behind every bookcase. At last he chose two volumes which he knew would bore him, but which would impress the new librarian beyond measure.

'Nietzsche,' he announced, as he banged the book, with the accompanying ticket, on to the counter. 'A good man. Hard to get into, but worth the fag. You read much?'

'I don't get the time,' she answered, 'I seldom arrive home till late, when I just want to talk, or nip into the pictures. Even then, I generally miss the supporting film. You interested in psychology?' she added, marking up his second choice.

'More or less,' he answered evasively. 'And that reminds me – reserve me a Freud, will you? F.R.E.U.D. It's always out when I call in.'

'All right,' she said, 'I'll do what I can. He's a popular writer, he is.' She pushed over a form. 'Fill in the name and address here, please.'

He did as requested, remarking: 'My friends call me Roly,' as he gave the paper back to her. 'What do your friends call you?'

'That's none of your business.'

Roland obliged her with a slanting gaze from beneath his hat brim, thinking, as he left, that she might be more promising when he called again. As he went down the steps, Mrs Maginnis, who was just in front of him, dropped her book and a couple of parcels.

'Thanks so much,' she said, as he retrieved them. 'Can't bend as I used to.'

'Nonsense,' he murmured gallantly, 'Nonsense.'

'Not so, young man, believe me. Aren't you Councillor Dexter's boy?'

'I am.'

'I thought so. I've seen you round here a bit, and I said to myself, 'that's a nice young fellow,' so I asked someone who you were. You're just like your dad, let me tell you. He and I used to have a joke together, sometimes.'

She started to walk along the street with him. Roland, immensely flattered, hoped that someone would see them.

'You were at Mrs Godshill's meeting on Sunday, weren't you?' he asked. 'I thought I saw you.'

'Yes, I was, and a fine lot of beasts they were to poor Arthur. I like a bit of fun, but some things seem to be going a bit far.'

'You're right,' he said, 'you're right.'

'I say' – Mrs Maginnis prodded him confidentially in the ribs – 'what do you think about this tub-thumping?'

'I don't know what to think.'

'No more do I. It seems to me that having religion ought to be as private as having a bath. You oughtn't to get up and have either of them in the middle of the common.'

Roland agreed. 'That's what I say. One doesn't, that's all.'

'Excuse me,' Mrs Maginnis said, 'I must pay a visit to the drapers. Give my regards to your pa, and ask him if he remembers Patty Maginnis. When I was a very young girl, you know, in the days when we wore our hair all puffed out over cushions – 'rats,' we used to call 'em – and you could put your finger and thumb round our waists, he and I used to play tennis together, on the place where the Lying-in Hospital is now. You ask him. He'll remember.'

'I will,' said Roly, waving his hand as he left her, 'you bet I will.' For a little while he amused himself by reconstructing a secret past for his father, but was forced to abandon this on the grounds of total improbability. After tea, all thoughts of the new librarian and of Mrs Maginnis deserted him, and he thought only of Elsie. 'She's beautiful,' he said to the dog, 'she ought to be in pictures.' Then, more truthfully, 'Or she would be beautiful if she had a bigger chin.'

He never doubted for one second that Elsie would meet him. At seven o'clock sharp he was by the pond, awaiting her coming. It was a night, he felt, for romance. The trees were dark on a floating sky. The island, on which the little boys were allowed to scramble naked in the afternoons, after their swim, was doubled in the clear water. I will say to her, he thought, 'I knew you would come. You look so pretty that I'm almost afraid to talk to you.' And she would answer, 'Do I?' smiling at him shyly. Then they would sit under the trees for a while, asking each other all sorts of questions, and when it got quite dark he would put his arms around her, and kiss her mouth. She would kiss him, too, and say: You're terribly strong. I'm half scared of you.' 'Don't be afraid, little girl,' he would whisper, 'I wouldn't hurt you for anything in the world.'

O sweet night!

When at last she came to stand at his side, ashamed, embarrassed, he jumped with the shock of finding her so near.

'Hullo.'

'Hullo.'

'I'm glad you came. I almost thought you wouldn't.'

'Why,' she said, 'I'm not late, am I?'

'No, no, of course not. I've only just got here myself. It's a nice evening, isn't it?'

'Very.'

'What would you like to do?'

'Do? Oh, I don't mind. Anything.'

'Well, I mean, shall we walk a bit, or sit down, or would you like to go to the pictures?'

'I don't care. Anything you want.'

'No, it's anything you want, Elsie.'

'Let's sit, then, shall we? I can't stay long.'

'Of course you can! You're not going to run away the moment I've caught you!'

Roly felt better. He was getting into his stride.

'I've got a lot of homework to do yet. I had a bother to get out as it is.'

'Don't let's talk about homework, or anything like that,' he said persuasively, 'We'll talk about us, shall we?'

She twisted her hands in her lap, saying nothing at all. She's stupid, Roland thought, Oh, God, she's stupid.

'How old are you, Elsie?'

'Sixteen.'

'All that! You don't look it.' This was cruel. Roland felt cruel.

'How old are you?'

'Getting on for twenty.'

'Are you in business?'

'No. I'm pretty much a gentleman of leisure, as you might say.'

Elsie thought about this for a little. Then she began to talk, rapidly, enthusiastically, about her plans for the future, of how she would leave school and go out to work, anywhere, anyhow. 'I'm tired of things,' she said. 'I want a change.'

Now he looked at her with interest. There was a faint line of colour in her face. Her eyes, nervously bright, seemed twice the size.

He put his hand on hers. This time she did not draw it away. She was unbelievably happy. The evening was quiet, and so delicate that a single word might break it in two pieces. The sun faded down to the ragged edges of the common. There was a watery light on the church spire, far away over the trees, and the lamps were lit on the path to the railway station.

63

'I shall never forget tonight. All my life I shall remember it.'

'Do you like boys?' he said.

'I don't know, really. I haven't known very many.'

'I don't like many girls. There were one or two, of course. Did you know Millicent Young? She went to your school. I used to go around with her quite a lot.'

Her tongue suddenly dried by an unreasoning pain, she murmured: 'Yes, I knew her.' Bravely – 'She's awfully nice.'

'Pretty, too. She knew a few things, I can tell you. You've got your secrets, I bet.'

'I don't know so much about that.' I must change the subject. I hate talking about Millicent.

'Are you fond of games, Roland?'

'Depends what games you mean,' he said, cunningly, 'I had my house cap for cricket and I wasn't a bad half back, but a fellow likes his fun in other ways, especially when he grows up.'

'I'm not bad at tennis.'

'We might play, sometimes, mightn't we?'

Sometimes. That's good. He's not bored with me, and he wants to see me again.

'I'd like to.'

'Shall we walk on for a bit? Are you getting chilly?'

'I'm quite happy here. Roland, have you got a cigarette?'

He was surprised. 'Sure. I didn't think, somehow, that you were a smoker. Try a Turkish, Turks on this side, Virginias on the other.'

It was nearly dark. As he lit a match, he was excited by the angles of her face, sharp and momentarily perfect in the yellow flame.

'Elsie.'

'Yes?'

He put his hands on her shoulders, looking straight down into her eyes.

64

'Nothing.' His courage had failed him, and so the moment passed by, bearing with it something she would remember for ever.

She said: 'I've got to be going, really. It's getting dark, and Mother worries if I'm out late.'

'Stay just a little while. We hardly know each other yet, do we?'

So she stayed, and they were silent together in the growing dark. When finally she arose, he put his arms around her. She would have run away, had she dared, but faint-hearted, she was quiet under his fingers. He bent his head to hers. At first she jerked her face away, but at last she raised her mouth to await his touch. He kissed her, shyly.

I shall never forget this, never, never in all my life. I know it's wrong to let someone kiss you when they've only just met you. It may be cheap, but it's beautiful, beautiful, and nothing can take that away.

'I've got to go, really, Roland.'

'Kiss me again, dear.'

Dear. This is for me. I am Elsie, and a man has kissed me and called me Dear. I love. I love, and I am Elsie.

'No, not now, please.'

'Yes, you will.'

Roly, roused by her denial, was nearly angry. He gripped her elbow, forcing her to stay at his side.

'I say yes.'

This time his kiss frightened her. Something was wrong and horrible. Oh, why did you kiss me again? Everything's spoiled, now.

'Please, Roland, I don't like it. Please.'

'Oh, all right,' he said, 'if you feel that way.' He released her arm. 'I'll walk with you to the road.'

'You needn't.'

'I will. It's late anyhow.'

65

As they reached the path, she dared not look at his angry face, white in the lamplight. I love, I love, she thought, and it's all lost. She hoped he would not glance down at her, for her eyes were wet with tears. She was ashamed of the two kisses now, as if they were dirty things, wicked things.

'This is my street.'

'I know it is.'

'Goodbye then, Roland.'

'Oh, goodbye. See you some time, I hope.'

'I hope so.'

Night, so suddenly forlorn, so scentless in the nostrils. Nothing to do now but go in. You've failed. He thinks you stupid and slow. Perhaps it's the other girls who act the right way, and you don't.

He walked as far as the gate with her. As she tried to smile a farewell, he said, unexpectedly:

'Aren't you going to kiss me goodnight?'

She paused a second too long.

'All right, if you don't want to.' He turned and left her very suddenly. With a drowning heart, she watched him go. All over, all lost. Blindly she went into the house. She had hoped to creep very softly upstairs and into bed before her mother could call her, but Mrs Cotton, hearing a creak from the loose board in the passage, came out of the sitting room.

'That you, dear?'

'Yes. I'm just going up. I'm tired.'

'Where have you been? With Joan?'

'No. Just sitting on the common. Goodnight, Mother.'

'Goodnight,' said Mrs Cotton, puzzled. She had been thinking about the girl a lot in the last two days. This bedtime silence was a fresh worry.

Elsie cried herself to sleep that night. Lying between two dawns, she dreamed of strange shapes and half happenings frighteningly divorced from her own sorrow. Waking in the dark, she heard her voice calling out: 'Never again, never again; men are beastly,' and she dreaded the morning, when she must go into the light, and, maybe, meet him as a stranger.

At this same hour, Mrs Maginnis, feeling beneath her night-gown, discovered a knot in her breast, no larger than a dried pea. For a long time she touched it, pressing its hardness with her fingers. Then she awoke her lover. Lighting the candle, she stared at him with fearful eyes. 'Feel,' she said.

Angry at being so suddenly aroused, he offered his hand impatiently to her guidance. 'I don't feel anything,' he said.

'Here, here, it's under your thumb.'

He rolled the swelling beneath his palm. 'That's nothing, Patty. A little cyst, or something. I think you can get them by a stoppage of the sweat glands, or something of the sort.'

'It scares me.'

'Oh, don't be a fool. Go to sleep, will you?'

He turned over, snorting his weariness into the pillow. Mrs Maginnis slept no more. She lay by his side, sick with the night heat and with her own fear, caressing the knot as if it were a child at her breast.

At this hour, Roly Dexter got out of bed and switched on the light. I'll read for a bit, he thought. So he put on his dressing gown, fetched the cigarettes from his trousers pocket and sat down to pick over the pages of the two unwelcome books he had selected from the library. They interested him far more than he would ever have imagined. Even when the reading lamp was a useless decoration in the morning light, he was still bobble-eyed over Havelock Ellis. I must see some more of this stuff, he decided, as he crept back into the sheets for a final hour's doze, it broadens a man's mind. It helps a man to understand life so much better. I'll have a look round for Elsie tomorrow night, he added to himself inconsequently. I'll ask Dad about Ma Maginnis at breakfast. I'll bet he goes hot right down to the collar stud. The best unpaid whore in town, Steve said. I wonder if he's ever... not he. He hasn't got the guts – or has he? I thought she looked at me rather funnily, as if she'd like to know me better.

He slept, then, and dreamed of the crippled hawthorns by the pond, of Elsie walking beneath them. She said something to him, so wise that he could not understand it. He tried to kiss her, but she dwindled in his arms until he discovered that he was holding a wooden doll. 'You're a whore,' he said to it, 'and I'll break you into firewood.'

'If you will sign the form here,' the doll answered him.

Mrs Maginnis Dislikes Doctors

'I'm not well, dearie,' she said anxiously, leaning her elbows on the cat's meat stall. 'Don't you think I'm looking queer?'

Ma Ditch looked at her. 'Careful of them lights, Patty. Your 'ands are nearly in 'em. Get down, puss! Your dinner's coming later. No, you look all right to me. What's wrong?'

'You don't think I'm a funny colour – a bit yellowish?'

'No, I can't say I do. Is it your liver? I suffer bad from the gripes, sometimes; get a bit of wind, you know – just 'ere – look, in me chest.' Ma Ditch swept away a satin bow and three strings of pearls to show the place. 'Mrs Parsons! Come 'ere a tick. Mrs Maginnis says she don't feel well. I think it's 'er liver. You're a martyr to biliousness, aren't you, ducks?'

Mrs Parsons looked modestly at her new bracelets. 'Well, just a bit, Mrs Ditch, but it's me 'ay fever that's really the trouble.'

'Cat-a-dog-a-me-meat-ah!' cried Ma Ditch, turning her attention to a prospective customer, 'What does your pussy want? Fine fellow, ain't 'e?' The man with the cat murmured something. 'No, I don't do that,' she replied, 'you can take Felix along to the vet. There's one on the corner of Willis Street. Pore little fellow!' she exclaimed to Mrs Maginnis, as he went away, 'I don't believe in that kind of thing. I always 'old that a cat's got a right to 'is fun, as much as we 'ave. What was you saying, Mrs Parsons?'

'About me 'ay fever.'

'Now, you take a look,' Mrs Maginnis said, desperately, 'Don't you think I'm a bad colour?'

Mrs Parsons peered short-sightedly into the bright face. 'Perhaps so,' she said doubtfully, 'but I can't really tell. 'Ave you tried 'ot water after meals?'

'It's not biliousness. I've got a lump come up, just under here. Feel.'

Ma Ditch, first wiping her hands on her apron, felt through the blouse. 'There is a little something.'

'It's a great hard lump.'

Mrs Parsons felt it too. 'That's nothing,' she pronounced cheerfully, 'I'ad one of them in me neck, and the doctor cauterised it for me. It was off in a few weeks.'

'Yes, you go and be vetted,' Ma Ditch said, 'like old Felix!' She roared so merrily at her own wit that Mr Parsons left his fruit to join in the fun. 'What's going on 'ere?'

'Nothing you would understand,' she replied, roguishly, 'you get back to your bananas.' He took no notice of her. 'Did I 'ear you say you were ill, Mrs Maginnis?'

'Yes. I've got a lump in my chest.'

He was concerned for her. The thought of The Admiral, without jolly Patty Maginnis to cheer it up of nights, was appalling.

'Now take care of that, my girl. Them things turn nasty if you don't watch out. You go along and see the panel.'

'I hate doctors!' Mrs Maginnis was vehement. 'They ask you what things you do, and then they tell you not to do them. I'm not going near one of them. You watch me.' She was defiant in her misery. As she stood there, she thought to herself: I know what's wrong. I know and they can't cure it. They just hack, hack, and on it goes just the same. When old Thompson was bad they could hear him screaming right down the street.

Just then, her dog, who had forsaken his mistress's heels, came bounding out of the poulterer's with something shiny and scarlet between his teeth.

'What's 'e got,' Parsons cried, 'a rat?'

'I don't know. Come here, Jim, come here. Damn and blast him, it's a hen's head! Dirty brute!'

She made a dive after him, but he eluded her fingers, tearing off under the stalls and through the legs of the shoppers. Away went Mrs Maginnis in pursuit, nearly knocking Ma Ditch into her own meats; away she went, breathless, red in the face, sworn at by the people with whom she collided. At last she caught him, dragging him out by his collar from beneath a stocking booth, when she managed to extract some of the mangled neck from his jaws. He had already eaten the beak and a few clinging feathers.

'God, you'll be sick, you will,' she panted, standing upright with the dog gripped between her ankles that he should not escape, her hat in the gutter, her gaudy hair blowing in the wind. As she gasped life back into her lungs, Mrs Maginnis, lustful for the sun, and seeing for the first time the mazing glory of light on the flowers and vegetables, was well once more.

She picked up the dog in her arms and went to rejoin Parsons and Ma Ditch. 'I've a good mind to kick him for his filth,' she said righteously, she who had never whipped an animal in her life, 'only I know he's going to get his punishment without any help from me. Look at him now!' – for the dog was retching already. 'Get down, old bloody muzzle,' she ordered, 'you get your sick over in the road.' Flopping down on to his quivering stomach, Jim obeyed almost immediately.

'Just like children they are,' Mrs Maginnis murmured, 'let 'em out of your sight for one minute and they go doing things they shouldn't. We haven't time to be ill ourselves, with them to look after.' She patted his fallen head.

'Put 'im on the lead,' Ma Ditch suggested, ' 'e'll be good now.'

71

'Right. Well, I'm going along. Oh, Mr Parsons, two nice ripe grapefruit, if you please, and a bundle of celery.'

'You take care of yourself, dearie;' Mrs Parsons touched her shoulder, 'and don't worry. You've probably only got a little wart.'

'Wart-oh!' said Ma Ditch, the wit.

'Thanks. Here you are, tenpence exactly. All right?'

'Only just.' Mr Parsons liked to be witty himself. 'Cheerio.'

'Cheerio, Ma. Cheers, you two. See you tonight, Mr P.?'

'You will, I expect, if my old girl don't want to go to the pictures. Do you?'

'No,' replied his wife, who wanted nothing he did not want.

Mrs Maginnis walked off with her bundles, cheerful once more. 'Cover it over quick, Jemima, cover it over quick,' she sang to herself, as she marched down Lincoln Street.

Her lover was standing on the corner, slacked against the lamppost as if he were an old coat hung on a peg. She felt a disappointment in him, something keen and new. In the night he was hotly male, with a chaining threat in his face, man to her woman, muscled Adam to her youthless Eve. In the morning he was just a thing who came to her for food and flattery, a shape with no shadows.

'Haven't you got a job yet?' she asked him, shouting down the space between them.

'No luck,' he replied, chewing the matchstick in his mouth. She came to him, laying her hand on his arm. 'Never mind. Can't always be lucky.' She pointed to the match. 'That's right, rattle the tin can, you old bastard! Wait a bit; you know I've got a cigarette somewhere in my bag, so you needn't show off. Here, I'll lend you fourpence – lend, mind you – and you can buy yourself ten Woodbines.'

He took the coins from her, black with rage that she should offer them. 'Ta.'

'Don't you "ta" me.' She pushed his shoulder kindly. 'If you'd got it, you know jolly well I'd take it off you, so what's the odds? You wait until your ship comes home, my boy, and you'll see. Now you hop in, and I'll make you a cup of tea.'

'Ta,' he mumbled again, following her up the steps of Number Twenty-Four.

'You look all in,' she said, snapping up the sitting room blinds, that she had forgotten the night before. 'Put your legs up on the sofa and I'll be with you in half a tick.'

Flinging her bundles with her coat and hat on to a chair, she put on the kettle and slid two slices of bread under the grill. 'You eat a good tea,' she called to him, 'and you'll feel better.'

He ate a good tea, but he did not feel better. He lay back on the couch, moodily silent, hating her plump hands that gave him money, and her loud voice that told him not to worry.

'Oh, you!' he said to her. 'It's all right for you to say "don't do this," and "don't do that." You're a wreck yourself.'

'I'm not,' she pleaded, 'I'm all right, really I am.'

'What about last night? Bloody little sleep I got. How's your chest?'

'It's well again now. Mrs Parsons said it was nothing at all. She knows someone who had a little lump like that, and it just went, all of a sudden.'

He said nothing, so she came closer to him, smoothing her hands around his face.

'What's the matter, dear?'

'Nothing. What the hell should there be?'

'There must be something wrong. Tell me.'

He pushed her hands away. 'I've told you. Nothing.'

She was unhappily quiet. At last she got up, and stood by the mantelpiece to face things bravely if they came.

'Tired of me?'

73

No answer.

'Don't be afraid to say. I've lots of friends. Are you?'

No answer.

'Are you?'

'More likely you're tired of me,' he evaded, 'You've been funny, lately.'

'Me? Me?' At first, not understanding him, she could have cried with relief. Falling to her knees by the couch, she put her arms around his shoulders, to hide her hot face in his coat. 'Silly boy, silly.'

Seeing no escape, he dragged his hand through her hair. 'Give us a kiss, then.'

Knowing what was expected of her, she unbuttoned her blouse, that he might thrust his fingers inside. Then they loved each other, angrily, miserably, he with the bitterness of failure, and she in the knowledge of farewell. They loved each other without words, for there was nothing more to say.

He left her early. 'I promised to meet a chap.'

When he had gone, she wandered round and round the room, the smell of his flesh still in her nostrils, and on her hands. Such a lot of things to do, she thought. Such a hell of a lot of tidying up that I don't know where to begin.

At eight o'clock that evening, she was just putting on her hat to go along to The Admiral, when the door bell rang. To her surprise she found Ada Mary on the step.

'Hullo!' she said, 'Fancy it being you! Come along in, won't you?'

The girl stepped past her into the empty room, and stood there teetering, staring about her.

'Sit down, ducks. How are you?'

'Very well, thank you.'

'And your ma and brother? They fit?'

'Very.'

'Take off your hat, do. You'll be more comfy. Why – what's the matter, dear? You're crying.'

'No, I'm not.'

'Oh, yes, you are. Wait a bit. What you want is a tot of whisky.' She went determinedly to her bedside cupboard.

'I don't drink, really I don't.'

'Oh, yes, you do. Come on. That's right. Now then, what brought you here?'

Ada Mary took a powder puff from her handbag, attempting to restore her slubbered face. 'Mother asked me to distribute the 'Thought for the Week' cards. I was just pushing yours through the letterbox when I felt terribly miserable and lonely, and knowing how kind you always are, I rang at the doorbell. It was an impulse.'

'You know what your ma thinks of me, don't you?' asked Mrs Maginnis, a little grimly.

'She's so often wrong.'

'She's not this time, not by a long chalk. But never mind about her. Look here, Ada Mary, you've got something on your mind. What is it?'

But the girl's resolution was gone. She stood up, taking her hat from the sofa.

'It was nothing, honestly. I don't know why I had to bother you. You've been awfully kind. I'm not going to stop any longer.'

Mrs Maginnis glanced sidelong at the desperate eyes. 'Okay,' she said, 'I understand. But remember this; if you feel rotten again, or worried about anything, I'm always here and I'll do my best to help. You want a rest. Go and see the doctor and try to get a certificate from him. A few days at home will do wonders for you.'

She walked with the girl to the door. Just as she was about to open it, she paused, with her hand on the lock. 'It isn't anything really bad, is it, Ada Mary?' she asked keenly, 'Something serious?'

75

'Oh, God, no; oh, my God, no, it hasn't come to that yet.'
Ada Mary was trembling violently. Mrs Maginnis pulled her
head forward and kissed her. 'Remember, I'm here.
Goodnight, old girl. Take care of yourself, and come back
any time you want to.'

She went in thoughtfully. Well, I don't know. Funny household, that.

The pink and gold clock on the mantelpiece chimed
nine. 'Blast it. Now I'm late.' She realised that she had been
sitting about doing nothing for nearly three-quarters of an
hour.

She set off for The Admiral. When she went into the bar,
she found Roly Dexter sitting in a corner nose to nose with
Teep, who was, as yet, sufficiently sober not to be single-
minded. 'It's the government,' he was saying, 'that's at the
bottom of it. What we want is more men with fight in 'em,
ready to spill blood if necessary. There's going to be blood
spilt too, before we gets our rights, and it won't be your blood
or mine. It'll be the blood of them bastards who sit in their
clubs, stuck behind the morning papers, saying 'we must do
this,' 'we must do that,' and telling each other how the People
wouldn't want their rights if they got 'em.'

'Blow 'em all dead,' said Mrs Maginnis cheerfully, desiring
to break up the party. Teep glowered at her and moved away
in search of another good listener.

'Hullo, you,' she said to Roly, 'don't see you here once in a
blue moon.'

'I generally go before you arrive. What's the matter – aren't
you well?'

To Mrs Maginnis, who was now under the impression
that, considering all things, she looked splendid, this was a
shock.

'Do I look bad?'

'Not too good, I thought, but perhaps it's the light.'

'I'm not very fit,' she whispered confidentially, 'got a bit of a scare last night. I found a funny sort of lump in my chest, just here, where I can't show a gentleman. Have a drink.'

'No, you have one with me. What are you taking?'

'Guinness, please. Like my name.'

He left her, to get the beers. When he came back, he asked: 'Have you seen a doctor?'

'I haven't,' she answered, 'and I'm not going to. I don't like them. My husband, Bert, his name was, had the T.B., so off they packed him to a 'sanny' on the East Coast. He was dead about a month after he got there, and it's my belief they froze him to death. Draughts, not enough bed-clothes, snow and rain blowing in on him. I shall never forgive myself for not making them leave him at home with me. I would have nursed him well again.'

'But that's the usual treatment for consumptives, isn't it?' Roly enquired. 'It's supposed to be good for them.'

'Well, I didn't like it, and I believe it hastened his end. At least the poor dear ought to have died comfortable. So you see why I'm not going to any doctor.'

Roly was stumped for any kind of consolation. Happily Mrs Maginnis changed the subject for him.

'What's a young man like you doing in here a fine night like this? You ought to be on the common with a girl, that's what you ought to be doing. Now then, the next is on me. I'll have a Scotch. Water, please. Have you got a girl?'

'Sort of,' he admitted, 'but I don't understand her very well. First she's nice and friendly, then off she goes, all 'La, sir,' if you get me. Half a tick. I must collect the drinks.'

Mrs Maginnis had a great many variegated drinks in a very short time. Roly, who drank moderately, watched her in wonder. At a quarter to ten, she offered to perform a sword dance for the assembled company. 'My grandpa was Scotch,' she assured Maisie. 'Here, Mr Wilkinson, lend me your stick.

Mr Parsons, your umbrella, if you please. Thanks. Now then, off we go.'

She untied her scarf, and with it hitched her skirts up from the waist. 'Willy!' she called to Sample. 'Let's have "The Keel Row."'

Mrs Maginnis was a lively dancer. Her feet, small for her considerable bulk, titupped nimbly around the improvised swords; her hands, one at her waist and one in the air, were red and lively. Parsons, wrapping a piece of paper around Maisie's pocket comb, accompanied Willy. Even the austere Wilkinson clapped his hands to the rhythm of the dance. Mr Teep was struck with the brilliant idea of shouting 'Hoots!' at regular intervals.

'Excuse me,' said Mrs Maginnis suddenly. Clapping her hand to her wet brow, she walked off very quickly through the door marked 'Ladies,' and the dance was at an end. Etiquette prevented much comment. When she reappeared, a little less ruddy than usual, she said 'goodnight' very quietly and left without delay, refusing Roly's offer to see her home.

Coldly unsteady, revolving extraordinarily coherent thoughts in the head that yet had no power to control her legs, Mrs Maginnis tacked down Lincoln Street. By a great effort of concentration, she let herself into the house with the minimum of trouble from her latchkey. Lucky I'm tight, she said to herself, because this will be the first night for a month he won't be here, and I don't like facing an empty room sober.

Holding firmly with one hand to the balusters, she managed with the other to light a small bead of gas on the stairs. That's better. She opened the door of her room rather tentatively, as if she wished to grow accustomed to the loneliness little by little. For a moment she thought he might have returned after all, as sick for her as she was for him, but the room smelt of emptiness and the lamp was unlit.

Mrs Maginnis, sitting down, dragged her feet out of her shoes. 'Cigarettes,' she mumbled, 'where the hell did I put them?' Then she remembered that she had given Roly Dexter her last, and she decided that it would be unwise for her to go right through to the main road in search of a machine. I'll stay where I am, quiet. Quiet. Better not lie down, either. I know what I will do, though. I'll play my gramophone. That'll cheer me up. She wavered over to the sideboard, fumbling for her records in search of one about love. She chose the least worn of her needles. I remember saying to him, once, 'There's a new needle on the market that plays a thousand times before you need change it.' 'Why should you worry,' he said – God, he could be bloody funny – 'Yours do that anyway.' And Mrs Maginnis wept for joy. It's late, she thought, Better not wake the neighbours, so she threw her coat over the horn of the old fashioned instrument. Feeling beneath this covering, she managed to start the tune, and settled back in her chair to enjoy it.

'When you and I were seventeen,' she sang, until the sentimental tears choked her. Know what you are? She asked herself severely, at this juncture. You're tiddley. Not drunk. Just plain, common, nasty tiddley. Now you get up, my girl, turn that noise off, and then go to bed. You can lie down all right, so don't kid yourself you can't.

She arose. As she did so, the floor dived beneath her, and she stumbled forward, throwing out a hand to save herself. Clutching the muffled horn of the gramophone, she stood upright to recover her breath. Here, steady on, old lady, steady on. She tugged at her coat to pull it away, that she might see more clearly to stop the record, but she tugged too hard, and the gramophone plunged forward to strike her a violent blow on the breast with one of its sharp corners.

Mrs Maginnis slid to the floor. As the instrument crashed down, the needle gave a last scream up the record. I hope no-one heard. They'll be coming from across the way to ask questions, and I can't talk to them. She touched herself with fearful fingers. The heavy box had missed her nipple by less than an inch, but she knew she was terribly bruised, and that the nut beneath the skin had been struck too. She could feel no pain. Sitting on the floor, her hands resting very, very lightly on her blouse, which she had not dared to undo, she awaited the moment when the agony should start.

The tears ran down her face.

'Oh, my dearie, my dearie,' Mrs Maginnis wept confusedly to the silent house, 'how could you, how could you hurt me like this?'

Saturday

'Now just see if you can remember this,' said Mrs Cotton.
'The twopence on the corner of the table is for the dustman:
when you hear him shout, let him come right through, and
whatever you do, don't forget to give him his money, because
they'll drop muck all along the kitchen and passage for two
pins. The two-and-three is for the laundry boy; I don't
suppose he'll call before I get back, but if he does, just give it
to him and take in the washing. I think that's all. Oh, if the
insurance man calls, tell him to come back on Monday. You
go and have your lunch down the street, and then I shan't
have you messing around my stove. Can you keep all that in
your head, or shall I write it down? No, I think you can
manage. Be a good girl now; I'll be home round about three,
and then perhaps we'll go to the pictures.'

She straightened her hat before the mirror. 'Why don't
you tie your scarf in a bow, Mother?' Elsie asked.

'No, thank you. I don't want to be mutton dressed up as
lamb. It's all right for you young ones. Goodbye, dear.'

And Mrs Cotton left on her journey to town, for the all-
important purpose of buying an autumn coat.

Elsie basked in the unwonted luxury of having the house
and its silence entirely to herself. It was Saturday morning,
that loveliest of lovely times, when everyone was working but
Elsie alone. Sunday was a dun-coloured bore: the streets
were dead, and no-one went out walking till four o'clock.
Behind the shutters people slept off their ritual dinners, and

no-one liked to play the piano or put on the gramophone lest someone else's nap should be spoiled. But Saturdays, with no more school till Monday, and everybody out in the streets getting in the weekend shopping, Saturdays were the festivals of the year.

Elsie got up from breakfast and cleared the plates away quickly, that there might be nothing for her to do whatsoever. Mistress of a mansion, sole dictator of the dustman and the laundry boy, she sensed her power. Looking out of the dining room window, she saw the little boys playing forbidden cricket in the road. On the far side Ada Mary walked, her basket on her arm. Elsie would have liked to ask her in, for the pleasure of receiving company on her own. How pleasant, she thought, how nice it would be.

She read for a little while, and smoked two cigarettes in succession. Then she wandered round the house, feeling the strangeness of each room. I would like to live alone, all by myself, with no-one to worry me, or make me do this and that.

The dustman came early, making several journeys through the kitchen to the garden. Elsie found an odd penny in her own bag, so she augmented his tip to threepence, which surprised him very much. When he had gone, she thought she would like to walk down to The Stalls and talk to all the people she knew. 'But I'd better stay in,' she said aloud, 'because the washing might come, or anyone might drop in.'

Startled by the sound of her own voice, speaking into silence, she felt a sudden touch of panic lest she should receive an answer. So she ran upstairs to sit in her own room with the door closed. Ten to eleven. I hope she won't be very long, after all.

After the momentary fright had died away, she became conscious of a desire to make use of her solitude, do something very interesting and exciting. Catching sight of her face in the glass, she thought: There are two of us now, two Mes, quite separate from each other. She looked up at her book-shelves. She had read everything and there was nothing old enough to be new to her. I wonder if I could run across to the library to get a book, without anyone calling.

She thought wistfully of the newsagent down Mornington Street, who had a small library of his own. Joan had told her that he possessed a copy of *Lady Chatterley's Lover*, which he kept in the cover of *Robinson Crusoe*, so that if you were in the know, you went over to him and said: 'Can I have Crusoe, please?' and you were charged sixpence a day for it. Elsie would never dare to go and get the book for herself. She yearned for the knowledge one day to come, and for the first time the things she had feared were beautiful to her.

For want of something better to do, she routed out an old diary, one which she had kept during her twelfth year, and nicked over the pages to see what sort of a child she had been.

'Tuesday, September 4th. Got up late, had hair washed. Chicken for dinner. Lucy in to tea, played dressing-up.'

I used to like dressing-up. I'd play it now, if I were not afraid of being laughed at.

Elsie took the printed cotton counterpane from the bed and swathed it around her. She liked the effect very much. Then she undressed, and wound it again about her naked body, with a tight fold around her breasts and a great fishtail behind. I look beautiful. She held the bed-cover before her, so that she could see the shape of her veiled body in the glass. How nice my hips are. My legs join beautifully at the top. She draped the material around her waist, knotting it just below the navel. Now I am a slave girl in the marketplace. The sultan will come by and claim me for his own. Going to the dressing table, she screwed her hair back over her ears, fastening it with a paste brooch. The result delighted her. She moved up and down the room, turning her head from side to side, drawing up the cotton to conceal her nipples, letting it fall again. I am beautiful. I am beautiful. Suppose he saw me like this. No one could resist me, as I am now, with my clothes off.

The ticklings of love, the excitement of her self-discovery, filled her with an energy so sweet, so violent that she stood on the tips of her toes and flung her arms wide.

Then the laundry boy banged at the knocker. Feeling, in a moment, cold and silly, ashamed that even her own reflection should have witnessed her humiliation, Elsie tore off the counterpane, unpinned the brooch from her hair, and scrambled back into her frock. Red in the face, she opened the door and paid the boy.

It must be nearly lunchtime, she thought, as she carried the washing into the kitchen. I must go out now. She could feel the quietness of the room upstairs, where she had revealed a secret to the looking glass. It was a hot day, so she did not bother to dress fully, but slipped her knickers on under her frock and put on a light coat. As she went down the road her shame departed from her, and she was gay in the sun.

In her purse she had, besides her lunch allowance, two shillings, her pocket-money for a week. When I go to work I'll have a lot to spend, all my own.

She went down the High Street, gazing in the shop windows. I want to buy something. She gave a threepenny bit to a beggar and her heart was lighter than ever. Soon she bought a string of red beads, another packet of cigarettes and an imitation flower to pin in her coat. Pleased by these purchases, she went down by The Stalls, to talk to the people she knew. From Parsons she bought a peach for her mother. She met Joan, then, and they talked together for a while on a corner.

It was just as she was nearing her own street that Roly stopped her, standing in her path like a headless shadow.

'Good morning, mum,' he said, humorously, 'carry your bundles?'

In his face there was no embarrassment at all. No-one would ever have thought that he had left her to suffer her first and keenest heartbreak. Elsie was bold with relief.

'Such tiddy ones!' she giggled.

'Let me take them, anyway. How are you? I haven't seen you for let me think, four days!'

'Five.'

'Monday, it was. Tuesday, Wednesday, Thursday, Friday – that's four, and we don't count today, because here you are. Go on, give me your burdens. Stand and deliver! Your parcels, or your life!'

'Thank you.'

'What are you doing, shopping?'

'Yes. Mother's up town this morning, and I'm all on my own.'

'Splendid. Let's go for a walk, shall we? No, I'll tell you what. We'll go in and have some coffee somewhere, or an ice, if you'd rather, and then we can talk better.'

Mute with pleasure, Elsie followed him. 'Where shall we go,' she asked, 'Brown's?'

'No, I don't think so. I don't like it much, and, besides, I know such a lot of fellows who go in there.'

She was momentarily disappointed. She would have liked to have gone to Brown's, because she knew a lot of people who went there, too, and she wanted them to see what a conquest she had made. But eventually Roland chose a teashop on the river embankment, where there were brave coloured sunblinds, and they went in.

'I say,' he said, looking at the clock, 'do you know it's ten to one? Look here, have a bit of lunch with me.'

She was dumbfounded by the largeness of this offer. 'Oh, no, I couldn't do that. I'd have lunch with you, but I couldn't let you pay. Mother gave me my lunch money, as she was out – I've got it in my bag.'

'You have it with me,' he ordered, finely, dominantly. 'What would you like?'

Elsie scanned the menu, seeing nothing thereon but a blur.

'Poached egg on chips, please,' she said, adding to the patient waitress, 'well poached.' 'That's the only way I like eggs,' she remarked to Roly, 'and I hate them in any form for breakfast.'

'Same for me,' he said to the girl, 'and we'll both have coffee. That all right with you?'

'Thank you,' murmured Elsie.

'Cigarette?'

'Please.'

He lit it for her. 'Well?'

Again she could not answer, for her happiness was transcendent. After all her crying, her shameful humility, here she was, sitting with him, having lunch (paid for by him) at a café by the river.

Oh glory! O second unforgettable moment! I love and I am Elsie.

'Quiet little thing,' he said.

'Am I? I was just enjoying the sun, and all this, and being with you.'

He was pleased. Most of the local girls were too wise to show that they were glad at him.

'I like being with you, too, Elsie. I say, I'm afraid I was a bit of a beast the other night – going off like that, I mean – only I sort of thought you were sick of me.'

'Let's not talk about it,' commanded Elsie, the temporary upper dog, generous to the defeated lover.

86

'All right,' he said. 'Then everything's OK now? We're friends?'

'Of course we are.' At this the tickling love assailed her once again.

They talked about nothing at all until the eggs came, silver and gold on the sizzling potatoes. After that, they had fruit salad and cream, and yet another coffee.

'Had a good lunch?' said Roly.

'Lovely.'

'What about meeting me tonight and coming to the pictures with me?'

'No,' Elsie answered, mindful of his pocket, 'not the pictures tonight. I'll meet you, though, and we'll walk.'

'We'll do better,' said Roly. 'I've got two free tickets for a flannel dance at the Town Hall which I wasn't going to use. Would you like to come with me?'

She caught her breath. 'Really?'

'Of course. I could meet you at the end of your road at half past seven.'

'Couldn't you call for me?' she ventured, 'Mother would love to meet you.'

Roly shied visibly. He dreaded mothers. Once you met a mother you were done. You had to watch your step, and pretty soon they asked you if you were serious.

'Oh no, I couldn't do that.'

'Why not?' She was on her guard.

'Oh, I don't know. I suppose I'm shy, really. People don't believe me when I say to them – 'I'm shy,' but it's true, all the same.'

She was soft with pity for him. 'I know. I'm just like that myself. Yes, of course I'll meet you on the corner. Let's go now, shall we?'

He paid the bill, fishing out a handful of silver to flash in her enchanted eyes. He left sixpence under the plate.

'Tipping – iniquitous,' he said to Elsie.

'Yes,' she answered.

He walked with her as far as Mornington Street. 'I'll leave you here. I've got to get back now.'

'Whereabouts do you live?'

'Lister Gardens.' He did not mention the number.

Elsie collected her small parcels. 'Thank you awfully for the lunch.'

'That's all right. See you tonight at seven-thirty.'

She ran away hurriedly, so as to leave the morning unspoiled. Another glance, another word – who knew what might happen?

When she got in, Mrs Cotton had returned, peacock proud in her new coat. 'How do you like me?' she asked. 'Look, two whole foxes in this collar, or so they said, and you just feel the lining. Not real *crêpe de Chine* of course, but so much tougher, and who looks at the lining, anyway? See this back. Doesn't it slim me? Guess how much I paid.'

'Oh, I don't know. I never can guess prices.'

'Just try. Go on.'

'Three guineas?'

'Elsie! Three and a half. This is a beautiful material, you know, and ought to wear for years. Now you've disappointed me.'

'Oh, Mother, I told you I couldn't guess prices. It looks lovely, anyway. You'll be ashamed to go out with me, now!'

Mrs Cotton laid her purchase away in its box. 'What have you been doing, dearie?'

'Reading, looking after the dustman, taking in the washing, and then I went for a walk. I met one or two people I knew.'

'Did you? Who?'

'Joan, and Mr Parsons, and a boy I know.'

'Who's that?' Mrs Cotton's voice was keen.

'Roland Dexter, the son of the town councillor. I've known him quite a long time.'

'Oh, have you? It's the first I've heard about it. How did you meet him?'

'One of the girls at school introduced me. Mother, he wants me to go to a flannel dance at the Town Hall tonight. May I?'

'Look here,' said Mrs Cotton, sitting down on the sofa, 'I think you're too young to start boys yet. I'd like to meet him before I give you permission to go about with him. Is he calling for you to take you to this dance?'

'Well, he wouldn't exactly call. He's so shy, you know.'

'He is, is he?' – grimly.

'Awfully. But he's very nice and quiet and everybody knows him. I'm meeting him on the corner at half past seven. Mother what does one wear to a flannel dance? Evening dress? No, surely not. I don't think any of my cotton frocks are good enough.'

'You could wear your blue lace, with the sleeves,' Mrs Cotton suggested doubtfully, falling right into the trap set for her.

'Then I can go?'

'I didn't say you could.'

'Oh yes, you did, oh yes, you did. Will you press the blue for me, darling, and may I wear your pearls?'

Later on in the afternoon, Elsie said: 'Mother, I'd like to have my hair set for tonight. May I?'

'Here you are.' Mrs Cotton hopelessly proffered two shillings. As her daughter went out, she faced the lowering future with her head down, and her mind glumly receptive to the necessary readjustment.

Elsie was at the corner of Stanley Street some ten minutes before Roly arrived. Hatless, her summer coat over the lace frock and her slippers in a paper bag under her arm, she looked anxiously up and down, fearful that the wind should ruffle her hair. As he strolled towards her, she thought how fine he looked in his grey suit and his dashing red tie. He stopped in front of her and admired her with his eyes. She flushed, fumbling with the clasp of her bag. At last he said, 'You look marvellous.'

'It's only my hair. I haven't had it set before. Do you like it?'

'You look like a film star. Honestly you do, and I don't flatter. You just ask anyone if I ever flatter.'

'You look nice, too,' she said.

This made him awkward. She would, he thought.

'Let's go,' Roly said, 'I'm afraid I'm a bit late as it is, but I cut myself shaving. Do you go to many dances?'

'A good few,' she answered wisely, wondering if she would give herself away before the evening was out, do anything the girls who were used to dances didn't do.

Her first trouble was the Town Hall cloakroom. There were so many girls there that she could hardly get in the door, so much bright light, so great a mist of flying powder that she was too dazed to fight her way to the mirror. As she gave up her coat, it seemed to her that she had changed on the journey, become smaller, and plainer. When I looked at myself in the bedroom glass I was lovely: no-one could look quite as nice as Elsie. Now everyone looks much nicer.

Eager to get as quickly as possible out of the crush of women, she hastily combed her hair and went down stairs again. There she saw Roly, in the vestibule, talking to a ginger-headed girl.

Now what shall I do? If I go down and speak to him he may be angry. If I don't, he'll wonder where I am.

Her heart dropped like a stone. Who is she? It's not my business, anyway. He knows a lot of girls, and why shouldn't he.

She hung about behind a pillar half way up the stairs, until he glanced up and saw her. Murmuring a few words to the girl, who walked away to talk to someone else, he joined Elsie.

'You're ready quickly. Some women spend years in the cloakroom.'

'I just powdered my nose. Was that a friend of yours?' she asked, hoping that her voice was casual.

'Yes and no. She's the new assistant at the library; I always talk to her when I go in there. Look here, if you're quite sure you don't mind, I shall have to give her a dance later on in the evening. A bore, but one must.'

'Of course,' she answered faintly.

Roly met so many people that he knew, during the course of the evening, and asked Elsie's permission to fulfil so many duty dances, that she was left alone a good deal. There seemed to be very few spare men, so she had to sit by the wall, trying to look very pleased and jolly, to look, in fact, quite delighted to have the chance of a rest. Her face grew tired with smiling, with nodding and becking at Roly as he slid by with someone else.

When he came to take her out for refreshments, he was amazed by the disappointment in her eyes.

'Dear,' he said, 'aren't you enjoying yourself?'

He ducked his head that he might watch her lips.

'Of course I am. Terribly.'

'Terribly is right. You're having a terrible time. What's the matter?'

'Nothing, I tell you. Only—' resentment took her. Courageously she added, 'I've seen precious little of you.'

He scowled.

'I know you've got a lot of friends of course,' she amended, hastily.

'Well,' he said, 'I haven't any more duty dances to go through now, except the one with the library girl.'

So she sat out that one, too. After that, Roly stayed at her side, martyred, ill humoured. Elsie chattered to him bravely.

Only ten, and two hours more to go. If I run up to the cloakroom, go to the lavatory and do my hair again, that will fill in ten minutes or so. Time's got to go. If only I could wish it wouldn't, it would.

They danced three times in succession, and she was glad that she was light on her feet, for she knew that as a partner she pleased him.

When she retired upstairs, Roly wandered into the corridor, where he met a man he knew. This was fortunate for Elsie, as the man commented on her prettiness. When she came down, therefore, she found a smiling Roland, a little deferential, easy-to-please. They were happy together for the first time that evening. If Roly had any regrets at all, it was that he had asked the ginger-haired girl to come to the pictures with him on the following Saturday. Because they were happy, twelve o'clock came long before they expected it.

'I'll see you home,' Roly said. 'It has been nice. Truly I've enjoyed it.' They walked home the common way, although it was late, and she let him put his arm around her shoulders.

'Don't let's hurry.'

'I must. Mother will only wait up for me.'

'Sit here with me, and have just one cigarette.' There was a clear, round moon. They sat under the hawthorns once again, in a pattern of black flowers and white. He kissed her three times, on her upper and lower lip, and lastly on the full of her mouth 'Elsie, darling.'

She put her arms around his neck, on this loveliest night in the world. Then he moved his hands down to her breasts and held them there, though he could feel in his fingers the withdrawing of her flesh.

'Don't.'

'Why not? You know how I feel about you.'

'Don't, all the same.' She shut her eyes in sorrow for the moment when she must be again untouched. He drew away from her.

'All right; kiss me, then.'

She kissed him in the warmth of gratitude that he was not angry with her.

'Tomorrow,' he said, 'by the pond. Same place, same time.'

'Tomorrow.'

As he touched her lightly for the last time, running his fingernail down the dark cutting of her throat, she whispered: 'I love you,' just so softly that he should not hear.

Mr Wilkinson Takes Two Plunges

It was from the girl in the library that Roly learned the news about Mrs Maginnis. 'She had a bad fall, or something, and hurt her chest.'

Roly, remembering the conversation in The Admiral, was much perturbed.

'I'm sorry about that. Is she lying-up?'

'Not she. She was in here this morning, looking a bit off colour, it's true, but as lively as a cricket in herself.'

Roly handed in his books. 'Two returned, none out.'

'Meet you tonight for the pictures?' the ginger girl whispered, tickling the back of his hand.

'Oh, sure,' he answered, wishing he had never encouraged her. One woman is enough for one man, he thought vastly, with a pleasurable vision of Elsie. She's my girl, all right. She'll do.

He left the library and went in search of Mrs Maginnis. He strolled up and down Lincoln Street for some time, for he did not know the number of her house. At last his patience was rewarded. She came hurrying along, wearing a proud new hat.

'Good morning. I was just looking for you.'

'Looking for me? You're a bit young, aren't you?' Mrs Maginnis giggled at him.

'I heard you'd had an accident.'

'Accident nothing. A little tumble. I hit myself here, but it's nothing to worry about.' She stared vaguely into the sky. 'Nothing to worry about yet, anyhow. I'm just waiting for it to hurt me, and when it does, my lad, you'll see. Come in a moment, won't you?'

Enchanted, Roly followed her into the house. This would be something to tell Steve.

'Heard the news about Maisie?' she asked him.

'No, what?'

'She's hooked old Wilkinson at last. You know Wilkinson, the miserable-looking chap from the candle factory. Maise has been gone on him for years, but none of us ever thought he meant seriously. He's always in debt – dogs, his game is. We're all wondering what he's going to use for money when they're married. Maisie's having a bit of a do round at The Admiral tonight – drinks on the house. Are you coming along?'

'Can't,' Roly said, 'I've got a date.'

'Oh, all right. You'll miss something, though. How do you like my place?'

He looked around him at the wallpaper, gay with ribbons and cornucopia, with bulging pomegranates and with noble birds. He admired the green plush bobbles round the mantelpiece, and the muslin curtains, neatly waisted with silken cords.

'Very pretty,' he said. Pointing to a picture over the fireplace: 'Who's that?'

'That's me, on my wedding day. I was a pretty *girl* then. I had so much hair that I could sit on it, real gold, too. That's Bert, there, with the whiskers. We used to like whiskers in those days. He was a good chap, Bert was. When he knew he was really ill, he said to me, Patty, old girl, if you don't get married again I'll come and haunt you. You have a good time with the boys.' How many men would have said that, I wonder.

'How's your girl?' she added, abruptly.

'She's all right, but I've got myself into a mess with another one as well.'

'That library cat,' said Mrs Maginnis, with conviction. 'I know. I've seen you two chatting together. If you'll take a tip, and I'm nearly old enough to be your ma, believe it or not, you'll give that ginger she the go-by. All scent and dirty neck, she is. You can follow her by her smell. Always messing around with the fellows, smirking herself sick over her scalps. You stick to little calf eyes.'

'You know everything, don't you?' Roly was in no way offended.

'I keep my eyes open,' she replied. 'Listen – you stick to Elsie – that's her name, isn't it? One woman's enough for a man. I've always believed in that.'

His expression betrayed him. 'Funny, this coming from me, isn't it?' she added.

He got up to go. 'Well, see you soon. I'm so glad to hear that you're feeling all right.'

'I'm OK,' she answered, 'till the pain starts. When it does, we'll see.'

When he had gone, she opened her blouse very gingerly. Her breast rolled out, like a money bag bulging with silver, and she cupped it in her hands to see the bruise. It was very slight now, and only a faint yellowing showed over the lump. 'It may be all right,' she said, doubtfully, 'we'll see, anyway.'

It was about this time that Mrs Godshill began to run the meeting alone, without the assistance of Arthur or Ada Mary. It was the popular belief of the neighbourhood that she had eaten her young. Ada Mary had suffered a nervous breakdown at work and was sent home, rather angrily, with the injunction to stay away until such time as she could resume her duties without periodical collapse. Arthur, with a courage born (though his mother did not even suspect it) of whisky, had refused point-blank to contribute further to the cause of religion. Every day he went out job-hunting and every night he arrived home, luck-less and enforcedly silent, for he was always incapable of speech. Ada Mary, out of the weakness of her heart, was paying for the whisky. She had saved a little money over a period of three years, and was happy to give it to Arthur that he might take what pleasures he could. That Mrs Godshill did not know of his latest hobby was due to her tremendous absorption in herself and in the sins of the neighbourhood. Despite the years, which she would glady forget, spent in removing her late husband from public houses, she never recognised a drunkard save when she caught him, as it were, in the act. So long as a man did not actually stagger or vomit before her eyes, he might be as drunk as Bacchus for all she noticed. So Arthur, who had learned, in something less than a fortnight, to hold his liquor, arrived home, palely and quietly paralytic every night.

It was Maisie who, in a fit of misplaced humour, sent him an invitation to her engagement party. She had not seen him since that exciting night in The Admiral Drake, for Arthur discreetly frequented the private bar of The Antlers, which was a twopenny bus ride from the neighbourhood.

'I know,' she said to Wilkinson, when they were discussing the celebrations, 'we'll ask old Arthur Godshill, just for fun. Who knows? He might even turn up!' To which suggestion her fiance, who had weightier matters on his mind, made no comment.

He was very worried. One night, when he was sombrely drunk, the idea of proposing marriage to Maisie had occurred to him with almost psychic lucidity; unfortunately he had acted on it without waiting to see how he felt when he was sober. So here he was, horribly in debt, without a hope of straightening himself out, engaged to a pink-and-white birth-day cake of a barmaid who loved him with suffocating inten-sity. The idea of wriggling out of this engagement did not occur to him. Somehow he had to go through with it, no matter what happened afterwards.

That night The Admiral filled up very early. Wilkinson, at Maisie's request, was there before opening time, ready to receive the guests. In honour of the occasion there were flowers in the vases – lupins from Parsons's back garden and sunflowers from Willy's. Maisie herself was wearing a new silk dress, as gaily patterned as Mrs Maginnis's wallpaper, and her left hand bore a marquise ring of exceptional sparkle. Wilkinson could never see it without worrying about the instalments.

The magic slogan, 'Drinks on the house,' had done its work in the neighbourhood, for The Admiral was crowded to bursting point before eight o'clock. At every fresh congratulation Maisie lowered her blushing face so modestly that she nearly lost it in her neck. Wilkinson sat quietly on his stool, murmuring, 'Thanks, thanks.' By nine, proceedings had taken a more formal turn. Willy had been permitted to perform a proper piano solo to which everyone listened in silence. Mrs Maginnis sang one of Vesta Victoria's songs, and Teep, to everyone's astonishment, stood up in his corner, banged for attention with his glass, and recited, 'I remember, I remember, the house where I was born.'

The greatest excitement, however, was still to come. Arthur arrived at The Admiral on the stroke of nine, with a bunch of violets for Maisie. The present of flowers was accidental, for he had found them outside the Palais de Danse, where a girl had dropped them: his arrival was not. He had received his invitation, and Mrs Godshill had found it in his trousers pocket. Red with fury, she forbade him to go, saying a great deal, at the same time, about God, the Devil, and Arthur personally. So Arthur, who had had no intention of accepting, put on his hat, dared his mother to follow him, and stalked off to The Admiral *via* The Antlers.

Maisie, concealing her amazement, thanked him warmly and stood him a drink. Wilkinson, finding himself neglected by the company in favour of the phenomenal Arthur, got drunk.

After a while, Parsons thought that Mrs Godshill's son might be persuaded to sing.

This found favour with all, and Arthur was requested to perform. Knowing no secular songs and determined to make a night of it at all costs, he crossed to the piano, and, leaning confidentially over Willy's shoulder, asked him if he thought he could vamp an accompaniment to 'Safe in the Bosom of the Lamb.' Willy, to whom this was child's play, showed his versatility by strumming through the hymn, to a chorus of approval from the room.

Arthur was halfway through the song before Ada Mary came in.

Peering nervously through the door, like a cat who expects a boot to be slung at it any minute, she called to her brother in a faint voice. He did not hear her at first, so she came up to him, looking neither to right nor left, and pulled at his sleeve.

'You've got to come home. Mother's ill. Arthur, stop singing, will you? She's ill. She's collapsed.'

He looked at her dimly, putting out a hand to touch her pale face and the snails of her hair, to see if she were really at his side.

Mrs Maginnis motioned Willy to stop playing. 'Here,' she said authoritatively, 'No more of that. Arthur's got to go. Sorry, and all that, but he has.' She put her arm around Ada Mary. 'Can you manage him, or shall I go with you?'

'We'll be all right,' Ada Mary replied.

Sobered by the silence, and by the sight of his sister, wretched with fear and embarrassment, Arthur went quietly.

As soon as they had gone, the noise broke out again.

'There's going to be a bloody lot of trouble in that family,' Parsons observed.

'There is,' said Maisie, 'and I only hope poor Ada isn't going to be the sufferer. They say no-one can do anything with old Ex Holy but her.'

'One has to be sorry for Ma Godshill,' someone said, 'He does let her down good and proper.'

'Good job too,' Parsons snapped, 'and serve 'er right.'

'Makes one think what a responsibility bringing up children is,' Maisie sighed, hoping, by this subtle means, to turn the conversation to herself again.

'Don't you say too much about children!' giggled Mrs Maginnis, rising to the bait, 'Won't be so long before you're a mamma.'

'You shut up.' Maisie shook a finger at her. 'Plenty of time to think about that.'

The interest swung round entirely now to the engaged couple. Their health was drunk many times and Wilkinson was complimented on his luck.

'I want quite a small house somewhere,' Maisie told the company, 'easy to run, you know, and not too many stairs. I'm going to have a blue drawing room with a walnut suite, and I shall make Harry buy me one of those dressing tables with a long glass and a stool attached, for the bedroom. I haven't asked him yet,' she added, laughing, 'but he's easy.'

It was at this point that Wilkinson decided to commit suicide. He went quietly to the lavatory and bolted himself in. His head was dark and stuffy inside. The walls closed in upon him, to recede once more. It was as quiet as the grave. Standing up on the wooden seat, he peered out of the small window, having some idea of squeezing himself through it and performing a death leap into the area at the back of the house. This, however, proved impracticable, firstly because his shoulders were wider than the opening, and secondly, because there was a drop of no more than eight feet, which would be insufficient to kill a child. He climbed down again.

There was nothing for it but to cut his throat. Fearlessly he loosened his collar and opened his penknife. Commending his soul to Jesus, Wilkinson shut his eyes, though it was as dark as pitch in the lavatory, and made a fierce dig at his neck. But before the knife could reach the skin, his hand had slowed itself up, and the result was a small and unimpressive nick beneath his left ear. This finished his suicide attempts. Putting the knife back in his pocket, he raised a finger to touch the thin trickle of blood which was running down to his collar. Then he put his head in his hands and wept for the misery of a world from which he was sure he would never have the courage to escape.

When at last he went back into the bar, his collar readjusted and a handkerchief knotted around the wound, he found that it was past closing time. The last customer had gone. Maisie ran to him, pale with anxiety. 'Oh, my God, Harry, what's up? You were so long in there. I had to say "goodnight" for you, and I was so worried I nearly sent Parsons to see if you were ill, or anything. What's the matter with your neck?'

'A boil burst,' he said simply, and laying his head on her comfortable shoulder, he started to cry afresh.

Maisie, terribly upset, clicked off the bar lights and led him into the back parlour, where a small fire burned always, no matter how warm the weather. 'What's wrong, Harry? Tell Maise.'

She sat him on the sofa, and took her place by his side. 'Go on, tell us.'

'I haven't got any money,' he moaned.

The revelation, in some queer way, disappointed her. She had expected something far more interesting.

'You're tight, dearie. You'll feel better in the morning.'

'I haven't got any money. I'm in debt up to my ears. You may as well hear this now, Maisie: I couldn't marry a guinea-pig.'

He told her about his run of bad luck, of the money he had lost, of the money he owed. Of his small attempt at suicide he said nothing, for he was bitterly ashamed of his failure. Maisie listened. Staring dry eyed into the fire, she saw her home fade away, with its fine dressing table and the blue-and-walnut drawing room. At last she thought of a plan. 'Look here, Harry, don't you say nothing of what you've told me to anyone. I've got a bit of my own put away and business here is good. We'll tell people that we've decided not to buy a house, but to run The Admiral together. There's enough in it for both of us, and nobody need know the truth. I'll pay off your debts as far as I can, and we'll start clean. What do you say to that?'

He could not answer her.

'I love you,' she said, forcing up his chin that he might see she was smiling, 'don't you know that? You're not going to get away from me, anyhow.'

Out of the depths of his humiliation, Wilkinson wept.

The house was very quiet. Maisie had not the heart to send her lover home. Upstairs her father, who had long retired from active participation in the business, slept soundly. She sat before the dying fire until her breast ached with the weight of Wilkinson's head upon it. After a while, he began to pull at her dress.

'Here, what are you doing?' she whispered.

'I'm so miserable,' he answered her, childishly. 'I want you badly. Come on.'

She was fearful. 'No, dearie.'

'We'll be married soon. What does it matter?'

And Maisie, her eyes wet with tears of pity, surrendered to him her virtue, so long and so fiercely defended, because he had need of it.

He left at a quarter to three. As he walked down the street, he found that the stars were going round like catherine wheels. His ankles were so weak that he could scarcely walk, but he dreaded going home. There will be no-one there, he thought. Of course, there never is, but tonight there should be, and there will be no-one there.

So instead of going up Mornington Street in the direction of Morley Road, he walked down the Parade and turned into Belvedere Row, which led to the river.

As he leaned over the bridge, it seemed to him that the river was so full of stars that there was no room for water. Anyone jumping over the parapet would not drown, but be impaled on a thousand spear points. This would be a very quick death.

He looked from right to left to see if there were anyone near him, but the embankment was deserted. He thought a little time away. A hundred miles from where he stood, Maisie was winding the clocks in The Admiral Drake, pondering her fall, facing a complicated future. In three or four houses in the neighbourhood there slept men who were waiting for the money he owed them. He laughed a little at the thought of this.

Then, splendidly courageous, he clambered on to the parapet. I'm still pretty tight, he thought, gloriously. Below him the river ran white.

Now for it. I'm not afraid to die. What sort of a man should I be to live off a woman till kingdom come? It's quite easy. In one more minute, down I go.

Then another thought suggested itself. If it were brave in him to kill himself, how infinitely braver it would be, with fear completely over, to abandon the whole idea! The lamplight shone on the helmet of a policeman coming slowly along the embankment.

Lion-hearted, his great decision made, Mr Wilkinson took the plunge. He climbed quickly down, and went home.

'Lie Long to Me'

On the Friday of the following week the holidays commenced and Elsie left school for the last time. It was a festival day, with a blue heat over the sky and over the hay drying grass. The common burned with summer; love lay at ease in the grass, little boys played cricket in the long field, while the green paint blistered on the twopenny chairs. Roland and Elsie sat by the pond watching the children paddle.

'If we get married,' she said, 'would you want babies?'

He frowned. 'No, I don't think so. It would spoil a lot of fun, and it might kill you.'

'I'm strong. I don't see why we shouldn't have a boy and a girl.'

He changed the subject. He had not actually asked Elsie to marry him, but the assumption that this would happen had developed imperceptibly in the course of three days or so.

'Look at that aeroplane,' he said. 'Would you like to be up there?'

'Yes. I shouldn't be afraid. But I'll tell you what I'd rather do: I'd like to have two wings fastened on to my arms and a little engine on my back so that could fly all by myself, like a bird. I often dream about that.'

'Oh!' He pointed his finger into her face. 'If you could hear what the psychologists say about that!'

'You and your Freuds and people,' she muttered. The last time the subject of psychology had arisen he had told her a host of terrible things that she never wished to think about again.

He rolled over on to his back, lifting his face to the sun.

'You'll grill the skin off your nose like that,' she said.

'You mind your own business. It's my nose anyway.' He flung out his hand blindly and hit her breast.

'Stop that, lunatic. You hurt.'

'Poor little girl!' He sat up. 'Kiss it and make it well.' She allowed his lips to touch the place.

'Happy, Elsie?'

She looked up at the bewildering trees, crossed with gold above her head. 'So happy, darling. So happy.' Then she said: 'Will you be jealous of me when we're married?'

'You bet I will. If I see you looking at anybody else, I'll take off your clothes and thrash you.'

A joy caught her. 'I think I'd like that!'

'If I took your clothes off?'

'No, no, of course not.' Elsie blushed. 'If you thrashed me.'

'Would you?' He stared into her eyes. She felt she had said something very wrong.

'Not really, of course.'

'Yes, you would.' He held her gaze. 'Would you be jealous of me?'

She bit her lips. 'Terribly,' she whispered. Then, 'But you wouldn't make me, would you?'

'I don't know what I'd do if you didn't behave yourself,' he teased.

'No, you wouldn't.'

'Silly.' He turned round to see if anyone were watching them, and kissed her quickly. 'Of course not. And you wouldn't go with other men to make me angry, would you?'

'Never, never!' she said loudly, 'it would be a dirty, mean thing to do.'

'I'd thrash you, mind,' he murmured, watching her, cat-like, to see the effect of his words.

'Darling, darling,' she said, closing her eyes, offering her mouth to his.

'Sh, sh – someone's coming,' he whispered, pushing her away.

The someone was Mrs Cotton. She had been sitting on a deckchair across the field, knitting and enjoying the sunlight, when she had recognised Elsie, by her orange beret, as one of two figures sitting on the grass by the pond. Coming over to them to make sure, she had her first sight of Elsie's young man.

'Why, hullo, Mother!'

'Hullo, dear.'

Mrs Cotton smiled awkwardly down at Roland, thinking he looked nice, and a gentleman.

'This is Roland Dexter. Roly, this is my mother.'

'How do you do.'

Roland scrambled up a little late. 'How do you do.'

'Elsie's told me a lot about you,' Mrs Cotton said, determined to let him know that there was no deceit or hole-in-the-corner business where she was concerned. 'I've been wanting to meet you.'

Roland mumbled something.

Mrs Cotton thought how pretty his hair was, how nicely his clothes fitted. Elsie's sixteen now, she assured herself, and knowing a few boys won't hurt her if I see them as well. 'It's nearly four o'clock,' she said, 'perhaps your friend will come and have some tea with us.'

Roly flinched. He saw himself dragged to the altar, neatly thrown and trussed by a determined mother. 'Well, I don't know.'

'Please!' Elsie cried, delighted by the orthodoxy of this invitation.

'I'd like to,' he said, 'only I'm afraid I can't stop very long.'

They went home. Elsie was beautiful with the excitement of letting her lover into her own house.

'Do you mind tea in the kitchen? We always have it there on Saturdays.' Start as you mean to go on, was Mrs Cotton's motto.

'Mother!' Elsie protested, ashamed for her mother and herself.

'I'd like it,' Roly put in, 'we seldom bother to lay it in the front room at home.' This was untrue, but he had once read a story he admired very much, in which a duke had drunk out of a fingerbowl to set at ease an unfortunate guest who had made this mistake at a dinner party.

This made them all feel comfortable, and tea was a pleasant meal. Afterwards, Mrs Cotton thought that Roly would go, so she put off finishing her evening's shopping accordingly, but as he had made no move in this direction by six o'clock, she said, 'Will you two children be all right for half an hour if I pop out to get a few things I forgot this morning?' Though she doubted the propriety of leaving them, she felt that she might safely trust Elsie.

'Of course we shall! You go along and don't bother to hurry back for us.'

So Mrs Cotton was watched out of sight down the road, and when she had quite gone, the lovers turned from the window to kiss.

'Come and sit on the sofa,' Elsie suggested. 'Do you like my mother?'

'I think she's very nice. She makes one feel so easy.'

Happy at this praise, she gave him a kiss on his cheek. For a little while they found nothing to say to each other. It was all so strange and new, being in a room together with a sofa to sit on, instead of the grass or a green painted chair. At last he began to play with her face and her breasts, and to kiss her

107

hardly. Straining with love, praying for the power to please him, she kissed him as he liked to be kissed. They slid from an upright position until they nearly rolled off the couch on to the floor.

'Look at us, slipping and sliding about,' Roly said, laughing queerly. His voice sounded very loud. He lay down at full length and Elsie sat beside him, facing the foot of the sofa.

'Put your legs up.'

'No.'

He tugged at her knees, but she remained sitting stiffly at his side, knowing she should not do as he asked. He pulled down her head to his and kissed her so strongly that she was afraid.

'Darling, darling. Lie long to me. Please, you're not afraid, are you?'

'Of course not.' She wondered if all her instincts were at fault.

He put his arm round her legs and dragged her up to him. The excitement fretting in both of them was so great that they dared not draw their lips away from the latest kiss. With the love in her body richer than she could endure it, she pressed her knees to his: their toes, stretched out to the end of the couch, touched. They lay there for a minute, their hearts knocking together, their breathing quickened with joy and fear. Suddenly she drew herself away. 'Cigarette, darling, please.'

He sat up at her side, his head in his hands.

'Roly, dearest, we mustn't. You know that, don't you?'

Presently he gave her a cigarette and lit one for himself. He was sick and dizzy with want, angry at her and at himself. Elsie, cold as a stone, sickened in her own heart. At last the darkness lifted. They dared to look at each other, and very gently kissed.

'I love you, Elsie.'

'I love you, dear, more than anything else in the world.'

Then, until Mrs Cotton came back, they talked about love and how, when Roly made some money, they might one day get married.

'Why don't you two open some windows in here?' she asked in a cheerful voice. 'It's very stuffy, and you both look as red as beetroots.' She pulled down the sash. 'There! Elsie, look at this linen I've bought – only six-pence a yard. I thought it would do to cover those two sofa cushions. Isn't that cheap? Feel it.'

'Very,' Elsie said, fearing to raise her eyes.

'Yes, but isn't it? Clark's summer sale. I saw a dress-length for you, but I didn't like to get it before you'd seen it. Are you staying for supper, Roland? You don't mind me calling you Roland, do you? You young people are babies to me. I've got some ham in the house and I've brought in lettuce for salad. There's some trifle left, too. It isn't much, but it'll fill a gap.'

'I don't think I ought to,' Roly said, 'I promised father I wouldn't be late tonight.'

'It's nearly suppertime now. Come along: it won't take me two minutes to get the cloth on.'

Roly kept his word, leaving immediately after the meal. Elsie saw him to the gate. As it was dusk and he remembered vaguely that they had been more than usually happy, he kissed her.

'Goodnight, Roly darling. Darling, we must never – be like that again.'

He was angry with her for mentioning it, for she had made him ashamed. 'We'll talk of it some other time, shall we? Goodnight. See you tomorrow, I expect.'

When she was in the house again, she half wondered what she herself had meant. There had been a moment: it had been the greatest, most beautiful, most terrible moment since the world began, and now she could hardly remember it. It was rubbed away as completely as the coloured oil in a wet road when a lorry wheel goes through it.

'Now that,' said Mrs Cotton as Elsie came into the kitchen, 'is a nice boy. I don't mind you knowing boys like that. Nice manners and good looking. Good style. Has he any money of his own?'

'Not that I know of. I believe his father pays him an allowance.'

'He should be well in some day. Yes, dear, that's a nice friend for you to have.' Anxiously: 'He is nice, isn't he? Never tries any nonsense or anything, I mean – kisses you, or anything? Because you will be careful, won't you? I know I can trust my little girl, but she is only a little girl, you know.' With which warning, and an unwonted smoothing of Elsie's cheek, Mrs Cotton went into the scullery to do the washing-up.

Roly walked about the neighbourhood wondering why he had so many things to wonder about. Elsie was sweet to him now, sweet and silly, but none the less sweet. His body ached with longing, not only for her but for the easing of his love. The moon hung low in a hot sky. In the shadowed doorways the furtive lovers said goodnight. He was just thinking about going home to listen to the wireless for an hour or so when he met Mrs Maginnis, returning early from The Admiral Drake. Whether it was the effect of the slanted moonlight or not, he could not tell, but it struck him instantly that she was looking pale. Dressed with unusual quietude in a black coat and skirt, her row of golden curls neatly curled over her hat brim at the back, she looked no more than thirty. He stopped her and they talked for a while.

'Me pale? No, I don't think so. It's this wishy-washy light. Been with your girl?'

'Yes. I went to tea with her and met her mother.'

'Beware of mothers,' Mrs Maginnis wagged her finger at him. 'They're up to no good.'

'How's your chest?' he asked, and giggled suddenly at the slogan-like query.

'All right,' she answered, 'I thought I felt a pain there tonight, but I couldn't be certain.'

He walked down Lincoln Street to her door.

'Will you come in for a bit?'

'Thanks,' he said, 'I'd like to.'

Her room looked smaller and more comfortable than it had done by daylight.

'Have a drink?' she asked. 'I can't turn on the gramophone for you, I'm afraid: I smashed it on myself the other night. Tipped it right over on to my poor chest.'

'Hard luck,' he said. She produced a bottle and glasses from the cupboard.

'Like whisky, ducks? I haven't any beer in the house.'

'Thank you.'

She poured out two stiff drinks. 'I left The Admiral early. I got the pip, somehow, worrying a bit about myself, I suppose, and all that. Soda? Say when. There you are.'

'Thanks.'

'Maisie's getting married in a fortnight from now. They were all joking about it tonight and making a lot of row. I couldn't join in somehow. How's your girl? Oh, I asked that, didn't I? Here, knock that one back and have another. Like to hear what's on the wireless?' She turned it on. 'Weather and news. I don't want to hear that, do you? Let's try a foreign station. Here you are – dance music. Slushy stuff nowadays, isn't it? I like it rather, though. Makes me think of all the fun I had when I was a girl. Used to go to two or three dances a week. They were dances then, too. We used to have programme cards, with a blue or pink pencil attached, and there were so many men about that we had to book up some of the fellows for the extras, or two for the same dance and see who got there first. How's your dad? He used to be a fine dancer. I used to see him and your poor ma before they were married, at the Town Hall hops. They were the best looking couple for miles around here. Another drink? Go on, it won't hurt you. Just a little one. And one for you, Patty, my dear? Yes, thank you. What was I saying? Oh, dances. Yes. Do you dance much?'

'I went to one the other night with Elsie.'

'Did she look pretty?' Mrs Maginnis, taking off her hat, patted her hair into shape. 'What did she wear?'

'A blue frock. Yes, she looked all right.'

'I had a blue frock – *nattier* blue, which was fashionable then, with a crossover bodice and velvet roses at my waist. That was when I had a waist. The fellows said I looked as pretty as a picture in it: I don't know, of course, but I'd hate to contradict them.'

'I'll bet you did.'

Mrs Maginnis looked at him through the soft blur of the room. His face was in shadow as he lay back in her big armchair, but his body was long and beautiful and his hands finely made for touching fine things. The dance band on the wireless was playing a thick, slow tune that brought the tears to her eyes.

'I'm very old to you, aren't I?' she asked Roly.

'Not a bit of it. I think you're pretty now,' he dared to say. Mrs Maginnis dropped her heart into the last straining cadenza of the tune. 'Don't be silly.' She filled his glass automatically, adding with a touch of pride: 'But I don't have to peroxide my hair.'

'It's pretty hair.' Roly looked at her from the dark of his corner. The lines of her face were smoothed away by the lamplight and her eyes were blue. Her hand hung slackly over the arm of the chair. Roly, as she intended, took it. The moment she felt the touch of his fingers she knew she was old and stupid, wicked perhaps, but she did not draw her hand away. Roly drew his chair near to hers and closing his eyes, kissed her fearfully on her mouth. Mrs Maginnis raised her free hand to push him away, but it rested on his shoulder.

'Get away, young Roland,' she mumbled through the veil, 'don't act silly.'

'I'm not silly.'

The pomegranates on the wallpaper swelled and bloomed; the seeds burst, ready for the dropping. The golden light steamed up and down the walls and across the ceiling. Mrs Maginnis stretched out her arm to the wireless, with some strange idea of breaking the spell, but he stopped her, knowing only too well himself that the moment would cease with the music.

Mrs Maginnis, putting her hands through his hair, felt the flesh of her own lover. She allowed the familiar fingers to touch her till the consolation of his return was a pain between her eyes.

Roly was a boy no more. He kissed her gently as if she were so young that his love might frighten her. As he walked home to Lister Gardens, he was as quiet and peaceful as the growing skies. The roads were smooth and long. The hedges stirred in a slight wind. It was not until he had been in bed for half an hour that he became sick and afraid.

'Elsie, I'm so terribly sorry,' he wailed into the pillow, feeling himself lost. His misery enlarged with the dawning. I've got to go away somewhere, he thought, find a job a long way off. I daren't face that woman again, or Elsie. He got out of bed to examine his face in the mirror by the light of an electric torch, and found that his eyes had changed. He smoothed the lids with his fingernails, afraid that when the sunlight came everyone would know his secret. He stared at his eyes once more until they frightened him so much that he shut off the torch and crept back in bed to hide himself in the dark. Wild ideas took possession of him: he would get up now and go away, long before the house awoke. I have about two pounds in my pocket; that should last a few days while I got work. I could leave a note. This plan possessed him to such an extent that he sat up, shaking with eagerness. Then the dread of going out into the streets overwhelmed him. The curtains bagged out into the room, the furniture grew hideously large, blackguarding him back between the sheets. When he laid his head on the pillow he heard a dance band inside it, first tuning up, then playing a song that was at once strange and familiar to him. He turned over on his side to escape the music, but it streamed back into his head through the other ear. At last he fell into an unhappy sleep.

In the meantime, Town Councillor Dexter lay wakeful in his room. He had heard Roly's key in the lock, and, on looking at the clock, had found that it was the suggestive hour of two in the morning. He wondered if he should speak to the boy at breakfast, but decided, after a lot of worry, that he had better not. He sought comforting analogies in his own youth. I was pretty harmless at his age, he thought, though I wasn't more than twenty when I first stayed out all night. If he's going to go that way I hope he marries early. It will keep Mm steady. He looked with mixed feelings at the picture of his late wife that hung on the wall opposite the bed. Mrs Dexter had kept her husband rather too steady for twenty-three years.

Mrs Maginnis Parts Her
Hair a New Way

Mrs Maginnis was fond of her bath, so fond, in fact, that she bathed every day, which made her something of an oddity among the other dwellers in Lincoln Street. They knew of Mrs Maginnis's daily baths because she made a point of telling them, feeling that whatever censure they might cast on her inner cleanliness they should be under no delusions as to the salubrity of her externals. This morning, as she lay on the bathmat doing her exercises in a rather cramped manner, for there was none too much room, and she was apt to bark her shins on the door or on the wash hand basin if she were not careful, she thought how delightful was the cleansing of the body. The sun poured through the window on to her knees, still pink and steaming from the hot water. She stuffed a towel along the bottom of the door to keep out the draught, and enjoyed herself thoroughly.

Today is a new day, she thought. And nothing that's happened will ever happen again. Baby-snatching, you dirty old whore, you. Never mind, he's the last. You're going to be a good girl, one of those good girls Ma Godshill's always talking about. It's a fine day and a fine world, and you're going straight on where you left off when you were sixteen. Jesus loves me, this I know. Shut up, Pats, I won't have that. You be quiet and get up off the floor.

Secretly, even to herself, she was dreading the moment when she should have to haul herself up by the rim of the bath, because then her head would split across, just once, to show her that she couldn't drink all that much overnight and get away with it. However, succeeding in arising with as little pain as possible, she went into the sitting room to do her hair before the overmantel glass.

Poor old Roly. Aren't you sorry for him, old bag eyes?

For a moment her self-cruelty upset her. It was too much. She ought to be ashamed of herself, being so brutal to poor Patty. Then, lighting a cigarette, she blew the night away through the tube, and a thousand and one nights after it.

'When I was the girl on the scooter,
And you were the boy on the bike,'

she sang to herself, as she dressed. She was as gay as a pink balloon bobbing between two worlds. She had begun love and ended love with neatness and precision. Youth had kissed her in greeting, youth had kissed her in farewell. She wondered how the outgoing youth was feeling at that moment, and, genuinely a little sorry for what she had done, she slapped herself on the buttocks as if in deprecation of a girlish escapade. She made up her face very modestly. Easy, my good woman, your pranks are over. You're dead and buried, with a wreath from Ma Godshill gladly slung over the tombstone, but O, what a lovely corpse you'll be! There's life in the old girl yet, my dear, there's life in the old girl yet. She sang merrily as she combed her golden hair. She did not touch her breast.

Life is new, she said, and it's a sunny morning. In celebration of her rebirth, Mrs Maginnis did her hair in a different way, knowing that this, above all things, was the best method of changing new lamps for old, dead fires for penance candles. Not that she was penitent. She was just another Mrs Maginnis.

She made a point of seeking for Roly. She found him eventually, trying to hide from her behind a bookcase in the Public Library. 'Hullo!' she called to him. He flinched. There were smears of sleeplessness under his eyes.

'Hullo.'

'How's your dad?' she asked, winking a fine blue eye at him. Then, her good deed done, atonement made, and a silent contract given that the past was dead and buried beneath a whisky mist in the house in Lincoln Street, Mrs Maginnis went her way, carrying three books instead of one, for she knew that time would hang heavy with her now.

Roly had rushed into the library to escape from her. Seeing her from afar as she came down the street, he had run to the nearest shelter, forgetting that another, if a minor, evil lurked within.

When Mrs Maginnis had gone, he saw that the place was empty save for the girl and himself. She came from behind the counter and led him, without a word, into an alcove.

'I want to talk to you. Where have you been all this time?'

'All?'

'I haven't seen you for days. Not since we went to the pictures.' She fronted him squarely, a ginger cat arching her back.

'I've been awfully busy, Gwen, really I have.'

'You have all right, with that girl from Stanley Street.'

'Is there any reason why I shouldn't go about with her?' Roly demanded, his eyes on the doorway, hoping with all his heart that someone would come in to distract her attention.

'None,' she said. 'Of course, it's no business of mine what you do. But I'd like you to know this: I'm not cheap, and I don't like being pawed and kissed by a fellow who goes with other girls at the same time.'

'You're a one-man woman, I suppose?' he said, dashingly. She was not amused.

117

'Never mind what I am. I just want you to answer this: is it her, or me?'

'Oh, don't be silly. I hate scenes.'

This stung her. Her little green eyes filled with tears of rage and humiliation. 'You hate scenes, do you? Well, you'll just put up with this one.'

Roly edged away, feeling less dominant, less handsome, than he had ever felt before.

'It's easy enough for you to sneer about scenes,' she went on, a bead of red appearing on her nose, 'but you think you can do just as you like with girls, and it's time someone told you that you can't. You're a cad, a dirty cad, and I wish your smudgy-faced girl joy of you. I wouldn't mind if you'd thrown me over for anyone decent, but she hasn't anything attractive about her. She's got a blank where her face ought to be, and I thought it was sickening the way, at that dance, she eyed you up and down: "Aren't you beautiful, Roly darling! How can the girls resist you?" Well, I can.'

'I only went out with you once, after all,' he put in.

'But you kissed me and said you'd never met anyone like me before.'

Roly thought of an idea. 'Powder your nose,' he said.

She burst into tears. 'You dirty little swine!' she gulped, 'You're a conceited, slimy brute. I hate you.'

Roly was frightened. He tried to put his arms around her.

'Take your beastly, smelly hands away.'

'Gwenny, don't be such a fool! I was only teasing. Gwenny.' He gripped her arms tightly. 'Gwen. Look at me.' She fought him away, but he dared not let her go. Almighty God, if someone came in. He was almost crying with fright himself.

'Gwen, lift your head up.'

She looked at him, shivering with the force of her tears. After a minute she slackened in his arms.

'Roly, can't you see why I'm so rotten to you? Can't you see why I'm crying? I love you, darling. I don't muck around like the other girls. I love you. I'd die for you. I'd crawl to you.'

'Gwen, don't be a damn fool.'

'I love you. Kiss me. Please kiss me.'

Roly heard the grinding of the swing doors. Hurriedly he kissed her mouth. Her arms shot up round his neck. She clipped her small teeth into his lip.

'Get away, dear, do. There's someone coming. Take my handkerchief.'

They were hidden from view by the curtain drawn half-way across the alcove. She dried her cheeks, dabbing a little powder on to her ruined face.

She's like a white rat with a long tail, running around your feet and tripping you up, he thought.

'Roly, do you love me?'

'There's no time to talk about it now,' he answered, as he had answered Elsie in relation to another matter, 'I'll see you tonight.'

'Where?'

'By the bridge, this side of the river, at eight.' He started to move away, but she caught at his sleeve.

'I'm sorry. Will you ever forgive me?'

'Oh, of course,' he said desperately. 'There's nothing to forgive. Don't be damn silly.'

'Really forgiven Gwenny?'

He stared at her, thinking he had never seen anyone so ugly in his life. 'Yes, yes, yes. Goodbye for now. Tonight.'

He left her hurriedly. The impatient customer was dancing his books up and down on the counter.

'Sorry, I didn't see you,' the girl said, going to attend to him.

Roly went weakly down the steps. 'Oh, Christ,' he moaned to himself, 'Oh, my sweet Christ.'

119

That afternoon he went to the pictures by himself. For the first hour, as he sat in the dark, he worried himself sick. The complications that had arisen in such a short while around his life, made him feel quite ill. I should like to stay here forever, he thought, in a corner so quiet that no-one could find me by flashing a torch into my face.

But the feature film proved a tonic. It dealt with the adventures of a young man of many affairs, who, after frisking from woman to woman in the jolliest manner allowed by the censor, finally found peace in a most improbable farmhouse, where he was shriven from his sins by his love for a pure and beautiful girl. Roly liked this picture so much that he was tempted to sit the programme round again that he might follow the career of this fortunate fellow once more, but when five o'clock came he found that he was hungry.

This offence of his belly, that it should vulgarly clam-our for food when his soul was so shattered, annoyed Roly extremely. However, he was forced to pander to it, so he went into a teashop, and ate a hearty meal of kidneys on toast. After that he felt better. Now what shall I do? he thought. If I go into The Admiral I shall have to face that woman again, and somehow I can't bring myself to see Elsie. I've been to the pictures. I've read all the books in the world. It's too early for beer, and even if the pubs were open I shouldn't want it. Now what?

To his father's surprise, he was back in the house by six o'clock, with the intention of staying in for the entire evening.

'Dad,' he said suddenly, 'is there any sort of a job for me at the Town Hall?'

'Job? Good God!' Councillor Dexter was lacking in subtlety.

'Why "Good God"? I'm fed up with having an allowance doled out to me, and I can't hang around all my life. Do you think you could use your influence to beat up something for me?'

'I'll certainly have a try. Your figures are good, aren't they?'

'Very good.'

'You wouldn't be paid much as a start. You realise that, don't you?'

'I shouldn't mind. I must do something definite. I'm fed up.'

His father looked at him curiously. 'I'll do what I can, Roly. I'm glad you want to work, you know, because . . .'

Roly pushed the dog with his foot, swore at it when it yelped, and then banged out of the room.

Mrs Maginnis sat in her bedroom, trying to do the evening crossword. It was so quiet in the house that she longed for something to move, to make any sort of noise. To this end, as her dog was out on some mission of his own, she crept upstairs to the top floor and borrowed the lodger's cat but when she brought him into her own quarters he refused to settle down, crouching in a corner with his eyes, like motor-lamps, fixed on her face. 'Blackie, Blackie, wuzzoo booful cat!' she crooned, but he only hunched his back and stared just a little beyond her, until she had the uneasy feeling that something he could see but that she could not was standing behind her shoulder. So she opened the door and shooed the disturbing animal upstairs again. As the clock chimed eight, she stuffed her fingers in her ears, lest it should urge her to put on her hat and go to The Admiral as usual. You stay here, Patty. You've got your crossword to do, and that nice book to finish. Quiet, you, my girl. You don't want to traipse down there when there's stout in the cupboard. Who wants to go out, anyway? It's raining. Listen to it, on the windows. All wet out there, all warm in here. Now then, let's see; what shall we do first? The crossword. 'Lightly,' in seven letters. Blast. The clock's stopped. 'Dickory, dickory, dock, The mouse ran up the clock.' Now I don't know what the right time is. Tell you what, Patty, pop on your hat and slip down to the post office to peek at theirs.

She put on her outdoor things and went out into the streets, where the soft rain was threading through the lamplight. It was so pleasant in the sweet-smelling night air that she walked very slowly, although she had forgotten to bring an umbrella. She stopped to look at the florist's window, and thought how much she would like a white carnation with asparagus fern to pin in her coat. And why shouldn't I have it, thought Mrs Maginnis, today is a new day and a new beginning. What's sixpence, anyway, for a nice flower? It was ninepence, but she bought it. How bright the streets are tonight. I'd like to take five pounds and spend it all in Woolworth's, buy beads, and earrings, and records for the gramophone, and sweets and pads of paper. She came to the post office. Scarcely noting the time on the big clock that could be seen if you stood right on tiptoe at the kerb, she wandered on and on, until, surprisingly, she found herself outside The Admiral Drake. 'Well,' she said aloud, 'I don't know how I got here, but here I am, so I may as well go in.' She went in.

'You're late tonight,' said Maisie, knowing nothing of the strange things that had been in Mrs Maginnis's heart that day. 'I've got news for you. By the by, have one on me. Now then. We're getting married next month – the fifteenth.'

'Congrats! Registry Office?'

Maisie looked at her with contempt. 'I should say not. I shouldn't feel properly married that way. St. Peter's, we're going to.'

'White wedding?'

'Well, no.' Maisie looked down at her fingernails. 'It isn't as if I was a young girl, and Harry thinks it would be better to have quite a simple do.'

'Bung-ho, and good luck. What are you wearing, then?'

'Same to you. Oh, a nice three piece, I think – blue, with a touch of beige on the hat and yellow roses.'

'You'll look a one, you will. Where's Mr Wilkinson?'

'He's got a bit of a cold, so he's gone to bed early with whisky and a hot lemon.'

'Have you got a house yet?'

'No. We've another idea. I'm not keen on putting in someone here, not with father the way he is, so I thought it would be better if Mr Wilkinson and I stayed on together, and ran the place between us.'

Mrs Maginnis smelt a rat. 'I thought you were so keen on a place of your own.'

'Well, I'm not now,' Maisie snapped at her, 'and I have my reasons.'

'All right. I'm not nosey.' Mrs Maginnis, nettled at being kept out of the secret, moved away. She sat down in a corner, as far away from Teep as possible, and stared into space.

Someone came to her side. 'Well, Patty,' said her lover, 'How's things?'

She jumped. 'Oh, it's you, is it?'

'What's funny about that? Have a drink?'

'No, thanks.'

'What's the matter with you? Got a smell under your nose?'

'I'm not talking to you,' she said childishly, temporising while she collected herself.

'Don't be a fool. Go on, have a drink.'

'Since when have you been able to buy people drinks?'

'Made a bit today.'

'How?'

'Showing a little interest at last, aren't you?'

She got up. 'Well, I'm going *home*. I've no time to waste on you.'

'Sit down. Who's the flower for? Me? Been to your wedding? Who's the lucky man?'

She raised her hands as if she would beat him away from her. This is the moment for action, Patty, she told herself, you're not going to fail right at the very beginning, are you? You tell him where he gets off. Now's the time to do it, while you're in the mood that you don't care if he chokes. Now's the time, Patty, old girl. Now is the time for all good men to come to the aid of the party.

'I'm going,' she said, 'and as for your funniments, you know what to do with 'em, don't you? I'm sick of you and your scrounging. You go and take a running jump at yourself.'

She was conscious that the whole room watched them; the tongues rolled around the dry lips, eager for signs of her weakening.

'I'm going home.' Her voice was breaking.

'I shall go with you,' he said.

And he did.

Heigh-Ho, says Roly

Maisie was married on a Saturday afternoon, and the sun shone brightly upon her as she came out of the church. She would have been entirely happy but for one or two small annoyances; firstly, that she had been unable to obtain tea roses to carry with her up the aisle and had been fobbed off at the last minute with common pink ones; secondly, that she was going back to The Admiral and not to the home of her own that she had, in her mind, furnished so completely from attic to cellar. However, she was being questioned less and less by her friends regarding her reasons for taking Wilkinson into unofficial partnership, and she was, therefore, becoming more and more resigned to her loss. She gazed with pleasure on her husband, thinking how dignified he looked in his new grey suit. No grinning ape business about him, she thought, he appreciates a solemn occasion when he sees one. Among the crowd watching her as she came out of church, were Elsie and Ada Mary. The latter should, by rights, have been at work in the draper's, but she had contracted such a bad cold that even Mrs Godshill thought it advisable to keep her away. Neither was looking on because of any interest in Maisie; they were both passing St. Peter's at the time and both thought weddings very pretty things. But when I marry Roland, said Elsie to herself, I shall wear white, and carry white flowers.

After Maisie had been pushed into the car by, her friends and deluged with rice by Mr Teep, who had risen to the occasion unexpectedly, Elsie spoke to Ada Mary.

'I've got a job now,' she said, 'I'm going to be a clerk in the Town Hall.' Ada Mary smiled nervously at her. 'That's lovely for you; they treat their girls awfully well, I believe. When do you begin?'

'Monday. I'm starting at twenty-five shillings a week. I got it by answering an advertisement in the paper.'

Ada Mary was conscious of a slight stirring that she did not recognise as class hatred. She had been working for nearly three years, and her wages were only twenty-two and sixpence. 'You're lucky,' she managed to say.

'Are you going down the road?' Elsie asked her. 'I'll walk with you if you are.' She wanted to talk so badly, and Ada Mary seemed as good a listener as anyone.

'Yes, I've got a little shopping to do.'

'What a bad cold! How did you catch that?'

'I don't know. It's my glands or something.' Elsie wondered how she might introduce the subject nearest to her heart. 'That was the barmaid at The Admiral Drake being married, wasn't it? I thought she looked quite nice, but somehow I'd want to be a white bride, wouldn't you?'

Ada Mary answered so softly that Elsie could not hear what she said.

'When I get married, I should like a veil and a train. What do you think?'

'I don't want to get married. Ever. I'm happy as I am.' The fierceness in Ada Mary's voice was startling to hear.

'You'll fall in love some day and think quite differently.' Elsie spoke with the wisdom of a *hundred* years. 'I know I said the same thing myself before I met Roland. Do you know Roland Dexter?'

'No. How's your mother, Elsie? I met her one sports day, but I don't suppose she remembers me.'

'She's all right. She and Roland are great friends. It's so funny – I always thought she'd mind terribly if I brought a boy home, but she likes him. You know,' she lowered her voice, 'I think it would be wonderful if we could get engaged, but mother always says I'm too young. I don't know my own mind yet, she tells me. Of course I do! I know that there will never be anyone else but Roland for me, if I live till ninety. It's queer – one moment you're still at school, and the next, you're thinking about getting married. Of course, you won't breathe a word to a soul about anything I've told you, will you?' she added, hurriedly. 'It's all very secret, and of course nothing's official or decided, but it is such a relief to talk to someone. You won't tell?'

'No.'

'I must go back now,' Elsie said, thinking her companion very dull indeed. 'I'll see you again sometime, I expect. Mind you tell me when you go and fall in love. You will, all right.'

'Goodbye.' Ada Mary left her abruptly.

That's a funny girl. Some people who go in for religion think it's wrong to be in love. Or she may have had a disappointment or something. She wouldn't be really plain if only she looked better, but she's always so pale.

As Elsie walked down the path along the edge of the common, Roland ran up to her.

'I've news for you.'

'You startled me out of my skin. What is it? I've news for you, too. Let me tell mine first.'

'Go on, then.'

'I've got a job at twenty-five shillings a week, in the Town Hall!'

He stared at her blankly. Then he roared out laughing.

'What's the matter, darling?'

'Such a coincidence! So have I.'

'So have you what?'

'Got a job in the Town Hall! Dad got it for me, but I get three pounds, my good girl, not a miserable twenty-five bob!'

He kicked away a football that had gone astray from a match in progress on the cinder track.

'We'll be together then!' Elsie was delighted.

'Well,' he said, doubtfully, 'not exactly together, I don't expect. It's a big building, you know.'

'But it will be wonderful even to work in the same place with you. Let's go home and tell Mother right away. You'll stay to tea, won't you?'

'I'm afraid not,' he answered, 'I've got to help Dad with some business tonight, and I'm afraid I shan't be able to stop.'

'Business! Business!' Elsie was nettled. 'You're always making excuses to leave me for something or other. I believe you meet somebody else on the quiet.' Had she believed this, she would not have dared to mention it.

'Don't be a fool. You know that's not true.'

'Well,' she said, 'I ask you! I see you for three days running, and then you don't appear for another three. I don't understand you. Look at the time when you first came home to tea! I didn't see you for a week after that.'

'Oh, it was just that things cropped up, you know. You're always imagining something or other.'

'Don't use that tone to me.'

'Oh, what in God's name are you talking about?'

'And don't swear at me, either.'

'Listen,' he said, 'If you don't like my conversation I won't speak at all. Just say the word, and I'll take myself away.'

They walked on in silence. The leaves were yellowing: the earth was soft with leaves. He laughed suddenly. Pressing her arm, he drew her close to his side.

'Silly.'

She laughed at him, too, happy that their brief unhappiness was over. She was so warm to him that she was afraid the love was too strong in her face, so she hung her head once more, and said, 'Darling.'

'Love me?'

'Roland, dear.'

A silence. Then, 'You are coming to tea, aren't you?'

He stopped. They had wandered on to the wooded ground behind the cinder track, and no-one was there to see them. Kissing her briefly, he said, 'Honestly, my sweetheart, I can't. I've told you why. You must believe me.'

Desperately desiring to understand, she touched his hand to prove that she understood. So they left the common and walked back to her home together.

Her mother was out, so they were unable to tell her the great news. They did not go into the house, for Mrs Cotton was adamant on this one point – that they should not be indoors together when she was not there.

'You've got to take young blood into account,' she would say to Mrs Phillips, who was an excellent conversationalist provided she were not called upon to talk. 'One gets carried away when one's young, and it behoves a mother to be careful.'

'Have you got to go right now?' Elsie asked Roland, wistfully, 'Or shall we go for another short walk?'

He looked at his watch. 'No, if you don't mind, dear, I'd better be getting along. I'll see you tomorrow afternoon. Shall I call for you?'

'No, I'll meet you on the cinder track. I shall be there at three.'

'Goodbye, then.'

'Goodbye, darling.'

He left her. In the public library, the assistant was putting on her hat. She got off early on Saturdays.

'Where's your young man?' demanded Mrs Cotton, when she arrived home. She was fond of Roly.

'He couldn't stop. He's got to help his father with some business tonight.'

Mrs Cotton was suspicious. 'Oh, has he. Funny, isn't it?'

Elsie was too full of her news to be much perturbed. 'Why should it be? Mother, what do you think? Roly's got a job at the Town Hall, too! We'll be there together.'

'That's nice, if it doesn't take your mind off your work. You must go in for business seriously, dearie, now I've let you leave school early. When does he start, the same day as you?'

'I didn't think to ask him. I suppose so. Mother, do you ever feel as though life is so lovely that something must happen to upset it soon?'

Mrs Cotton was not in the mood. 'Bother him,' she said, 'I'd got seven crumpets for tea, and a box of tarts. Couldn't you have made him stop for just an hour?'

'He was awfully busy.'

'Oh, was he. Well, I wish he'd told you that yesterday. I've got enough food for a school treat here.'

After tea was over, Elsie felt there was nothing left in the world to do. She fidgeted round the house, reading a few pages of a book, playing spasmodically on the piano, until her mother was out of patience. 'For Heaven's sake, why don't you put on your things and go out for a walk? Why don't you call on Joan? You haven't seen much of her lately.'

Elsie had avoided Joan purposely. She was afraid that the subject of Roly might come up. 'No, I don't think I will. Oh, damn that boy.'

'Elsie, Elsie,' said Mrs Cotton, weakly. Her suggestion, however, proved to be a forecast. Joan dropped in for supper at eight o'clock, honey-bland pleased to see Elsie.

'You're quite a stranger,' she said, 'you haven't been near me since you left.'

'I've been so terribly busy job-hunting and whatnot. I've got work at last.'

'At last! From the way you talk, one would imagine you'd been fighting your way round the labour exchanges for years. Tell me all about it.'

Elsie told her. 'Isn't it good? And the best of it is that I shall be working with . . .' Her voice trailed away.

'Working with whom?'

'Did I say working with someone? I must have been dreaming, or thinking of something else. Supper time! Come on. Draw your chair up.'

'How's Roland?' Joan asked unexpectedly, just as they arrived at the cheese and coffee. Elsie's heart jumped. 'Oh, do you know him?' Mrs Cotton enquired, 'He's a nice boy, isn't he?'

'No, I don't really know him myself, but I heard people say they'd seen him about with Elsie.'

'I only met him quite recently.'

'And you never said a word about it? Isn't she horrible, Mrs Cotton, concealing all those exciting things from me?'

'I don't know that there's anything exciting about it. It's just nice for Elsie to have a boy as a friend, you know. There's nothing else in it, of course.'

'No, of course there isn't,' Elsie put in, rather hastily.

'Oh,' said Joan. 'But you're deep,' she went on, 'you might have told me that you'd met him. It was really me that introduced them, Mrs Cotton. I pointed him out to her, you know, because I thought he was rather taken with her.'

'Cheese, Joan? Have some more coffee; Mother's got a cupful left over on the stove.'

'No, thanks.'

'Are you quite sure?'

'Oh yes, thank you. Did he just come up and speak to you, Elsie?'

'She was introduced to him,' Mrs Cotton said, proudly, 'I shouldn't like her meeting boys casually, though I do try to move with the times.'

'Oh, was she. I see. How nice.' Joan kicked Elsie's ankle, under the table, to show that her discretion might be relied upon.

After the meal, when Mrs Cotton was clearing the table, Elsie suggested that it might be pleasant in her bedroom. The two girls went upstairs.

'I say, you are an oyster,' Joan exclaimed, 'after all, it was really through me that you noticed him at all.' Elsie made no answer.

'Never mind, I forgive you.' Taking a cigarette from her case, Joan smiled expansively. Elsie, emboldened by this delightful understanding, talked about Roland for a long time. 'He's a dear,' she said warmly, 'and I am really in love with him. We want to get married one day, only don't say anything about it, will you? It's terribly private.' Joan was silent. Then she said, 'Elsie.'

'What?'

'Oh, nothing.'

'Go on, tell me.'

'It's really nothing at all.'

'It must have been. What are you so red about? Do tell me, Joan. Whatever it is, I shan't mind.' Her heart beat in anticipation of what was to come.

'I can't.'

Elsie got up, and put her hands on her friend's shoulder.

'You've begun, so you must go on. Please. Hurry up! Can't you see you're worrying me? Joan, is it about Roland?'

'Well. Look here, we've been friends for a long time, haven't we?'

'Yes. Go on.'

'You know I wouldn't tell you anything if it weren't to help you, don't you?'

'Oh yes, yes. Do go on.'

'Well. Look here – No, I can't.'

Elsie was quiet. The room became intolerably hot. Joan made up her mind.

'Elsie: I may be sticking my nose in things that don't concern me, but you just ask your Roland about Gwenny.'

'Gwenny?' It was as though her heart had stopped.

'The girl in the public library. I've seen him about with her quite a lot, and I thought you ought to know. Or perhaps you do know. I say, you're not angry with me?'

'Angry? No.'

Elsie felt so sick that she would have run away had she not been ashamed of her weakness. 'No, I'm not angry. It was nice of you to tell me.'

I'd like to slap your fat face across so hard that it split. 'I expect he's got his reasons, anyway.'

'Oh, I expect so, darling. But I don't want to see you made a fool of, that's all. Remember – ask him about Gwenny. What's the matter? You're surely not going to cry?'

'Of course not. Don't be more of a damn fool than you can help.' Pause. 'I wonder what the time is?'

Joan, a little afraid of what she had done, though she had enjoyed herself at the time, took the hint. 'Time for me to go, I suppose.'

As she left the house, Joan said: 'I expect it's all right about your Roland. Don't you worry. Promise me you won't.'

Mrs Cotton, hearing an unnatural silence in the bedroom, went upstairs to investigate. There she found Elsie sprawled over the window seat, shaking with sobs.

'Why, my dear, my dear? What is it? Tell mother?'

Elsie lifted her head. Her mother was horrified at the sight of her red and swollen face, of the eyes, squeezed small by grief. 'Where's Joan? Has she gone? My dearie, surely she hasn't been saying anything to upset you?' She drew Elsie's head into her lap. 'Quiet. Quiet. Wait a minute – I'm going to give you some sal volatile.'

She mixed a hasty dose and gave it to the unresisting girl. 'Now tell me why you're crying.'

Too weak to protest, Elsie related all that had passed between herself and Joan. Mrs Cotton, terribly upset, torn between the desire to find and slay the traitor Roland and the desire to kick Joan to death, could at first find nothing to say. At last she dried Elsie's face with the corner of her apron, and unusually inspired, lit a cigarette and handed it to her.

'Don't you worry about what that piggy little beast says,' she advised, trying to put conviction into her voice. 'Just nasty jealousy, that's what's at the bottom of her tattling. I won't have my little girl made miserable like this. As for Roly, you haven't heard his side of it yet. For all you know, he may have been friends with this girl for years before he met you, and after all, you two aren't engaged or anything like that. You're still a baby and you shan't be fretted. Now be sensible, and stop crying. You'll see him tomorrow and then you can ask him frankly about this Gwenny girl. I'm quite sure he'll be able to explain everything, and you can tell that spiteful, fat Joan what you think of her.'

'She wanted to help me,' Elsie whispered. 'People only act for the best, really.'

'Oh, did she? Well, you just keep me away from her, that's all.'

On the morrow, when Sunday dinner was over and done with, Mrs Cotton lent Elsie her new silk scarf, saying: 'You go out and meet him, looking nice, as if you hadn't a care in the world. You're worth six of him, anyway.'

So Elsie went on to the common to find him. She stood watching the meetings for a time, waiting for him to come. Mrs Godshill was back on her rostrum, with Arthur and Ada Mary performing their usual offices. She had found an excellent method of controlling the former. Whenever he went, as she called it, 'on the drink', she had a collapse, and then blackmailed him, by the last rags of his filial piety, to stay at her side. Today she was leading the hymn with her customary vigour.

'Jesus loves me,' she bellowed. Elsie, weakened by her own unhappiness and by a very bad night, felt the tears stinging her eyelids. Jesus loved everybody in the world save herself. She dried her eyes, adding another layer of powder to her face.

Roland came up behind her and gripped her shoulders.

'How long have you been here?'

'Only a few minutes.'

'Well, shall we watch, or walk?'

'Let's walk. I want to talk to you.'

Elsie did not intend to defer the dreadful moment longer than possible. He caught sight of her face, and was disturbed. Now what? he thought.

'All right. We'll go and find a seat behind the tennis courts. What's up?'

'I'll tell you soon.' She fought to hide the trembling of her lips. They went down the long path in silence, dead to the painted racket of Sunday afternoon. The boys and girls, strolling hip to hip, passed by. The children, balancing on the rim of the drinking fountain, fought for the two iron cups.

Roland and Elsie found a quiet place between two wooded hillocks. 'Let's sit on the grass,' he said, 'it's quite dry. Come on, darling, out with the terrible news.'

'It's not news. It's something I've got to ask you.'

He turned cold, wondering how much she knew. Dear God, it musn't be that woman.

'Hurry up, then. Have you discovered that I'm keeping up two homes?' He blushed at his own bravado.

'Roland, what about Gwenny?'

It might have been worse.

'Gwenny? Oh, yes – her.'

'Someone told me you were going around with her. Is that who you hurried off to meet, last night?'

'Somebody's got a bloody nerve. She's the library girl. I've known her for ages; she's more like a sister than anything

135

else. Truly, darling, she is. I don't care a damn about her, but I have to see her sometimes.'

'Why didn't you tell me, then? Why didn't you?'

'I knew you'd misunderstand.'

'Is she in love with you?'

'Well, you see, I don't like to hurt her.'

'But you'd hurt me! Don't you see what a fool I've been looking to everybody? I think you're a cad. Does she think you're in love with her?'

'Oh, good God!' he said, 'Oh, Christ, are you the Spanish Inquisition? Oh, for crying out loud!'

'Don't use that language to me!'

'Well, don't be such a fool, then. Listen, darling,' he put his arm around her waist, 'I did see her last night, and I lied to you, but perhaps you'll forgive me when I'd tell you why. I saw her to tell her that I always regarded her – as a sister, as I said – and that I'd never feel about her in any other way, so we must never go around together any more.'

Now I've got to get rid of Gwen, or there will be trouble, good and proper. Still, sufficient unto the day, thought Roly.

'Did you tell her you were in love with someone else?'

'Well, not in so many words. You see, she was so worked up.'

'You've got to tell her, if ever you see her again. Will you?' Her cheeks were wet now. He kissed them. 'Of course, my darling. Happy now?'

'Almost. I can't be happy all at once. I've had such a shock.'

'Let's go home, shall we?' he asked her tenderly. 'I want to make you quite happy.' He smoothed her breasts to their tips, as if he were moulding a clay figure. Then he saw a common keeper, straddle-legged, regarding them with disfavour. 'Come on,' he said quickly, 'let's get back.'

As they passed the meetings on the return journey, Mrs Godshill was preaching on the love of God. Elsie, with Holy's arm locked through her own, cared not a whit for His love.

136

When they got back, they again found Mrs Cotton out. 'We'll go in, just the same,' Elsie said, daringly, 'she can't be very long.'

Again they sat on the sofa in the front room, and again they were bold enough to lie side by side, as if in a bed. When they heard Mrs Cotton's key in the lock they sat up, mute with love, and neither looked at the face of the other.

'How long have you been in, children?'

'Ten minutes.'

'Well, I suppose you want your tea. Come and help me get it, Elsie,' said Mrs Cotton, impatient for the news. When they were in the scullery, she shut the door and whispered: 'Well, what did he say?'

'It's all right. She's been chasing him around, as far as I can make out. He saw her last night to tell her there was nothing doing.'

'Oh, he was lying, then?'

'Only because he didn't want to worry me.'

Mrs Cotton, still unsatisfied, was forced to leave the matter as it stood, for Elsie, with shining eyes had rushed back to join him.

At teatime, Roly became quite brazen. He held Elsie's hand beneath the cloth in such a frank manner that Mrs Cotton's disapproval melted in the sweetness of the hour. He even drew the conversation round to marriage.

'I believe in marrying young,' he said, surprised at his own confession. 'What do you think?'

'There's young and young,' Mrs Cotton replied cautiously, 'Leave it too late – no, but I shouldn't like to think of my Elsie, for instance, going away for a long time yet.'

'She'll have to go some time.'

'Well,' Mrs Cotton was a trifle menacing, 'if and when she does, I hope the man treats her properly. If he doesn't, he'll have me to reckon with.'

Roly did not leave until eleven o'clock that night. He sat with Elsie in the drawing room, listening to dance music, showing her some new steps, and kissing the top of her head when Mrs Cotton was not looking.

'I love you,' he murmured, as she said goodnight to him at the door, 'Really believe in me now?'

'Of course,' she answered, her eyes blank with love.

So he went off up the road, enjoying the whiteness of the night, deferring the moment when he should have to puzzle out the problem of Gwenny.

Every Tub on Its Own Bottom

It was in the following spring that Elsie, hearing, through Mr Parsons, of Maisie's wedded felicity, began to regard marriage as a concrete affair instead of an agreeable mirage, or simply as a pleasant subject of conversation between Roly and herself.

One night she said to her mother, 'He's asked me to marry him.'

'My God,' said Mrs Cotton, startled into unaccustomed expletive by the suddenness of this news. Weakly she added: 'Don't be so silly. You're both too young to think about that yet awhile.'

'How old were you when you were married?'

'Seventeen; but then, we were quite old women at that age when I was a girl. You've only got to look at my early photos. Since when has Roland talked to you about this?'

The question worried Elsie a little. She had spoken of being engaged very often with Roly; they had even wrangled over the respective merits of church and registry office, but she could not recall whether he had actually proposed to her or not.

'Oh, quite a while ago.'

'Well, I don't want to hear anything more about it for some time.' Mrs Cotton tightened her upper lip to show that she meant business.

Elsie, silenced by the itch of love, dared not pursue the subject. She said goodnight to her mother and went upstairs, clasping her hot water bottle to her like a little girl hugging a doll. Bedtime was now a secret joy. Lying in the half darkness, the faint square of window before her eyes broken with stars, she conjured up pictures of her own between waking and sleeping. Sometimes she would imagine that she was having violent quarrels with Roland, all ending in the most beautiful reconciliations. Sometimes he would be the one to say 'forgive me,' at other times it would be herself. The loveliness of her humiliation would work in her mind until she dreaded the sleep that must tear these images from her. Sometimes he would insult her, and she would stare back at him, bravely angry, knowing that her defiance would only make their mutual surrender the more sweet. Sometimes she would strike him, gazing, afterwards, with fear into his dreadful eyes, but before he could grip her shoulders to force his kiss upon her lips, her thought would flow to small things, to the work to be done on the next day, and the letters to be written. She had one dream more beautiful, more terrible than any, and she drew it very seldom out of the dark. It was that she and Roland were being married. She would start very early in the day, passing through the last lovely awakening and the detailed journey through the hours, until she found herself on the threshold of fear. She had never dared to prolong the dream to its ending, for she was afraid of it.

For many months she had been happy. She saw Roly on Tuesday and Thursday evenings and all day Sunday. On Sunday he came to lunch and tea. She felt, subconsciously, that the best way to be happy in love was to ask no questions. I know he loves me, and so I never ask him this or that. If he tired of me, he'd tell me.

She had, however, a muffled terror of his pocket book, bulging with papers, zealously guarded, that he would slip back so secretly into his coat if it chanced to protrude. It angered her that she could find no small mysteries of her own with which to torment him. If only he weren't so sure of me, she thought, if only he weren't so sure.

Roly was happy too. He had managed to keep Elsie and the library girl successfully apart without hurting the feelings of either, which struck him as a course both honourable and politic. He had little affection for the latter, according her only one evening in ratio to Elsie's three, but he could not free himself from her. Also, she excited him a little. They quarrelled savagely whenever they met, parting with a bitterness that was never entirely conclusive. There were always explanations to be given, final decisions to be reached, and so the meetings went on. 'You still run after that girl,' she would say accusingly, knowing nothing but hoping he would think that she did, and always he would be able to allay her suspicions by the simple method of saying to her: 'Do you really mean that? Because if you feel you don't trust me, surely it would be better if we called everything off.' Then she would rush at him with thin, childish cries of contrition, laying her cheek to his, covertly loosening the neck of her dress that her flesh should move him.

Roly, despite all this, was getting a little tired of his complicated existence. Of Elsie he was genuinely fond. Though they worked together in the same building, they seldom saw each other, as their office hours did not coincide, and the rare delight of meeting her once in a while on the stairways, or in a corridor, made her doubly desirable to him.

Things might have gone on very pleasantly had not a night in early May exposed Roly's deception.

It was Wednesday night. The weather was warm for springtime, and the buds were bursting very early on the trees. Elsie had gone out for a walk across the common before bed. As she passed between the little hills, the teasing love in her body made the night lovely to her. The sky was full and starry. Elsie knew the Plough when she saw it; there was Charles's Wain, now, like a little wheelbarrow, cutting its way through a dark blue field. There was a cloud so strangely shaped that it looked like a man. The grass was damp with recent rains, and the lights along the path were doubled in the wet stone.

I wish I were not alone. If he were here, we could look up together; he could kiss me, and we could look up again.

She felt herself growing to the sky.

I am getting so old. I would like to have a baby soon, so that when he is seven or eight, people can say to me, 'Surely you're not the mother of a great boy like that?'

It was so simple to walk in the grass. It made life simple, and to be simple was to be happy. So Elsie was thinking, when she saw Roly sitting with the girl on the dark bench beneath the chestnut tree. She would not have seen him at all had it not been for the sweeping headlight from a passing car that had shown him to her. For a while she dared not move. She wondered what to do. She could not go up and speak to him. She was afraid to go home, with a long night and day to live through before the blessed agony of explanation could be faced.

Roly had been foolish that evening. As a rule he and the girl took a bus ride out to the Great Park where no-one was likely to see them. On this occasion, however, he had been so late in meeting her that there had been no time to go very far afield, and he had risked a walk on the common instead. It's a chance in a thousand, he thought, or even a chance in a million.

Elsie stood so still that she felt the years flying under her feet. She watched Roly and the girl. She could not see them very well, for fingered shadows were between her and the chestnut tree, but it seemed to her that the two of them touched and kissed.

She turned and ran for home. At first, a blind rage steadied her feet. I wish he were dead, with earth in his mouth.

Everyone knows about it but me. I'm the fool. I wish I were dead.

Only when she found she was crying did she realise her misery. Shaking as if she were sick, storming with tears, she went to her mother.

'Dearie, dearie, tell me. Are you ill?'

'Roly. I wish he were dead. I'd like to kick him to death, stick my heel in his filthy mouth. Mother, darling. Help me.'

'Stop crying, my little girl, Mother's here. She's with you. Tell me, quickly.'

Elsie set her teeth in the back of her hand. Our Father Who Art in Heaven, Hallowed be Thy Name. Gentle Jesus, meek and mild.

'Calm, my dearie, calm.'

'Yes.' Elsie sat back on her heels, gasping for breath. 'Yes, I'm calm now, very calm. I won't cry any more. I saw him on the common with that girl.'

'What girl, my dear?'

'From the library. He said he'd given her up. He hasn't.'

Mrs Cotton, dumb in the face of so much unhappiness, could only run a strand of Elsie's hair through her fingers.

'Never mind. He's young, and of course he doesn't know his own mind yet. Nor do you. There are lots of other men in the world. It has always been my dream to see my little girl nicely and safely married to someone really decent. You take my advice and show that young man of yours that you don't care a pin about him. That's the only way to make him toe the mark.'

There was silence between them for a long while. Then Mrs Cotton suggested that they might have a cup of tea.

'Tea,' Elsie mocked, resentful of such an intrusion into her misery, but she drank it gratefully.

Roly parted from the library girl that night with a joyful heart. She had told him the welcome news that her family were moving to Acton next month, and that she would have to find work in that area.

'You'll still meet me, though, won't you?' she pleaded, fiercely clawing at the lapels of his coat. 'I couldn't bear it if you forgot me.'

'Of course I will,' he answered, rash with tenderness, giddy with relief, and he clipped her to him until she cried out.

With this affair so neatly concluded, Roly went to meet Elsie on the following day with righteousness in his heart, and a new tie, worn as a gage of liberty, around his neck.

She had been waiting by the pond for a long time, and her greeting stupefied him.

'I'm not going to stop,' she said, 'I only came to tell you that I'm never going to see you again.'

He knew instantly what had happened. As he made no answer, she continued, 'I saw you last night with that girl.'

'If you'll listen to me,' he said, 'I can explain.'

'You'll listen to me first. I suspected it for a long time, and now I know. I'm going to forget all about you but – but I hope we may remain friends,' she added, suddenly desiring to compromise.

'How can we if you're not going to see me again?' he said, hoping to make her smile.

'Never mind that. You can go back to that red-haired thing and tell her I sent you. I thought you cared about me, once.'

'Darling, Elsie darling, I'm never going to see her again. She's leaving the neighbourhood.'

'You liar!' she cried to him, her fair round face ugly with grief. 'I believed you once before. You get back to her – beastly, man-chasing little thing that she is, and I hope you'll both be happy. I shall be better without you, too. I thought I loved you, but I'm sure now that I didn't. I always knew you were hiding something but I didn't let you know it, do you see? I knew. I was just waiting till you gave yourself away.'

'If that's how you feel,' he said, angry in his turn. He left her then, hurrying across the Parade, his shoulders hunched and his head down. He was expecting her hand on his arm at any moment. This time he would not give way to her easily. She should crawl on her knees before he'd forgive her. After all I've done for her, he thought vaguely, choking with his own nobility.

Elsie stood staring after him, the drivelling tears in the corners of her eyes. Digging her heels into the soft ground, she forced herself to stay where she was. She was so lonely that a physical cold settled upon her. She longed for the near-ness of his body, for his gripping knees and the locking of his mouth.

Our Father Who Art in Heaven.

When she got home, Mrs Cotton said, 'Well?'

'I sent him away.'

'And a good job too. What did he say?'

'He said she really was leaving the neighbourhood this time, but I wouldn't listen to him.'

Mrs Cotton said nothing.

'Mother, I was right, wasn't I? Say I was right. You don't think I should have given him another chance.'

'No, I don't. Certainly not. There's lots of time for you, and it will do him good. Anything we may do to men is only just payment for all they do to us. Tea?' she added diffidently.

Elsie cried into her cup.

'Don't you go to work tomorrow if you aren't feeling like it,' Mrs Cotton suggested anxiously, 'I can easily write a note and tell them that you've got bad neuralgia.'

'No, I don't think I will.' Elsie was dimly comforted. Her wretchedness, at least, was appreciated.

She went up to bed early and sat for some time looking into the mirror, to see if life had changed her very much. She was afraid to lie down, for tonight there would be no pictures to make her happy.

Roly arrived home in a very bad temper. He felt himself, for once, defeated. But she'll come round. She'll come. Just give her time. Then, for the first time, he thought, though he had spoken the words aloud very often, I love you, Elsie. He ate a hearty meal, thinking, the while, of the excellent answer he should write to the letter she would certainly send. 'There is no basis for love without trust. I want to see your faith in me in the future.' That was fine, that was gracious. It would be pleasant to write to Elsie, anyway. Though he had received a few notes from her on various occasions, he had been chary of answering them. But now he knew where he stood. 'Love,' he decided to add, 'is tried by suffering. We shall have our ups and downs, of course, but if you will have implicit trust in me we shall win through.' Roly had matriculated with honours in English.

Halfway through suppertime that evening the maid came in. 'May I have a word with you, Mr Roland?'

'Of course.' He sat back in his chair, quite the young master.

'It's your father. He came home early looking awfully white and queer. I asked him if there was anything wrong and he said, "No, it's nothing," but I thought I ought to tell you.'

'By all means,' Roly said, carefully. 'You're quite right, Annie. Where is he now. I didn't know he was in.'

'He's up in his bedroom. I asked him if I'd better get a doctor, and he said I wasn't to be silly. All the same, I thought you'd better hear about it.'

'I'll go and have a word with him. I expect it's his indigestion.'

The girl, her responsibilities transferred, went out.

Roly found his father lying on the bed, reading *Tristram Shandy*.

'What's up, Dad? Annie told me you weren't well when you came in.'

Councillor Dexter was annoyed. 'Damn nonsense. It's like her interference.'

'But you left work early.'

'I had a funny turn – a little pain, you know, but it soon wore off.'

'Oughtn't you to see Stoker?'

'Look here.' His father sat up, laying the book on a chair. 'I'm not quite a fool. When I want a doctor I'll get one myself. I can use the 'phone, can't I?'

Roly looked at him doubtfully. 'You look quite all right.'

'I am all right, so don't worry me. How's the job?'

'Not bad. I can't stick old Watts, though.'

'Nobody can, but he's a good man at his job.'

'I want some more money, too. When do I get a rise?'

'No rise in all the world,' said Councillor Dexter, groping for his pun.

Roly went downstairs in a worse temper than ever. He looked at the clock, calculating that there would be just time enough for him to go round to The Admiral. The lapse of time had healed his aversion towards meeting Mrs Maginnis. Suddenly he felt the need of her advice.

When he arrived he found her in the corner with Teep and her lover. When she saw Roly she arose, holding out her hand to him.

'Well, well, well; who's the little stranger?'

'I am, I suppose. How are you?'

'Never better. How's the girl? Have a drink.'

She walked over to the bar with him, where Maisie and Wilkinson were serving side by side.

Roly told her about Elsie. Mrs Maginnis, forgetful of her lover, nodded a bright head in solemn tribute to the sorrows of youth.

'Ah, well,' she pronounced at last, 'every tub on its own bottom. You let little Elsie go her ways for a bit, and you go yours. A change will do both of you good. And then, perhaps, a bit later on you'll patch things up. I told you what would happen if you went around with that little Smeller. Red-haired people always are strong, they say,' she added unnecessarily. 'Still, good luck to both you and Elsie, and when you do kiss her again, give her one for me.'

'Blow 'em all dead!' cried Teep, by way of recalling her to the group.

'Coming,' she said, picking out a daisy from a vase on the bar and waving it at him. 'Cheerio. Remember all I said.'

She walked back to the corner.

'How's married life?' Roly asked Maisie. She tossed her head at him, smiling secretly. 'You ask him.' Roly did not care to ask Wilkinson, who was looking more dour than usual, so he swallowed a second beer quickly and went home.

Mrs Maginnis, gazing after him, mourned for her dead. 'Who's he?' her lover enquired suspiciously, jealous, not for the withdrawal of her love but the withdrawal of her bounties. 'Town Councillor Dexter's boy. He's a nice lad, he is. Got a nice girl, too, but they've quarrelled. I remember how I used to row and row when I was young. Those were the good times.'

'I don't wonder you rowed,' he said, 'you'd get anyone's goat.'

'You ought to be ashamed of yourself, you ought.'

'What do you mean?'

'A kid like that. I'm twice his age.'

He turned away, calling her a name. Mrs Maginnis, with no-one left to talk to but Teep, who had a vast stock of new ideas for the government of the country, dreaded the coming night, when there should be quarrelling without sweetness, war without peace.

'Time, gentlemen,' said Maisie, conveying, by the tone of her voice, both raillery and regret. Wilkinson, tired and eager for his bed, clanked a row of empty glasses.

'Time, gentlemen,' echoed Mrs Maginnis to her lover, taking the lobe of his ear between her fingers. 'Come on.' He brushed her hand away. 'Don't muck me about. I'm coming.' He strode to the door, leaving her to follow in his wake.

He liked to stride a little in front of her whenever they walked down the road together, for this gave him a feeling of mastery. It was a constant annoyance to him that she would never give him the doorkey, for he had therefore to wait on the step while his lady, the guardian of the gate, stepped before him to permit his entry.

Ada Mary, who had been watching in the shadow of the house opposite for Mrs Maginnis's return, could have cried with disappointment. With the man there she would be unable to claim audience with her friend, and Ada Mary badly needed help. Not that she had anything specific to say, for no-one in the world could aid her, but the very act of saying nothing to Mrs Maginnis brought relief. She watched the house until a light appeared in the first floor window, and the man drew down the blind. Then she went back to Haig Crescent, where Mrs Godshill, who usually retired early, was waiting up for her.

'You've been out with a man,' Mrs Godshill said, positively.

Ada Mary made no reply. Going into the scullery, she stacked the supper plates and put on a kettle of water for the washing-up. Mrs Godshill followed her.

The girl went about her business as if unaware of her mother's presence.

'I said, you've been out with a man.' Ada Mary decided that it was no use saying no.

'Yes,' she said, 'Why not?'

Mrs Godshill found herself wondering why not.

'Careful of those dishes,' she temporised, 'and not so much slap bang.'

'Why not? The man, I mean.'

'Because it looks bad, and because I don't trust you further than I can see you. Avoid the very appearance of evil. Your brother's brought enough shame on me. Are you going to start?'

'Shame, shame, shame!' Ada Mary faced her. 'Is it wrong for a girl to know a man? Don't you ever think I might want to get married and settle down?'

'You're not the marrying type. You be content in the service of the Lord.' Mrs Godshill finished.

Ada Mary waited until she had gone. Then, satisfied that her mother was safely shut in the dining room, she crept to the foot of the stairs, calling, 'Arthur!' very softly.

He came out of his bedroom and beckoned her up to him. Sitting on the edge of the bed, Ada Mary gazed at her brother.

'You're looking so ill, dear.'

'I am ill. I'm not going to last so very long.' He came to her, running his fingers over her pinched profile, from forehead to chin.

'What are we going to do?'

'I don't know,' she said, looking round at the prisoning walls.

'Nor do I. Shall I light the gas?'

'No.'

She could see him clearly enough in the glow of a lamp from the street outside. He had developed a strange habit lately, of sitting with his eyes closed, as if he were too weary to look at things any more.

'Take down your hair.'

As she removed the pins, it fell in thin, light strands about her shoulders. He knotted his fingers in in it. 'Ada Mary do you think she's all right?'

'All right?'

'Sometimes I think she's going mad. She's terrible lately, always watching, watching, watching, watching you and me, watching herself. Dear, what shall we do?'

'I don't know,' she said, and still she did not tell him of her grief. 'There is nobody left in the world but you. Everyone in the street is dead and buried. You're the only living person,' he said. He loosened his hold of her hair, and ran his hands nervously up and down her shoulder blades. 'Are you alive, Ada Mary, or are you dead too?'

He frightened her. Drawing away from him she said: 'I must go down now. Mother thinks I'm doing the washing-up. Goodnight.'

'Goodnight, dear. Come back to me.'

'Goodnight.'

As she moved to the door, he saw the warmth in her, and still he did not understand.

Without troubling to undress, he lay down on the bed, drawing the eiderdown over his body. Below him the house rocked with noise, with the clattering of crockery and the banging voice of his mother. He heard Ada Mary cry out as if in anger. Mrs Godshill, retreating upstairs, shouted back at her, and a door on the landing slammed so violently that the hanging Christ on the mantelpiece fell down. Arthur arose and replaced it on the shelf, upside down. Then he crept back into bed, to shiver and shake with laughter at his wit.

In her own room Ada Mary walked up and down, praying to a God in whom she no longer believed. Something must happen, she thought, and very soon. Something will happen, because I am unhappy, and no-one has the right to be as unhappy as I am. Wait just a little while, Ada Mary.

'Wait just a little while,' John said to Leda, 'and things may straighten themselves out.' She rolled across the bed as if in pain, burying her face in her arms. 'It's the end of us,' she murmured. He did not hear her, for her voice was muffled in the sheets.

'We'll manage somehow,' he continued. 'If her damned action goes through undefended, in a nice, quiet manner, they may not even find out about you at school.'

She sat upright to stare at him as he sat by the gasfire in his pyjamas. 'Of course they will, you fool, and when they find out, I shall be sacked. Then who's going to keep us?'

'I think,' he said, 'that you're rather insulting to me, Leda. Haven't you any faith in my work?'

She was sick with her despair. 'If only she hadn't found out! How did she do it?'

'She's Argus-eyed,' he answered gloomily. Then he came to sit at her side. 'Tell you what, don't let's talk about it any more, shall we?' He jerked his head forward with a gesture she had once found lovely. He crossed his legs beneath him. 'I'll read to you for a bit. Would you like that?'

She made no answer. He dragged down a pile of manuscript from the bookcase. 'Here you are – I don't think you've heard this. I wrote it about a year ago, and it is really incomplete. It was intended to form the nucleus of a fairly long narrative poem called *The Second Day*.'

He read to her, and because he had a beautiful voice she forgot his poetry. After a while she became tired. John had been reading for twenty minutes before he discovered that she was asleep. Flinging the papers on to the floor, he crossed the room and clattered about the wash- stand that he might wake her. It's high time I moved on, he thought. The intellect of a weevil.

'Don't stop, darling,' she called, frightened out of her dream.

'It's all right. I'd nearly finished when you went to sleep. Always tell me if you don't want to hear my work, and believe me, I shan't be offended. I always hope that when I appear before the Judgment seat it will never be necessary for God Almighty to lean down and say: "J.R., you have committed the ultimate crime of being a bore."'

'I wasn't sleeping, darling, honestly. I just like to close my eyes when I listen.'

He turned out the fire, kicking the manuscript into the hearth.

'I think that poem is one of the best things you've done.'

'Don't worry, my dear, I'll never bore again. I often wonder whether Rhoda really enjoyed listening to me. She always said she did, but you've made me doubt it.'

Switching off the light, he got into bed. He lay extravagantly far from her, his nose almost touching the wall, his limbs drawn away from contact with her own, as if he feared contagion.

Holiday

'You're looking peaky,' said Mrs Cotton; 'are you feeling all right?'

Elsie thought for a moment. 'I suppose so. Yes, I'm well enough.'

'You don't look it, then. A whited sepulchre, that's what you are. You haven't been working too hard at the office?'

'No, I don't think so. Of course I haven't. Don't fuss. It drives me mad.'

'If that's how you feel,' Mrs Cotton said with decision, 'it's high time you had a change. You're nervy.' She pulled down the lower lid of Elsie's eye and examined it closely. 'I think you're a bit anaemic, too. You're not still worrying about that boy, are you, dearie?'

Elsie said, 'Be quiet, will you, Mother?'

'That settles it. Tomorrow, off you go to the doctor and we'll see if he won't give you a certificate, so that I can take you to the seaside for a week. Would you like that?'

Elsie nodded. 'I am tired,' she said. 'I haven't the energy to do anything, and I'm not sleeping well.' With a gesture rare in her, she turned to her mother for comfort. 'Do you know,' she said, after a minute had passed, 'I think it's not so much Roly I miss, it's someone to touch and kiss me.'

Mrs Cotton was shocked. 'Rubbish. You're far too young, as I've told you . . .'

'Yes, I know, you're always telling me.'

'Let me finish, if you please. You're far too young for that sort of thing.'

Elsie moved out of her arms to pace across the room and back again.

'You want a change of air. If you don't pull yourself together, my dearie, you'll lose all your looks and get those ugly hollows in your cheeks.'

'I can't be uglier than I am now.'

'What on earth do you mean? Who said you were ugly?'

'Do you remember when I was six, and could spell very well for my age, the day I went to Mrs Phillips's party? How I was playing with Kathleen and Mrs Phillips said to someone who was there, "Yes, she's a nice child" – referring to me – "but it's a pity she's so U-G-L-Y"?'

Mrs Cotton, remembering very well, burned with fury at the thought of it. She had never entirely forgiven Mrs Phillips for this lack of caution.

'Yes, I know, the old cat. But she only liked chocolate box children. As if you were ugly! I remember you coming home with me with your little face all worried and weepy, and saying: "It's not true, Mother, is it? I'm not ugly, am I?" You were always a most interesting child, and now you've grown up you've got all your father's good looks.'

'I do know,' Elsie said with a thin smile, 'because you've told me about it, that when you took me out in the pram strangers never looked in at me and and said: "Oh, what a pretty baby!" It was always: "Oh, what a quaint child!" Quaint. That's what I was. Quaint. Thank heavens I'm not like Joan, though. People are always saying: "What a bonny girl Joan is," and that means fat.'

'I'd like to see a bit of fat on those bones,' Mrs Cotton muttered, feeling for Elsie's ribs. 'Perhaps I ought to feed you up a bit. Could you drink a glass of hot milk at bedtimes, do you think? It would be so good for you.'

155

'I hate it. It's so silky.'

'You are a trial. How can I get you fit if you don't do anything to help yourself? Doctor for you tomorrow. We'll see what he has to say.'

He said that Elsie was suffering from anaemia and nervous debility. 'Yes, take her away for a week, if you can. There's nothing much wrong – a lot of girls are like that at her age – but a dose of sea air might freshen her up.' He readily gave her a certificate.

'I'm glad,' Elsie said as she walked home with her mother. 'I don't feel awfully well, really.'

'I know you don't; I can see that by your pale face and your twitchiness. Now, where shall we go? We can't venture far afield in such a short time. What about Brighton? It's very pleasant in the spring.'

'Anywhere. I don't mind.'

So they went to Brighton, to stay at a small private hotel where there was a balcony with striped sunblinds.

'Good home cooking,' said Mrs Cotton, at the first meal; so she settled down to an enjoyable week.

The morning after their arrival, she took Elsie for a walk along the front. The weather was bleak, even for early May, and the shelters were crowded with shivering people.

'Never mind the cold if you're wrapped up warmly,' Mrs Cotton said, 'this fine fresh air is doing you all the good in the world. Snuff it up, Elsie, as I do – one, two, three – Snuff!' They walked along, breathing in the air like wild animals scenting the approach of an enemy.

'I'm so cold,' Elsie gasped, finally, 'do let's go in and have a coffee somewhere.'

'Look here,' replied her mother, 'I brought you down here to get the sea into your lungs, not to fug indoors.'

'But aren't you cold? My nose feels as though it's going to drop off any minute.'

Mrs Cotton, herself chilled to the marrow, yielded after the minimum of decent reluctance. They found a café where there was a palm lounge and a small dancing floor. Elsie chose a chair by a radiator.

'Look at the bright sunshine outside, and us stuffing in here.'

'Look at the people in the street all dashing in out of the cold,' Elsie said sharply. Then they laid aside all sense of guilt and sat there until it was time to return for lunch.

'Let's come here for a tea-dance tomorrow,' Elsie suggested as they left. 'No tea-dance for you if it's fine,' Mrs Cotton asserted. 'We're going to walk all the way to Rottingdean along the cliffs.'

That evening Elsie stood by the window, looking out on to the promenade. The fading light was blue and transparent. The coloured sunblinds, dim in the gathering dusk, flapped at the coming of a light wind. The tide, laying a white ribbon along the beach, broke in troubled semitones over the pebbles as it washed to and fro, and the pier lights stretched out into nothingness, pointing the way to a mysterious dark wherein nothing lay hidden. I wish Roly were here. I'd like to walk with him, tonight, right along the front. There will never be anyone else for me.

It poured. They woke to the sound of drenching rain.

It must have been soaking down for hours, by the look of the pavements. Rain before seven,' her mother said, hopefully, 'clear before eleven.'

But it did not clear, so they went to the tea-dance. 'Are you going to buy a ticket for a partner?' Mrs Cotton asked.

'I don't think I dare. Suppose I don't dance well enough?'

'Don't be silly, it's their job. Think of all the fat old duchesses they have to hop around with. I think it's horrible to see an old lady like that one, with the velvet hat, trying to do the new steps.'

'There aren't any new steps nowadays. You just slide.'

'But that's just it; they don't slide,' Mrs Cotton remarked with unusual penetration, 'they bounce. You can tell they're used to the polka. Go on, dearie, buy your ticket from the girl at the desk and try to get that dark young man. He looks a good dancer.'

He was a very good dancer indeed, and he made Elsie extremely nervous. When she returned to her mother she said: 'I hated it, and it cost me a shilling! He wouldn't say a word the whole way round, except 'Yes,' and 'No,' till I felt like asking him for eightpence change. Wouldn't you think he'd be glad of someone young after all those old hags? I'm going to watch now. I don't want to try a professional again.'

As she sat over tea, she wondered if someone might not ask her to dance. There was a fair man having a solitary meal in a corner, and she thought that he would like to approach her if he were not shy. She mentioned this to Mrs Cotton, who said sagely, 'Well, I'll go along to the lavatory for a few minutes. Perhaps it's me he's frightened of.'

'No, don't leave me, Mother.'

'Don't be such a silly girl. I'm not going to spoil your chances.' Gathering up her coat and her bag, she went off before Elsie could stop her.

The music began again. Elsie lit a cigarette, trying to pretend that dancing did not interest her. Then she powdered her nose, using this as a pretext to focus the young man's face in her mirror. To her horror, she saw him rise and make his way over to her. Although this was what she had wanted, she had to fight an impulse to run for cover in the ladies' room before he could reach her. Now she could see before her his shoes, his stiff legs. At last she had to look up.

'Would you care to dance with me?' he said.

Not knowing how to answer him, feeling that 'Yes' was abrupt and 'I'd love to' was over eager, Elsie silently arose and laid her hand on his shoulder.

They danced well together. As he bent his head to hers she found he was much older than she had thought; there were delicate lines about his mouth, and his hair was tiredly yellow.

'I wanted to ask you before,' he said, 'but I didn't dare.' Again she found no words to say.

'Are you staying down here?'

'Only for a week.'

'What a short while! You ought to make it a month at least. I shall be here for a month. Are you fond of dancing?'

'I love it.'

'Is the lady you were sitting with your sister?'

The absurdity of this made Elsie laugh.

'No, my mother, of course; but I'll tell her what you said. She'll be so pleased.'

When the music stopped, he said: 'Might I come and sit at your table? I'd like to dance with you again, and I can't keep on popping back and forth across the room like a rabbit, can I?'

'No; please come if you want to. Look, there's Mother.'

'I'd better tell you my name if I'm going to be introduced to her,' he said easily, 'and ask you yours.'

'Mine's Elsie Cotton.'

'I like it. It's nice and fresh. Mine is Charles Leake, which isn't so nice. It makes you think of plumbers, doesn't it?' She laughed. They walked back to the amazed Mrs Cotton together.

He and Elsie danced several times before it was time to go. While they were waltzing together he said: 'Look here, I must see you again. I didn't like to mention it before your mother, though she's not a bit frightening, but will you have tea with me tomorrow?'

'I don't really know. It's nice of you.'

'Please, Elsie.'

'All right, I will.'

'I'll meet you by the clock at three, shall I?'

'I'll have to tell Mother.'

'Oh, of course! I was going to tell her myself only I just wanted to ask you privately.'

Mrs Cotton was not enthusiastic. 'Well, I don't know,' she said valiantly, wondering just how much this generation permitted, afraid that she was badly behind the times. 'She's very young. I hardly like . . .'

Elsie kicked her ankle.

'You know she'll be safe with me, don't you?' asked Mr Leake honourably. 'Why don't you come with us? That would be very nice.'

Mrs Cotton, relieved beyond all measure by this remark, said, 'no, she would not come herself, but that Elsie must be in by six. He saw them both back to the door of their hotel. As they went upstairs, Mrs Cotton's misgivings revived. 'I do hope I was right to allow you to meet that man again. You're only sixteen and I may be doing very wrong.'

'I can take care of myself, darling. Please don't worry. He's nice, isn't he?'

'He seems a gentleman,' her mother said doubtfully, 'but you can't always tell. He's years older than you. I don't think he's much under forty, as a matter of fact. Baby snatching, I call it.' Elsie was excited. 'Men are much better than boys,' she announced with the authority of vast experience.

'You're not to go far with him, mind, and you're to be right inside here by six, no matter how much fuss he makes. I must say he seems straight enough. That won't stop me from worrying until you get in.'

As Elsie dressed for dinner in her semi-evening frock, Mrs Cotton thought how much better she was looking already. I do hope he's all right. He seems decent. Surely Elsie can take care of herself.

In bed that night, Elsie woke her mother out of the first profound sleep to ask if she did not think Charles a lovely name.

'No,' said Mrs Cotton, resigning herself to mental distress for many hours to come. For a little while she had forgotten the worry that must attend tomorrow. She turned over, switching her plait into Elsie's face.

'I wish you'd have that horrid fungus cut off, Mother, it's not modern.'

'I don't want to be modern. You did know where you were when I was young. Go to sleep, will you?'

She had, as she anticipated, a bad night, but the morning sun reassured her. Elsie would come to no harm. Not only did Mrs Cotton discuss Mr Leake with some excitement at breakfast, but she even went to the length of taking her daughter into the town to buy her a new hat.

'You may as well look pretty,' she said. 'If this man helps you to put that Roly out of your mind, so much the better.'

'Roly,' said Elsie disparagingly. And to herself she added – Charles, Charles, Charles.

As she left the hotel Mrs Cotton sent a prayer after her departing figure. Then she retired to the lounge, although the day was fair, to fill in the hours somehow until the girl's return.

Elsie found him waiting for her in a large saloon car. 'Oh!' she said.

'I thought we might go for a drive as it's so fine.'

She was dubious and a little afraid. Joan had told her terrible stories about men in cars.

'Not too far.'

'Not too far, then,' he echoed. 'Hop in. You look very pretty. Where would you like to go?'

'Anywhere.'

As they drove off, her heart beat fast.

'How old are you?' he asked.

'Sixteen.'

He was surprised. 'I thought you were much older. Guess my age.'

She shrank from the attempt. 'I couldn't.'

'Try.'

'No.'

'All right. Prepare for a shock. I'm forty-one. That's much more than twice your age. Are you horrified?'

'Why should I be?'

'That's nice of you.'

He looked at her diffidently. Then he said: 'You are old for your years, you know. Are you experienced?'

'I don't understand.'

He saw her eyes. 'Never mind. We'll go up here, shall we, and look at all the counties jumbled up together?'

They admired the view from the windy hills, and had their tea above the Dyke. Afterwards he said: 'Shall we drive further on, or stay here for a while?'

'I don't mind. Please choose for me.'

'We'll drive on.'

He stopped the car in a lane. 'Tell me about yourself.'

'What shall I tell you? You tell me things.'

'I'm quite unexciting. I'm an estate agent and I live in Croydon. I've been under the weather lately, so they packed me off for a long change. Take your hat off.'

'Why?'

'I want to see you properly. That's better. Now I've told you everything about me. It's your turn.'

'I'm a clerk in a town hall, and I've been ill, too. Not very ill. Just anaemic.'

'Now, I wonder why that is? Elsie, have you ever been in love, or are you too little?'

'I have,' she said, staring straight out into the shadowed lane. 'I'm not now.'

'I'm glad.'

He put his arm round her, drawing her to him so gently that she was not startled. She pressed her cheek against his shoulder. Slipping his hand inside the collar of her coat, he laid it on her neck. He moved it a little lower. Still she did not stir, so he looked at her in surprise. When at last he kissed her, she neither refused his lips nor responded to them. At last, pressing her hand, he took his arms away. Without a word he started the car.

'We'd better be getting back, Elsie. We're late.'

'How late? Please hurry! Mother will be terribly worried.'

'Because she thinks I'm such a nasty bit of work, I suppose?'

'What's the time?'

'I shan't tell you, because you'll only fret if I do.'

He drove back to the town furiously. When at last he stopped the car outside her hotel he said, 'It's ten to seven. What is your mother going to say?'

Her eyes filled. 'She'll be sick with worry.'

'Well,' he said, 'I haven't been so dreadful after all, have I?'

'Of course you haven't. Thank you for everything.'

'Give me your home address. I may not be here after tomorrow.'

'You said you were staying for a month.'

'I had a letter this morning telling me that I might have to cut my holiday short. Are you sorry?'

'Very, very sorry.'

'Give me the address. I've got a good memory.' She told him, and he repeated it several times that he might not forget.

'Goodnight, Elsie; perhaps goodbye.'

'Goodbye,' she said inattentively, her eyes on the balcony window, from which she hoped her mother had witnessed their return.

He was gone almost before she realised it. Then she felt she had been unkind, that something had been done amiss. Roly? She enquired of herself. Charles?

She was barely inside the door when Mrs Cotton seized her. 'Elsie! How could you! If you only knew how I've been feeling! It was terrible. I thought of all sorts of things, where I could get hold of you, if the police could help. I think you're thoughtless, and cruel. You know what it cost me to let you go.'

'It was the car. We went out quite a long way and forgot about the time.'

They went into the deserted lounge. Mrs Cotton, lying back in a chair, closed her eyes.

'Mother.'

'Don't talk to me.' She had seen more frightfulness in that last hour than ever before in her life – Elsie, carried away to God knows where, to houses that never gave up their dead; Elsie raped by a sexual maniac, Elsie murdered by a homicidal maniac, Elsie, raped and murdered by a maniac both sexual and homicidal. Mrs Cotton had seen Elsie lying in a ditch, her clothes torn from her body and her throat cut. She had seen her in a lonely place, fighting with the last shreds of a dying strength.

All this she had seen, so she decided that, as a punishment for her daughter, she would not open her lips again that night. This intention, however, was defeated by her natural curiosity. In the middle of dinner she laid down her knife and fork, saying angrily: 'Well, aren't you going to tell me anything about it?'

'There's nothing much to tell. We went up to the Dyke, had tea, and then drove home.'

'That couldn't have taken you all those hours. What else?'

'We just talked.'

'I hope he behaved himself? No funny business?'

'Of course not.'

'Well, does he want to see you again? For Heaven's sake, be a bit more communicative. Isn't it sufficient that I've been nearly mad with worry, without you hiding things?'

'There's nothing to hide, really. No, I don't think I shall see him again. He's been called back to town.'

'So he says. Well, I shall sleep easier for that, anyway.'

Elsie made no comment. Mrs Cotton, taking a second look at her, said: 'Never mind, my dearie. No man called Leake could be much good, anyway. What would you like to do tomorrow?'

'He said I looked pretty.'

'There you are, then! What more do you want? Now perhaps you'll stop grousing about your face. Your father and I did our best for you, you know.'

Oh, Elsie, smile, won't you?

'We'll have to see how the weather is, Mother.'

'You must get some fresh air before we go home. I can't have you turning up at the office all washed out, just as you were before. Still, it has been cold and nasty.'

The weather was very bad during the rest of the week. Elsie and her mother spent the last four days running from shelter to café, from café to cinema. Mrs Cotton bought herself a new woolly to wear under her coat.

On the last day they went to the pictures. Afterwards Elsie suggested that they should have tea in the restaurant adjoining the cinema. 'We could watch the dancing for a bit.'

They had barely been seated for ten minutes before she saw the man, dancing with a tall woman.

'I don't like it much here, do you, Mother? Shall we go somewhere else before they take our order?'

She could not bear the idea that Mrs Cotton should see him and know her humiliation.

'I don't see anything wrong with the place. I think it's very pretty, with all these pink lamps along the walls. I shouldn't like to pay their electric light bills, would you?'

'I'm chilly.'

'Well, let's go and sit in the corner where we'll be screened by all those palms. You know, I'm thinking of buying a plant for the drawing room window at home. One of those small cactus things would look pretty, wouldn't it?'

'Yes, quite all right. Come on; we'll change our seats if you think it's warmer over there.'

They sat in the corner where they could neither see nor be seen. Mrs Cotton grumbled. 'What's the use of listening to the music and not being able to watch what's going on?'

'I was cold over there.'

'You're not sickening for a chill on top of everything, are you?'

'No; there was a draught, though.'

Elsie ate a poor tea. 'Go on, it's hours before you'll get anything else, dear,' Mrs Cotton advised her. Then she said, 'Your looks are improving, you know. You're getting more bridge to your nose. Now, if only you could coax a little colour into those cheeks . . .'

'Oh, don't harp, Mother; don't harp.'

'Well, it's for your own good.' Mrs Cotton parted the fronds of palm standing on their table, as if she were peering through a forest. 'Look, Elsie, look! There he is!'

'I saw him.'

'He's dancing with a woman, and they're coming round our way now. She's a bit old in the tooth, but then, so is he. I suppose he found you a bit young for him. Tyke!' Mrs Cotton added, in a tone that surprised Elsie a good deal.

They finished their tea in silence. Elsie's heart broke to the aching music. Roly, she said to herself, then, Charles, Charles, Charles.

'He took my address. Would he have done that if he hadn't wanted to see me again?'

'A blind,' her mother said, darkly. 'Oh, my dearie, what's the matter now?'

166

'I'm miserable.'

'What for? Heaven knows I'm doing my best to give you a good time.'

Elsie leaned across the table, her eyes pregnant with the coming revelation.

'I think I ought to be married. I want a man.'

'You're talking like one of *those women*, dear. I can't let you say things like that. Anyway, it sounds like the films.'

The girl said nothing. She crumbled a cake between her fingers.

'Waste. That cost me threepence.' Then, 'Do you know what I'm going to call you? "The Man Who Laughs," because you're the girl who doesn't. Would you like to go back?'

He passed by.

'Please. I've got a bit of a headache.'

They returned home on the Saturday. While they were in the train, Mrs Cotton said, tentatively, 'Do you feel you were a bit hasty with Roland, dear? Because if you do, I expect he'd be only too glad to make it up. If you're unhappy, why don't you write to him?'

'I couldn't do that.'

'Well, find some sort of excuse. Has he lent you any books? You could write to him asking if he'd call and fetch them.'

'He hasn't.'

'Do as you think best, then. It does seem silly, though, for you young things to quarrel just as if you were engaged or married.'

'Mother, sometimes I could hit you.'

Mrs Cotton took this literally. In consequence, she sulked for quite a long while, staring, without seeing anything, at the shifting countryside. It's funny, she thought, how one's children grow away from one. Elsie's starting to make an enemy of me. 'Sometimes I could hit you,' she said. That means that she thinks of me as a nuisance, instead of as a friend.

All those cows lying down in a field. Doesn't that mean rain or something? I should like a little house right out in the country where I could live with Elsie, but I suppose she wouldn't care about it. Those cottages there, now. They look absolutely isolated from the train, but of course they couldn't be, because the train sees them and forgets about itself, but they have to sleep all through the noise of the train and watch it rush by. She'd be bored though; always wanting to get back to town. She doesn't really like the country. Nothing of Will in her but the looks. He was the type who'd lean over a gate for hours chewing a straw and staring at nothing. Elsie's all me, as a matter of fact. I liked a bit of fun as a girl, but we didn't talk so loosely then. I didn't know half she knows when I went to Will; I thought he was being a beast. Perhaps our first year would have been happier if they'd told me more.

There's a spotted horse in a field. Oughtn't I to wish? That's what they call a lucky horse. Quick now – I wish for Elsie to make a good marriage to a man who will be kind to her. When you're young you wish for yourself, but when you get old you wish for other people. Wishbones, mince pies, cutting cards to fortune tellers, I always wish the same thing for her. It's too early to hope for results yet. If only I knew how much she knew. She said someone was a nancy boy the other day. I wonder if these young people know what the words they use mean, or whether they just parrot what they've heard. That's rather funny. I parrot, thou parrotest, he parrots.

'Ready for work, darling?' she asked aloud, suddenly eager to be friends. Elsie answered her vaguely.

'Oh, do listen when I talk to you! Are you ready for work on Monday, I said?'

'I expect I shall be, when the time comes.'

The view from the carriage window changed. Here and there a row of brick dwellings sprang into view, trimly gardened, 'Real Homes at Easy Terms.' Then the outskirts of the town straggled into sight, eyeless houses multiplying like trout, with washing napping on the lines. How ugly they are, Elsie thought, hundreds and hundreds of backs of houses, all exactly the same, and yet every one of them is there because someone loved somebody else. I suppose. But that's silly; I'm here because of that, and mother is, and the guard and the engine driver.

'Charles Dickens, Builder and Contractor.' She craned her head to see the sad name until the hoarding was lost from view.

They arrived home a little after six. 'How different the house looks when one's been away from it, even for a short time! All the rooms seem larger.'

'Letter for you here,' interrupted Mrs Cotton, who always inspected the mat the moment she entered the house, no matter what time it was. She never lost the habit of hoping that there would be something exceptionally exciting in the post.

'It's from Joan.' Elsie opened the envelope.

'She should write, she should, after the way she upset you. What's up with her?'

'Wait a minute. I haven't read it yet.'

'Nasty fat writing she's got. All round and stuffy, like she is. What is it? Anything important?'

'Roly's father's dead.'

'No.'

'He's dead. She heard it from the sister of a boy Roly knows.'

'What of it?'

'A heart attack, Joan says. Mother, what shall I do? I must write to him or see him, somehow. Poor, poor Roly!'

'Give me that letter.' Mrs Cotton read it carefully. 'There's a funny thing! Apparently he'd had two attacks before.

Nobody knew anything about the first, but Roly found out something the second time. The old man wouldn't see a doctor, so he just got carried off.'

'Mother, do you think I could write to Roly? What does one say? It seems awful to write consoling letters, but everyone does it. It must be dreadful to be reminded of a loss every time you open an envelope. If you ever die, Mother, I hope no-one will write to me.'

'I hope they do!' said Mrs Cotton vigorously. 'I'd hate to think I was forgotten before I was cold.'

Elsie sat down, throwing her hat on the floor.

'Poor, poor Roly. And I was so beastly to him.'

'Look here, you gave him what he was asking for, and it'll do him good in the future. I say, he ought to be well in, now; he'll have all the old man's money. I suppose it will be in trust for him till he comes of age.'

Presently she said, 'Perhaps you had better write him a little note, dearie. It would be sure to please him. Let's have something to eat now, and we'll think it out together.'

Elsie sat in the growing dark. 'I love,' she said, speaking the two words delicately. Knowing that when she was in bed she might draw her visions to her again, focusing them as clearly in her head as if they were painted scenes, she was happy.

At last I know. I love, and I am Elsie.

'O Saisons, O Châteaux!'

She wrote him a warm, brief letter to which he did not reply.

Now he is hurt, she thought, and how miserable he must be. Suddenly alone, and I myself deserting him. He needed me and I failed him. I wouldn't listen. Now he is so far away that I can't fetch him back, or maybe I can.

Tomorrow he'll write to me.

Elsie saw him in the darkness, his face to the wall. There was rank death in his room and no voice answered when he cried aloud in his sleep. Lonely, lonely.

'Mother, he must answer. He will.'

But he did not write.

So, after she had tarried for fourteen days in a wilderness of her own making, she went to see Joan.

'Have you heard anything of Roland?'

'I thought you were more likely to hear things than me.'

'We quarrelled, just before I went away. I wrote to him, but he hasn't answered.' She was afraid to look at Joan's face lest it triumph before her eyes. 'Haven't you heard how he is?'

'Well,' Joan said, happily prolonging her store of information, 'he's very cut up, I believe. His aunt is coming to live with him – that's his father's sister, not his mother's, and she's trustee for the money until he's twenty-one. Isn't he lucky? He'll be quite well off in a year from now; he was twenty last week.

'Oh, and there's more fun; a rumour is going round that Leda's living with that man – do you remember? The one we saw her with.'

'I don't care if she is. It's Roly I'm so worried about.'

'Did he chuck you or did you chuck him?'

'It was my fault. I didn't have faith in him.'

'Well, I told you,' Joan said mendaciously, 'that he was no good.'

'If only I'd trusted him! He was just a little weak, you see, and I thought it all so serious. As if I'm not as bad! When I was away . . .'

She told Joan about the man with the car. It was an interesting story, and Elsie, forgetting her sorrow in a momentary warmth of pride, made it more so. 'And now you see.'

'You are lucky. You ought to feel like a dog with two tails – a man that age, I mean. But it ought to have gone farther. It would have been awfully exciting to see what happened next. Elsie, if you were terribly keen on a man – would you?'

'I don't know. Sometimes I think I would.'

'But you'd feel dreadful afterwards, wouldn't you? I'll tell you what: if either of us ever – do that, let's not keep it a secret from each other.'

'I couldn't talk about it, if you could. Joan, it does so hurt to feel yourself growing up!'

'You needn't boast. I'm two months older than you are.'

'I'm not boasting.'

'I say, I'm leaving at the end of this term.'

'What about matric?'

'I'm not going to try. Go on, don't hide things. What did you and Roly row about? You know I won't let it go any further.'

Elsie told her. At the conclusion of this recital Joan said: 'Serve him right.'

'Never mind about that. I feel absolutely wicked. All this misery for him, and then me behaving like that. I shall write again.'

'You'll be a fool if you do.'

172

As Elsie left the house, she met Mr Parsons.

'Good evening, Elsie,' he said, 'Ma all right?'

'Yes, thank you.'

'You've been away, 'aven't you?'

'Yes. I wasn't very well.'

'You don't look it, either. 'Ave you tried 'ot milk every night before going to bed? That's 'ow I pull my wife together when she's queer.'

'No, but I'll remember what you say.'

'You know Ma Ditch, who 'as the pussy-butcher's? Well, she's been in a very bad way. 'Ad boils all over 'er neck. One of them got so sore she 'ad to pop a bottle over it and draw it out with steam. Awful mark it left, too. Minnie 'elped 'er do it and it nearly made 'er sick. Oh, I know what I was going to say: isn't it bad about old Mr Dexter? Good chap, 'e was. 'Ard luck on 'is boy.'

'Yes, it was a shock to everyone. Look, I musn't keep you standing about, Mr Parsons. Remember me to your wife. Goodnight.'

She returned comfortless, seeing in herself a greater sin than time could rub away.

And he was so fine: he wouldn't cheapen himself in my eyes by arguing. He trusted in my trust.

'He's been round here for you,' Mrs Cotton called to her as she went into the house, 'he couldn't wait now but he may be back later.'

Elsie stopped breathing and thinking. The world slowed up like a roundabout after the penny ride.

'Well, now are you happy?'

The world moved on.

'What did he say? Was he nice? Is he looking bad? Did he tell you what he wanted to see me for?'

'He looked quite ordinary. He's not in black, but he has got a diamond sewn on his sleeve. He was quite nice to me, said what a shock his father's death was to him, and asked if you were all right. Now look here, he may be back any minute, so if you don't want him to starve, you'd better pop round to the ham-and-beef shop for a few sausage rolls or something. They keep open late.'

'Quick, then, give me some money. No, don't bother to search for the housekeeping purse. I've got a couple of shillings in my own bag. If he calls before I get back, don't let him go! Tell him I'll only be a second. Do I look all right? Is my nose shiny? Where's my black hat, in case I meet him outside?'

'Go on, hurry up. You don't want your black hat. The one you have on is good enough.'

Elsie ran to Mornington Street, her heart bursting with expectancy. I won't give in too easily. He'll only think the less of me if I do. Roly likes strong people, people who don't cry. The first time I cried he was upset and unhappy; the second time he was annoyed. You can only cry at a man once.

I feel terribly sick. I wish I could go straight to bed without seeing him.

She found a crowd of people in the shop. Crazy with impatience, she shouted out her order.

'One at a time, lady,' said the assistant, firmly.

' 'Ow people shove!' a woman complained, fixing Elsie with her eyes. 'People should wait their turn.'

The road home seemed very long. She was held up by a line of traffic as she tried to cross Mornington Street; as she turned into her own road, a group of children impeded her by playing 'touch' around her, as if she were a tree. Breathless, bright-eyed, she ran into the house, slamming the hall door behind her.

'Is he here?'

'You'll have that door off the hinges, if you're not careful,'

Mrs Cotton complained, 'you can't play games with these old-fashioned houses. There's a crack in the step and a bad settling round the kitchen window as it is. No, he isn't. What have you brought?'

'A half of biscuits and four sausage rolls.'

'A quarter would have done. Where are the rolls? I don't see them.'

'They must be there. I thought he packed them in with the biscuits. Oh, damn, oh, damn; I must have left them on the counter!'

'What on earth are you playing at? You'd better run back and fetch them. Oh, there's the bell. You, can't go now. He'll have to put up with what there is, and if he doesn't like it, he can lump it. Shall I answer it, or will you?'

'I'll go.'

'Powder your nose then, quickly. Careful, you're like Joey the Clown now. Let me wipe some of it off. There he goes again. Impatient isn't he? Take him in the front room; there's a fire.'

Elsie opened the door to him.

'Hullo, Roly.'

'Hullo.'

She thought how tall he was. His head nearly touched the roof of the porch, and she could not see his face for shadows.

'Come along in. How are you?'

'Oh, I'm not so bad.' He sat down, taking out his cigarette case.

'Roly, I'm so terribly, terribly sorry.'

'Thanks. Have a cigarette. I haven't got a match, I'm afraid.'

'I have. Here.'

'Thank you. I got your letter. I meant to answer before, but things were in such a mess, what with the arrangements, you know, for the funeral, and getting Aunt Rose down, that I couldn't find a minute.'

They both looked into the fire, finding no words to say to each other. Mrs Cotton thrust her head in at the door.

'Roland, tea or coffee?'

'Oh, whatever you're having. Tea, I think. Don't go to any trouble.'

'It isn't. We always make it for ourselves just about now.' She went out.

'How are you, Elsie? I was sorry to hear you'd been ill.'

'I'm all right now. Darling—' Then she saw that his eyes were red with crying. 'I didn't know your father,' she went on, diffidently.

'He was OK. We got on all right, and it seems funny without him. He went very quickly. I don't think there was much pain. I don't really know, of course, because Annie found him, and she . . .'

'Don't talk about it, please, Roly, please.'

'I'll be all right in a tick,' he said.

The itch of love stole along her fingers. She locked them tightly together, hand to hand, lest she should reach out to touch his face.

'Can we just have the reading lamp, Elsie? This light's so strong. It tries my eyes.'

'Of course, dear. Is that better?'

'Much.'

'Roly, I'm sorry about last time we met. I didn't understand, then.'

'Oh, God, will you now?' he thought, remembering that two of the library girl's letters remained unanswered.

'Never mind about that. It's all right.'

'Really all right?' She looked at him, searching his face for comfort. I suppose it would be indecent for him to kiss me at a time like this.

176

'Yes, of course.' He put his arm around her shoulders, suddenly. I love you, Elsie darling. Darling Elsie, I do. Aloud he said: 'I've only got you now, you know.'

She was shaken by the headlong sweetness of the moment.

'And I'm always with you, darling. Never, never forget that.'

He kissed her, gently at first, as if he were exploring a new world. His lips roved over her mouth. She clung to him. Opening her eyes, she was terrified at the nearness of his own.

'Elsie, my Elsie.'

'Never, never leave me.'

'Never, dear.'

'You need me, don't you?'

'I do.'

Mrs Cotton, burdened with a heavy tray, knocked on the door that somebody might open it for her. Roly jumped up.

'Thank you. Pull the piano stool forward, Elsie, and we'll have it on that. Sugar, Roly? I forget.'

'No, thanks.'

'That's good. Never taking it ourselves, I always forget to bring the bowl for other people. Well, how are you feeling?'

'Not too bad.'

'Does your aunt look after you nicely?'

'Oh, quite. I don't like her much, though. I wanted Margaret, mother's sister, to come. She and I always got on well.'

Elsie drank down her tea quickly, hoping to set him an example. Go away, Mother, go away. Can't you see I want him to myself?

'You and Elsie friends now?' Mrs Cotton asked, tactlessly.

Roly pretended he did not understand her question. 'Friends? Oh yes, of course. Why not? We always are, aren't we?'

177

'A little bird,' said Mrs Cotton.

Mother, for God's sake shut your mouth.

'Roly, aren't you eating anything?'

'Yes. I'll have a biscuit, if I may. I'm not really hungry these days. I suppose it's the upset.'

'You've no idea how I was when Elsie's father died! I felt I simply couldn't swallow a thing for days. Luckily my sister was with me, and she insisted on me drinking a cup of beef tea, every two hours. You can imagine how hard it was for me, having to answer all sorts of callers, and do my bits and pieces around the house, with Elsie only a baby. I don't believe she hardly remembers her daddy.'

'Mother, will you, will you go away? I'll make you, I'll wish you away. The thought in my mind is going into yours. I'll push it in as though I'm driving a screw into a wall. In you go, in, in.'

'Elsie, what are you staring at me for? Have I got a smut on my face?'

'No, darling.'

'I thought there was something wrong with me! I'm sorry we weren't home for the funeral, Roly.'

'That's all right.'

'Of course, we didn't even know till we got back.'

'Of course not.'

'I suppose there were some beautiful flowers.'

'Yes, very.'

Now will you please go? I'm not willing you, I'm just begging you. Go. Go. I'll think of something else; if I keep thinking about her she'll stay. A watched pot never boils. Leda. They say she's living with a man. I never thought, somehow, that schoolmistresses could be in love. She seemed very old to me, when I was small, but now I know she's young, and that somebody is in love with her. I wonder if Leda loves as I love. I was once in love with her, and now that I am in love with a man myself I know that there is no difference at all between the two feelings, except that the first dies suddenly, in a second, and is all forgotten. Once Leda asked us to do an illustration to any Shakespeare play, and I drew Cleopatra in her golden barge. I remember that the barge was much too small for her, and Leda laughed and laughed. 'You might as well put her in a soup tureen,' she said. And I said, 'Well, look at the Venus in that picture you showed us, standing on the shell. She looked as though she were going to fall off at any minute.' 'But then, Botticelli is just a little better artist than you are, my child,' she said, and I said I didn't see that that was the point. She was quite angry, and I thought how beautiful she looked.

The sitting room door banged. Mrs Cotton had gone out with the tray.

Elsie looked at him. He looked back at her. Neither of them knew where to begin. Then he pulled her on to the sofa by his side and they came together.

'Love, love, love.'

'Elsie.'

'I can hear your heart. Is it wrong to love like this?'

'I don't know. I don't think so. How could it be, for you and me? We could never be wrong. Your hair smells so nice. I think it is fairer than it used to be. No, we're not wrong, though other people mightn't understand it.'

The stream of love rose to the fountain head.

They lay panting, neither of them knowing the other, strangers to all else but the uneasy joy in their own bodies. At last he said, 'Sit up.'

'It was like this before.'

'You were right then, only I didn't realise it. I want you all, darling, not only this little part of you. Elsie, when I'm twenty-one, will you marry me?'

'Yes.' They were quiet together. Then she laughed for joy, light awaking within her.

'Can we be engaged?'

He looked down at his feet, awkward, unhappy. 'I don't know.'

'Let's be. That is, if you want.'

'Of course I want, but—' He evaded her eyes. Then at last he hid behind the screen of his recent sorrow. 'I couldn't do anything definite just yet. You see, it's so near on father's . . .'

'Yes, I know.'

'You see, I'd have to ask permission and all that. We'd better wait until you're seventeen. Your mother would think you too young. People would talk.'

'Mother would understand, and I hate people.'

'For my sake, darling, wait.'

'I'll wait a hundred years.'

'Not a hundred, just one. And let's go on loving, just as we do now. We don't want people to know about us, do we? It's better, somehow, having it a secret between you and me.'

'We musn't love so much, though.'

'Oh, I don't know, dear. Why not? We can't get our happiness any other way, and I wouldn't ask you to – you know what I mean.'

'To sleep with you.'

He was startled. He looked at her. Her face was flushed and her eyes bold.

'Elsie, darling.'

'That's what you meant, isn't it?'

'Well, yes.'

'Surely we can be honest when we're together. I'm not a child any more.'

'A lot of people would say you were,' he murmured, frowning a little.

'As I said, I hate people. Roly, isn't that what you meant? That you'd like to sleep with me?'

'I suppose so. I'm sorry.'

'Don't be. Of course you want to! You couldn't love me if you didn't.'

'You know a lot, don't you?'

'I'm growing up,' she said, with a touch of dignity that instantly excited him.

'Elsie, you wouldn't – would you, darling?'

'Oh, no, I wouldn't,' she answered, 'but I'd like to.'

Her eyes dropped before the surprise in his own. Strange suspicions chased each other like grey moths through his mind. At last, understanding that her love was stronger than his own, he kissed her gravely.

'I love you.'

'And I love you.'

He left her at ten o'clock. 'Will you say goodbye to your mother for me? I've got to go now, because Rose frets about the place if I'm not in. I shall be damned glad to see the back of her and have the house to myself.'

'Would you be happy alone?'

'If I couldn't have you, of course, silly.'

Mrs Cotton, peering through the crack of the kitchen door, saw them kiss goodnight. Half pleased, half distressed, she wondered what she should say to Elsie. She had no chance, however, to say anything, for the girl went upstairs to the bathroom, and Mrs Cotton heard the click of the key in the lock. Too moony with love to talk, I suppose. Well, she might do a good sight worse than him. I only wish she hadn't been in such a hurry, though. I hoped I'd have her by me for a long while, yet. Mrs Roland Dexter. Elsie Dexter. Elsie Katherine Dexter. Here, there's lots of time for that. He may turn out a shifty little rotter. Watch and pray. That's all we mothers can do. Watch and pray.

'I'm in a jam,' Roly said to a friend, whom he met on the way home. 'I don't know what to do. There's a girl I'm very struck on; as a matter of fact, I want to marry her some day, but I've got myself into a mess with that little bitch who used to be in the library and I can't get out. It's women,' he said despondently, slouching against a lamppost, 'blast the lot of them.'

His friend, who was very young indeed, regarded him with admiration. 'You'll come to a bad end, old man, you will. You're a bloody Don Juan.'

'I was,' Roly admitted, bowing his head in recognition of a fearful past, 'but I'm through with all of it now.'

'Why can't you shunt the library girl? It seems to me that all you've got to do, now she's moved away, is to tear up her letters and hide from her. Try a long, black beard.'

'It's not so simple as that. You see,' Roly looked round to see that no-one was within earshot, 'you see, she was more to me than a friend.'

The other intimated that this news, though distressing, in no way surprised him.

'I never cared a damn about her really, but she was such a little dinger, and whenever I threatened to leave her, she started crying. It was on Wimbledon Common that it happened.' He stared into the evening, as though he saw frightening visions there. 'She was particularly up and doing that day – pleading, badgering – it was enough to finish any fellow. I suppose I was tired, or something, and didn't feel up to squashing her tricks, so I just gave her what she wanted.'

The friend, although he was young, had a card up his sleeve.

'Why worry?' he asked, casually, 'It isn't as if you were her one and only. I know half a dozen lads who've had her.'

Roly, to whom this was news of a staggering order, yawned as if suddenly tired of the whole discussion. 'Oh yes, I know that. But I felt, somehow, that it was up to me to help her, if I could. Still, you're right in a way. If I'd been the first it would have been different. Well, cheerio. I must push along.'

When he was round the corner of the street, he gave a stamp of joy. Lister Gardens was dark and quiet, so he jumped up at the trees to relieve his feelings. That's the end of you, my girl, that's the end of you. One, two, three, four, that's the end of you.

He thought he would go in and tell his father about it. Then he remembered that there was no-one to tell save Aunt Rose, who would neither appreciate nor sympathise.

The house was quiet, as if death still lay in an upper room. Frightened, he called: 'Rose! Rose!' She came hurrying out of the kitchen. 'Yes, what is it, Roly?'

'I thought you were out.'

'Of course not. You're late, aren't you?'

'I went round to see Mrs Cotton and Elsie.'

'Well, go and eat your supper. There are some mutton sandwiches on the table, and you'll find a bottle of beer in the cupboard, unless you'd rather have something hot.'

'Thanks. The beer will do splendidly. Don't you wait up for me.'

'I'm not going to. I'm very tired. I've been going through your father's papers tonight, and you wouldn't credit the stuff he's hoarded up all these years. There's a bundle of letters in the desk which you wrote to him while you were in hospital. Would you like to have them?'

'No, thanks. Just throw them away. Anything by the last post?'

What a funny boy he is, she thought, with some disapproval. You would have thought he wanted them. 'Yes, there's a letter for you on the table.'

He went into the kitchen. Propped up against a pile of sandwiches was a letter from the library girl. He glanced through it quickly. Then he frowned. She was a damn nuisance. 'I want to see you specially,' she wrote, 'it's important.' The word 'important' was three times underlined.

I suppose I'd better see her once more. He found, in the dresser drawer, an old picture postcard of Swansea. He scribbled on the back of it: 'All right. Meet you at the War Memorial on W. Common 7.30 tomorrow. Cheerio. R.' I'm not trekking out to Acton. She can just come up my way.

He sat down to his meal. He had just finished the beer when he thought aloud: 'Oh, my sweet Christ, it couldn't be that! No, it couldn't be.'

In Belvedere Row, John laid his head in Leda's lap,

'A child, my darling,' he murmured, 'as lovely as you are. Shall we make a poet of him?'

Never had news been more distasteful to him than this. But here – thought John – we are, and we must make the best of it.

She gazed over his head to the green-painted wall as if she expected to find writing there.

'I'd better resign at once,' she said, 'I'm finished. Even if your damned wife did drop her action, I should be done for. How are we going to live, John?'

'Trust me. Mary,' he added, gently.

'John, John, stop being so beautiful about the whole thing, and see if you can't think out a means of livelihood.'

'Be patient, Leda-Swan. Do be patient. My book will be out soon.'

'And my baby will be out first.'

'Don't, dear. Don't talk like that, please.'

'I've got a little money in the bank,' she said, 'about three hundred. I'd better leave the school immediately and go down to my sister's, though God knows she won't be sympathetic. You can follow in a few days when I've calmed her down, and we'll decide what to do. I suppose we'd better take a flat, somewhere, while the money lasts. And then ...' She was past crying. Now she could only sit in silence, waiting for her voice to return to her.

'We'll be all right,' he said. 'What about this house?'

'Luckily for me, the lease is up next month.'

He went to the desk. 'Shall I read to you? I've been working on a poem for the last week, and I think you'll like it. Shall I? Or are you too tired, Leda-Love?'

'Go ahead,' she answered. To herself she said: Everything will come right, Leda darling. Have faith. Perhaps something can be done. She listened to her lover's voice. At least the sound of it was sweet to her. But oh, if he were dead and my baby were dead! Then I could go on as I used, teaching children who loved me and were afraid of me, going out every morning without hope but without fear, coming in each night undesired, but unharmed.

> *'The ultimate nativity,*
> *The womb of Mary in the grave,'*

he read.

'John.'

'What is it? Listen, darling, I love you at all times save when you interrupt me. What is it?'

'Couldn't you read another poem? That one is so topical.'

'I'm going out,' he said.

'Where?'

'Walking. Anywhere. My nerves are on edge.'

'And where do you think mine are?'

'Darling,' he said, taking her hands, 'I know, I know. But after all, the main responsibility rests on me, doesn't it?'

'Good God. How?'

'I hope to make my way for three people now, instead of for myself alone. It isn't pleasant for me to feel that I might have to live on your savings. After all, I am a man.'

'Are you?' she said, wonderingly.

He picked up his hat and left her.

Leda knew that he would come back. He would leave the child cheerfully enough, but not the three hundred pounds. The room stank of him. His clothes were all over the bed, over the backs of the chairs. There was a bundle of his manuscript in the washbasin and another bundle stuffed behind the clock. What a price to pay for him. I would give the rag-and-bone man threepence to take him away. But I've got to keep him now, cleaving unto him for ever and for ever. John in the same grave with me, John hiding behind my back on the way to the Judgment Seat, John whining at me to find him the most comfortable quarters in Hell.

She forgot about him then, until, once more, she heard his key in the lock.

The Silver Nutmeg

Maisie, sitting in the window of her first floor drawing room, that lay directly over the bar of The Admiral, was pleased with the afternoon. Wilkinson slept on the sofa, his face covered by newspapers as if it were a parrot cage. The window boxes, satisfied with their minimum quota of rain and an unusual amount of sunshine, bloomed cheerfully. Maisie could see two ways, down Mornington Street and along the Parade. The row of shops owned by Mr Teep, whose grocering was but a sideline, was pretty in a coat of fresh paint. There was a new orange sign over the hairdresser's door, bearing the blue inscription, 'Perms From One Guinea.' The fruit shop had a new brass rail along the window, the café proudly displayed some new cretonne curtains.

'Nice to be alive, sometimes, isn't it?' said Maisie to a deaf Wilkinson.

The trees along the Parade were bright with uniform greenness, as if a child, disdaining matters of specie, had drawn the same brush over all of them. Beneath them, in deckchairs, sat the mothers and nursemaids, rocking perambulators to and fro.

'Things have turned out well for us, haven't they?' she asked. 'Just think how worried we were only last year, and here we are now, all comfy, with business bucking-up. It's nice to be Mrs Wilkinson, I can tell you. Married women get far more respect, don't you agree? Harry, don't you agree?'

She saw that he was sleeping.

'Oh, Harry, you're not much of a companion, are you?'

She frowned. Then, realising that this was but a small evil in a welter of good, she turned back, to watch the traffic sweeping round the corner. She went on talking, although she no longer expected an answer.

'I like the "Go" lights better than the "Stop." They're such a pretty colour. I wonder if I could wear a dress that shade, or whether it would be trying to my skin? My hair's got a touch of red in it, really. There's one of the children, coming home from school! Then it must be nearly four. Harry, Harry, wake up if you want your tea! It's all laid, and I've only got to boil the kettle.'

She admired her own modest face, reflected in the silver teatray which had been given to them as a wedding present by several customers of The Admiral. I wear well, you know, but then, we never did wrinkle much in our family.

'Harry!'

She noticed with displeasure that his face was covered with the sports page, and that certain names in the greyhound racing news were ringed with blue pencil. Now that has got to stop. I've paid his past debts, but I won't pay his future ones. She switched the paper away.

He arose suddenly out of a dark sea.

'What's the time? I was just having a nap.'

'I could see that. It's nearly four, young man, and time for tea.'

'Good.' He stretched himself until the muscles of his chest bulged out. Maisie admired him silently.

'I'm hungry. What have you got?'

'Salmon paste, watercress and the last bit of my seed cake. Harry, there's something I want to ask you.' Drawing her chair to his side, she sat in comical judgment upon him. 'Now look here, Prisoner-at-the-Bar, just why have you ringed those dogs?'

'Dogs? Dogs?' he asked innocently, opening his eyes very wide, as he always did when he was lying, or evading an issue.

'You know what I mean, all right. Are you betting again?'

'Me?' Had she not known him so well, she must have quailed before the reproach in his eyes.

'Yes, you. Now, Harry, be a good boy and don't do it. We may be making money, but we're not making that much. Promise me you won't.'

'Maisie, I gave you my word before.'

They played a short game of staring each other out. Maisie won.

'It was only one dog I was keen about,' he said. 'Harelip the Second. I haven't put any money on yet. I was just going to risk a couple of bob.'

'Well, don't,' she said, decisively. Getting up, she made the tea. He watched her glumly as she poured out, with her pretty, married grace.

'You'll be sorry if it wins, old girl.'

'I shall not. I shall only think to myself, 'Well, it might have lost,' so that's enough of your nonsense.'

He ate his meal in silence. Then he stole a look at her, to see that she was unusually grave. As she saw his eyes upon her, she smiled, putting her head right on one side, so that her pink chin creased into her face.

'We are happy, aren't we, Harry?'

He could not resist her.

'You bet we are. Would you like a new hat, by the way? Your brown one's looking a bit dished.'

She was amazed. 'Where did you get the money for new hats? Harry – dogs?'

'No,' he said, truthfully, 'I've got a bonus. Only five quid, it's true, but I've been saving it as a surprise for you. Pleased?'

'Pleased!' she exclaimed, delighted beyond measure that he should have some pocket money of his own, for she knew

189

how, despite the inadequacy of his salary, he hated to make demands upon her. 'I should say I am! But you don't want to go buying things for me.'

'Oh yes, I do. I like to see you looking smart, though you might not think it.'

'Oh, Harry!' she said, 'Oh, Harry!' He liked to hear her say his name, for she affected a charming hesitation over the 'r's.

She kissed him. 'I am happy. I love my snuffy old husband, too.'

'Here, what do you mean by snuffy?' he asked, pretending anger, 'I'll spank you if you say things like that!' As she danced away from him, he gave her a resounding slap on the bottom. 'You're no gentleman!' she cried. 'You ought to be ashamed of yourself, wife beating!'

They were having a lovely time, when the doorbell rang. 'Damn,' said Maisie. She ran down to answer it. 'Why,' Wilkinson heard her call, in a sweet, false voice, 'it's Mrs Maginnis!'

Actually, she liked the sun-haired lady considerably better since she had found out that her husband did not.

'Come on upstairs!'

Mrs Maginnis peered coyly round the door. 'Anyone at home? Oh, Mr Wilkinson, am I disturbing your tea?'

'No,' he mumbled, unsmilingly, 'we've just finished.'

Maisie offered Mrs Maginnis the best chair. 'Well, how are you? You look well. And how's George?'

'He's left me again, and for good, I think. Still, we can't have all of the luck all of the time, can we, ducks?'

'I'm sorry. Would you like a cup of tea? It hasn't been made long.'

'Thanks, I don't mind if I do. What pretty china! Wedding present?'

'From Parsons,' Wilkinson said.

'Nice of him, wasn't it?' Maisie was delighted by any praise of her household goods. 'He chose it so carefully, too, asked me what colour I'd like, and when I said a pink background, he went all over the place to find it for me. Look, there's the vase you gave us!'

'Oh yes!' Mrs Maginnis smiled.

'We always say that corner's just made for it, don't we, Harry?'

He muttered something.

Mrs Maginnis was gratified. 'I'm so glad you like it, Maise. Well now, tell me, do you really think I'm looking well?'

'Are you getting a bit stouter?' Wilkinson asked, wondering if this was expected of him.

She looked at him sadly. 'Oh, Mr W., you nasty man! Now I shall feel just dreadful.'

'He doesn't know what he's talking about,' Maisie put in. 'I think you've lost, if anything. You look very fit and your skin's lovely. I wish I had that nice healthy colour!'

'Between you and me, it's Box that does it, but we shouldn't say that in front of the men, should we? Giving away all our little secrets!'

Crossing her fine calves, she sent a naughty glance to Wilkinson. 'Well,' she resumed, 'I'm glad you think I'm looking OK. I thought I was a bit sallow. Seen anything of young Roland lately?'

'Very little; I think he's only been in twice since his dad died. Oh, and speaking of that, you've been deserting the old firm, Mrs Maginnis.'

'It's George,' she explained, 'I had such a lot of trouble with him before the final break came.'

Maisie was startled to see the change in her face. It was as though age and ill-health had swept across it in a single moment.

'Perhaps you are looking a bit tired.'

'No, I'm not tired, but I'll tell you what it is.' She looked significantly from Maisie to Wilkinson, who was staring at her, cow-like, disinterested, across the Moorish table.

'Don't mind him,' Maisie said, 'we never have any secrets. Unless, of course, you'd rather talk to me all alone.'

'I'm going,' Wilkinson announced. His paradise had been ruined anyway. 'I'll just go down to the bar and see that everything's all right.'

'I'm so sorry!' said Mrs Maginnis, 'I'm afraid I'm *de troppe*, or whatever they call it in France.'

'Not a bit of it,' he replied, with a glare. He went out, banging the door savagely to indicate that his resentment still persisted.

'Now.'

'Maisie, you remember me telling you about my chest, that little lump I found? Well, I'm almost sure it's bigger, and last night it began to hurt a bit, which it's never done before. I'm awfully worried, ducks, and I had to tell someone. I thought you might help.'

Maisie stood up. Laying her hands firmly on the other woman's shoulder, she gave her a little shake.

'Patty,' she said, forgetting the ceremony of years, 'You just listen to me. You go off to the doctor, quick quick, and see what he's got to say. You can't monkey about with these things.'

'No.' Mrs Maginnis was adamant. 'No, I won't go near those quacks, not if I die for it.'

'You'll die if you don't.' Maisie instantly wished the words unsaid.

'Yes, that's what I shall do, and God knows how bad it will be. But no-one can do anything, so I'm just going to pray. Ma Godshill once called me 'Godless woman,' at one of her twopenny meetings. Well, she wasn't quite right. This is just one occasion when I do damn well pray.'

Her face changed again. In a second she was as bright as a button. 'Maise, you're a dear, and it does me a lot of good just to talk to you. I'm glad you and Mr W. are so happy. Now tell me, I want to see a good show one night; could you and the husband come to the Empire with me?'

'Oh, see now, you should come with us.'

'No. I said it first. We'll have a little party, shall we? That is, if he won't mind. I don't think he likes me much.'

'Yes, he does,' Maisie answered, very heartily, 'We're both very fond of you. He calls you,' she said, improvising grandly, 'our Spot of Sunshine.'

Mrs Maginnis, not believing this for one instant, smiled politely. 'Well,' she went on, 'let's fix up, shall we? Second house on Tuesday night? Or – wait a bit – can you both be off together?'

'Dad might be able to put in an hour or two, and young Harry would help him. I don't know how The Admiral will like being left to Dad and the potboy, though. I think people like to see me and my Harry.'

'I'm sure they do. But we must have our fun all the same, musn't we? I want to see some pretty girls dancing; I like to see a leg as much as a man does, you know. Did I ever tell you that I was on the stage myself? Well, I was. I was in panto at the age of sixteen. I left at twenty, when I married Bert, or I might have made my name. Dance! I could high kick the cobwebs off the ceiling. I never had a proper part, of course, only a line here and there. Once when I was one of the attendants on the Prince in 'Cinderella', I had two whole lines to say. 'The mysterious Princess is here, O isn't she a pretty dear?' and when we took it on tour after the Lyceum run, I understudied Dandini. I haven't forgotten all my old steps, either. Take a look at this.'

Rising from her chair, she lifted her hand to shoulder level and kicked it up. Maisie watched the china.

Mrs Maginnis performed three more kicks in succession, two with the right leg and one with the left. Then she sat down again, breathless, triumphant. 'Well, not so old as I look, eh? Once upon a time I could do six kicks on each leg, without panting, too!'

'Hurrah!' said Maisie, relieved that the exhibition was at an end, 'That's the spirit.'

'I could do the double shuffle at one time. Let's see if I can remember it: Um-cha-cha-cha, UM-cha, Um-cha-cha-cha – that's it.'

Mrs Maginnis shuffled so gaily, with bumping of head and breast, that Mr Wilkinson came upstairs to see what all the noise was about.

'Having a game?' he enquired.

'Just trying to recapture my lost youth, dearie; showing your wife how I used to dance in my panto days.'

'We were making up a little party for the Empire on Tuesday night, Harry,' Maisie said, tentatively. 'You and I and Mrs Maginnis. Would you like that?'

'Who'd look after the bar?'

'Dad and young Harry.'

'You know your dad hasn't left his room for weeks.'

'Well, let the boy run it on his own. Come on, do let's go! I haven't been out at night for ever so long – not to the halls, in fact, since you and I – remember?'

The recollection melted him. 'All right, if you'd like it.'

'I'll be going now,' said Mrs Maginnis. '1 know you two don't get much time on your own. I shall see you again before Tuesday, I expect, Maisie, but if for any reason I don't, I'll call in here at half past eight.'

'That'll be fine. Goodbye, Mrs Maginnis, and good luck.'

'Good luck? Oh, I see. I'm all right, so don't you bother your head about me. I just got a bit nervy, that's all. Goodbye, Mr W., be a good boy.'

'Bung-ho,' said Wilkinson, glumly. Mrs Maginnis went off laughing to herself. The idea of Maisie's husband being anything but good was very funny indeed.

She had some shopping to do. That morning she had amazed the bank by drawing off the remainder of her small account.

'Leaving the neighbourhood?' enquired the clerk. 'No, just got a few bills to meet.' Reckoning that the bills must be disproportionate to her income, he wondered a great deal.

Mrs Maginnis bought two new dresses, a hat, a coat, and three pairs of shoes. We're going to have fun, my girl, she said to herself, and right away, too. We've enough to keep ourself in luxury for the rest of our days, now.

When she arrived at The Admiral on Tuesday night, she dazzled Maisie by the splendour of her attire. Wilkinson looked at her with more than customary disfavour. Now Maisie will be wanting things like that, and we just can't do it. Royal blue, indeed. She ought to be wearing black at her age. This was hard on Mrs Maginnis, who was not so old as all that.

'You look a treat,' Maisie said, eyeing enviously the lizard shoes and the grey hat. 'I wish I could wear a sailor like you can.'

'Is it all right? I think it's a bit 'chase-me-girls', really, but I like to show my hair at the back.'

'Spreading yourself, aren't you?' Wilkinson asked. 'Perhaps I'd better go upstairs and change into my dress suit. You'll be wanting us to walk behind you, now.'

'How he does go on!' said Mrs Maginnis, squeezing Maisie's arm. 'Well, I thought I might as well look smart in my old age.'

'You old!' Maisie cried. 'Why, they'll have to shoot you on Judgment Day.'

'No, I don't think, somehow, that I'll make old bones. Now then, boys and girls, are we ready?'

Maisie went first into the bar to give final instructions to the potman. 'All right,' she said, as she rejoined them, 'all set.

Come on, Harry, you're going to have a night out with the girls. A thorn among roses, isn't he, Mrs Maginnis?'

'Steady now, you'll make him blush. Oh look, it's raining.'

'Have to walk to the corner and get the tram,' Wilkinson said.

'Not me.' Mrs Maginnis hailed a taxi. 'Trams for a high-class party like us? I should say not. Hop in. This one is on me.'

'Oh, we can't do that!' Maisie was horrified.

'Here, whose 'do' is this, yours or mine? The Empire, and step on it,' she said importantly to the driver.

Wilkinson sat between them, anxiously watching the taxi meter. 'Come into money, haven't you?' he asked.

'Ah! I wouldn't tell you if I had. Afraid of getting my house burgled.'

The cab drew up at the theatre. Mrs Maginnis over-tipped the driver.

'Shall I get seats?' Wilkinson asked, feeling that something of the sort was expected of him.

'You can collect them, if you like,' she answered, 'They're booked in my name at the box office.'

'You think of everything!' admired Maisie. Suddenly she said: 'Well, just look at that!'

In the side turning, just in front of the stage door, Mrs Godshill was holding a meeting. Arthur was squeezing the damp keys of the harmonium. His mother was trying to lead six or seven unwilling bystanders in a hymn. Ada Mary, strange to tell, was trying equally hard to take a collection.

'That means,' Mrs Maginnis said, eyeing the group curiously, 'that they're on their uppers. Collections, indeed! I wonder what they're supposed to be collecting for? I suppose things are a bit tight, what with old Arthur out of a job and the girl always sick. Poor Ada! Doesn't she look queer?'

The rain was stringing through the lamplight. Mrs Godshill, yellow as a bone, wiped the water from her spectacles.

'Here, wait for me a mo'!' Mrs Maginnis ran forward to take Ada Mary's shoulder, just as the girl was about to rejoin her brother. She put ten shillings in silver into the red bag. 'Here, that's for you, so don't go giving it to any church funds.'

'Thank you very, very much!'

Mrs Godshill glared at them.

Mrs Maginnis nudged Maisie. 'Take a look at that girl, will you, and tell me if I'm seeing things,' she whispered.

Maisie looked. 'I don't see anything odd.'

'Oh, well, I expect it's just me.'

'A palace of pleasure can be a hall of vice,' shouted Mrs Godshill, originally. 'You who spend your money in a theatre or a picture house, to have your ears assaulted by filth and your eyes by fleshly spectacles.'

'Try an optician!' Mrs Maginnis called, unable to resist a joke.

'What do you know of the misery of thousands who 'ave no food to eat, no bed to lie on?'

'The trouble of it is,' whispered Mrs Maginnis to Maisie, 'that it's all so bloody true. But then, what good can our seat-money do to the starving thousands? The only way to help is to give donations to institutions who'll distribute it properly. It's no good helping the individual,' she added, to assuage a pang of remorse for all she was spending on herself.

Just then, Ada Mary fainted.

'Stand back! Give her some air!' Arthur cried, trying to lift her. Two men came forward and picked her up. 'Better take her in here,' one of them suggested, nodding towards The Rose and Crown, which stood on the opposite corner.

'She don't go into no pub!' Mrs Godshill shrieked, eyes ablaze, umbrella waving.

'Well, there's no chemist open, and this is the quickest.'

The men pushed her aside, butting her in the stomach with the limp body of Ada Mary, and carried their burden into the public house.

Wilkinson, who had been waiting in a queue, returned with the tickets. 'What are you two standing about in the drizzle for?'

Mrs Maginnis snatched her ticket. 'You two get along in. I want to see that that girl's all right.'

She disappeared into The Rose and Crown, and did not come to her seat in the dress circle until the first turn was nearly through, for which she was glad. She was depressed at the sight of a large and elderly lady, who should have retired to an armchair years ago, lifting, with one hand, a small and elderly husband, who, hanging head downwards in her grasp, shouted 'Yip!' and 'Vulla!' at intervals. Into Maisie's lap Mrs Maginnis thrust a large box of chocolates. Wilkinson stirred uneasily. The next turn was much better, consisting of songs, backchat and tap dancing from the famous Three Brothers Chick. 'Remember?' Maisie whispered, touching her husband's hand. The best act, however, came before the interval, when an old-time variety star sang all her greatest successes, inviting the audience, by a flicker of an eyelid or a gesture of the hand, to join her in the chorus.

Mrs Maginnis sang lustily. Maisie sang too, in a thin, embarrassed soprano. But Wilkinson gave them both a surprise, by sitting bolt upright in his seat and bumbling through every number in a resonant bass.

'Oh, she met me at the bottom of the Old Stone Steps
With 'er little Christmas Pudding in 'er 'and,
(Are you with me, boys?)
With 'er little Christmas Pudding in 'er 'and.'

During the intermission, Wilkinson, feeling he had relaxed far too thoroughly, strove to make up for it by buying drinks all round, and swallowing his own in a deathly silence.

'Isn't he a one?' said Mrs Maginnis, regretfully. 'I wish I had someone like that around the house to make me scream with laughter all day long.'

He glowered at her. The bell rang.

'Come on, let's get back,' said Maisie. 'We don't want to miss anything, do we? There's a sketch coming on now, too.'

After the vigour of the old star, things fell a little flat. Mrs Maginnis thought about Ada Mary. Maisie thought about Mrs Maginnis's new clothes. Wilkinson thought about Harelip the Second. However, they remained until the very end, sitting patiently through an exhibition of plate-catching by a group of Chinese jugglers.

'Funny,' Maisie said, after the National Anthem had been played, and they were fighting their way to the exit, 'It's almost a miracle, all that tossing and catching, with a whole dinner service at a time – and it was china, too, for one of the plates smashed – but we don't think anything of it, do we? It isn't as if we could do it ourselves.'

'Thanks for the evening,' said Wilkinson, remembering his manners.

'It was lovely,' Maisie cried, 'and very nice of you, too. Will you come into The Admiral with us, when we get back, and have just a drop of something in the back parlour?'

'Thanks,' Mrs Maginnis said, 'but I think I'd better be going straight home. I've got a wee bit of a head.'

She felt, all at once, very tired indeed. She would go to bed and read for a while, or perhaps think out something especially exciting for the next day, something that would make her forget such things as headaches and the treacherous nut in her breasts. There's not much time now. There are plenty of things I want to do before the balloon goes up.

She left them at the door of The Admiral. As she went into her own house, the clock on the mantelpiece was chiming twelve. 'You be quiet,' she said to it, 'Cinderella's home again. What fun we girls do have.'

She flung her hat and coat down on to a chair as if she could no longer bear the sight of them.

When at last she was in bed, with the candle blown out and the smell of tallow hot in the room, she took the spare pillow, against which no head rested, and brought it into the crook of her arm. With her face pressed against the cotton case she slept soundly, but for a long while after she had started to dream her lips were moving up and down the cloth, as if she were seeking vainly for a mouth in a face that was featureless.

The next morning Roly, who had stayed away from work on the pretext of a headache, called upon her.

'Little stranger!' she said, as she opened the door, 'Out of the everywhere, into here. Come in, and don't look at my dressing gown. You caught me on the hop.'

'How are you?' he said. 'How's the chest?'

'OK. Never felt better, and my little trouble has nearly gone. Now then, what have you come about?'

'Oh, nothing in particular.'

'Don't you tell me that. You've something on your mind and you want a bit of help. Is that it?'

She looked at him straightly, observing the worry in his face. What a kid it is still. All soft on the cheeks, and doesn't shave properly to prove it could grow a beard if it tried.

'More or less,' he answered, rubbing his hand up and down the deep indentation in his hair. 'I'm a bit in the cart.'

He told her how he had met the library girl the previous afternoon. 'She kicked up such a fuss. Said I couldn't possibly leave her after what I'd done, though I know damn well I wasn't the first.'

'Roly, she's not expecting?'

'Thank God, no, but I'm in a jam all the same.'

Mrs Maginnis, her blue eyes screwed up to nothing, thought the matter over. 'Now see here,' she said finally, 'the only advice I can give you isn't exciting, and you've probably thought of it yourself, but it's the only advice that is going to help you. What I say is: lie low. Don't answer letters and don't see her under any conditions. You'll find she'll let you go all right. If I know anything of her type, she won't want her people to get onto what she does in her spare time. Lie doggo, and you won't have any more trouble. Have a drink? It's early, but none the less welcome.'

'Thanks, I will. And I'll take your advice about Gwenny. If I could get properly shot of her I'd be as happy as a sand boy.'

'Another tip. I shouldn't be seen coming in here, if I were you. People know me of old, and they'll say things that aren't true, even though I'm old enough to be your mother. I am, you know. Nearly.'

'People always think the worst,' he said, indignantly, momentarily forgetful of the night when she had taken the first of his youth away. 'If you think it would be better for me not to call, I won't, but I shall miss you.'

'I do think so. Come on, drink it off. You look as if you needed it.'

'One thing more,' he said. 'Elsie. I'm thinking of marrying her next year. Shall I tell her?'

'About the girl? You'll be a damn fool if you do. She feels just the same way as you do about life now, but because she's a woman and isn't allowed to do anything about it, she'll break her heart if she hears your story. It isn't jealousy of another woman that makes a girl so upset when a fellow confesses an affair, Roly, it's envy that he can do what she can't.' She paused for a while. Then she said: 'If I go on as I'm going, I shall begin to feel like the lady who writes the "Advice to Lovers" corner in the weekly mags.'

'You're a help to me, honestly you are. Well, I think I'll be going. See you sometime.'

'Of course you will. I shall be in The Admiral most nights.'

'And I'm glad to hear about you feeling better.'

'Oh – that. Cheerio.'

'Cheerio.'

He left her. She moved hesitantly to and fro, as if there were something forgotten that she must do. She went into the bedroom to dress herself in her new clothes, and they gave her no pleasure.

Someone knocked at the door. When she opened it, Roly pushed a bunch of white narcissi into her hands, and went off down the street again before she could barely thank him.

She carried them indoors. The scent was so strong that her mind moved back twenty years, moved so swiftly that she cried out with the pain of it. Then she put the flowers in a vase, standing them in the window where the light could fall upon them. One of them fell out on to the floor. Mrs Maginnis ground it into the linoleum with her foot, as if she were setting her heel in the face of a dead enemy.

It was on the following Sunday, a wet, blowing day, that Ada Mary, after the meetings had dispersed, contrived to step unseen from the narrow stone jetty into the pond, to drown in no more than six feet of water. No-one had witnessed the tragedy, for the boys and girls who walked together on the cinder track had been driven into shelter by the violent rain. One man afterwards related in The Admiral that he had noticed someone standing out on the pier, but thinking nothing of this had passed on, without witnessing the suicide.

On hearing the news, brought to her as she sat talking to Maisie on Monday evening, Mrs Maginnis went very white, gripped the rungs of her chair, and, for a while, said nothing at all. She had been at the meetings on Sunday, laughing at a fine disturbance precipitated by the boys to annoy Mrs Godshill; she had spoken to Ada Mary, touched her hand.

At last she said: 'How did they find her?'

'Well,' Maisie whispered, lowering her voice that she might speak reverently of death, 'she didn't come home, and she didn't come home, and at first they just thought she was staying to supper with a friend, though they didn't know who she knew. Then, when half-past twelve came and still she wasn't in, Arthur went out and rang up the police. Mr Davies heard of the excitement – though perhaps I oughtn't to put it like that – and he told them he'd seen a girl who might have been Ada Mary standing out on the jetty just after that awful shower of rain. So off they all went to the pond, and there she was, with her poor face showing through the water and one of her legs caught somehow in the stonework under the pier.'

'Just like the girl in 'Amlet,' interrupted Ma Ditch, who had once been to a play.

Maisie leaned forward right across the bar, her feet off the ground, her mouth within an inch of Mrs Maginnis's ear.

'Listen, I don't want to mention it before all the others, but there's a queer sort of rumour going about.'

'You needn't tell me anything,' said Mrs Maginnis, her voice hard in the sympathetic silence of the room. 'Give me a double scotch, will you, Maisie?'

She drank it at a gulp, listening to the general conversation without hearing it. The red and green fairy lights above the bar flashed and darkened, swelled and shrank.

'Not much to look at, was she?'

'Nice, though. Best of the bunch.'

'One's almost sorry for Ma.'

'And Arthur.'

'She always looked as though she 'ated the 'ole 'oly business.'

Mrs Maginnis arose. Majestic in her grief, grandly unsteady, she pushed through her friends.

'Going, Patty?'

'No, she's not, are you, Pats? Come and have a knock at the skittles.'

'Goodnight all,' she said, loudly. They stared after her as she went.

'What's up with 'er?' asked Ma Ditch. 'Not upset about Ada Godshill, is she? There's a fine one, walking out on us like that.'

'She was very fond of Ada,' Maisie said, belligerently, 'wasn't she, Harry?'

He nodded. 'It's the shock.'

'Well,' Ma Ditch grumbled, being unappeased, 'fancy Mrs Maginnis with the 'Oly Rollers. Whatever are we coming to?'

'Perhaps it's 'er chest,' suggested Parsons, always sympathetic to illness. 'Do you think it's that?'

'Bosh,' Ma Ditch rejoined, 'People don't walk out that funny way because they've got a pain. They say, "Oo, something 'urts," or "Oo, I do feel queer," but they don't just walk out.'

'Bosh,' said Parsons, in his turn.

Mrs Maginnis, beating her hands to her side, wandered up and down the Parade. Coming close to the cinder track, she saw a crowd of people standing beneath the lamps that ringed the pond.

Ghouls. Ghouls. Ghouls. Aren't they sorry she isn't there for them to gape at? That's what they want, a nice, horrible corpse. Poor Ada Mary. I might have done something, but then, what could I do?

She saw the night sky as if it were the drowning waters into which the girl had stepped. A cloud that might have been a white face bloomed out of the dark. Even now a light rain was falling.

Peeking and prying. I can almost hear them. This is the stonework, here below, that she must have caught herself in.

She looked like this, she looked like that, when they dragged her out. Unsound mind. Yes, they'll say that at the inquest. Unsound be damned. She was as sane as I am. 'Thank you very, very much.' That's what she said when I gave her ten bob. And yesterday at the meeting, when I spoke to her, she said, 'No, there's nothing you can do,' and I said, 'You can come and see me if you need help.' That's what I said and that's what she said, and in she went. There were hundreds of people round about, and not one of them saw her jump.

Suddenly determined, Mrs Maginnis went over to the pond, pushing her way through the small crowd on the jetty. She walked to the end of it and looked down. Several people stared at her curiously.

Feeling she ought to say something, she mumbled a few words she had remembered out of nowhere.

'Holy Mary, Mother of God,' she prayed, 'Holy Mary, Mother of God.'

The coroner brought in the sympathetic verdict. The inquest was short, and very little was said. Nevertheless there was great rumour and considerable scandal, so, by the end of the week, there were 'To Let' boards at the gate of the house in Haig Crescent, and Mrs Godshill and Arthur had already moved away.

'We shall miss them, funny lot as they were,' Parsons said, meditatively. 'They were part of the neighbourhood, some'ow. It's as if we was a row of teeth with one black gap in it now.'

He was so pleased with this simile that he gave a purchaser of grapes two ounces overweight.

He Opens a Pocket-Book

She loved to walk as he walked, in step with him, straining to his side. When they came to the ditches she would hold his hand and leap with him, so that they both arrived on the right foot, ready to stride on without interruption. The sky shone through the leaves. On the hills there were silver birch trees, thin as the air; in the hollows were clumps of toadstools, smelling of an old, sweet decay, crushing softly beneath the shoe.

She was nearly as tall as himself, so that he need not bend down to speak to her. 'You're lovely and thin,' he said, 'You could hide behind the trunk of that tree and no-one would see you.'

'Don't you like me so?'

'I think you're beautiful.'

They came to the sandbanks. 'When I was little,' she said, 'I used to run down these as hard as I could go, and up the other side.'

'All right, let's run now.'

Putting their arms around each other's waists, they careered down the steep hill. He could run faster than she could, and dragged her with him till she panted for mercy. He pulled her up to the top of the slope opposite, and they kissed. Below them lay a stretch of wood, and beyond it the waters of the little lake where the waterfowl dived for fish. From tree to tree crept the little boys, bondsmen to civilisation during the week, bandits on Saturday. The weekend lovers could not be seen, for they had chosen the dark places to lie in, with leaves before them and above.

He took off her hat, to see the colours that the shifting sunlight made in her hair.

'I don't want to talk here,' she said, 'do you?'

'No.'

She stood closely at his side, feeling the rub of his shoulder to her own, the rub of his hip.

'If I kissed you again, do you think anyone could see?'

'I don't care if they do.'

'Nor do I.'

They turned to face each other, that they might touch.

'Well,' he said at last, 'I suppose we shouldn't do this on the top of a hill, should we?'

'It's only a little hill.'

'But hundreds of people that we can't see may be able to see us. Let's find a quiet place.'

Hand in hand, they searched for somewhere.

'This will do.'

'Oh, no, everyone could look in.'

'Well, this then.'

They sat down. 'No,' she complained, 'it's too bumpy, and there are children behind the tree. Look, there's a boy right up in the branches!'

So they searched on, trying this place and that. At last they found a patch of grass, screened by hawthorns on one side, and by three small hills, covered with bushes, on the others. It was fresh with recent rains, and smelt sweetly.

'It's damp,' she said, laying her palm to the earth.

'We'll sit on my mackintosh. Cigarette? Oh, look at me! I've only brought two.'

'I've got a full packet somewhere. Here you are.'

'Let's finish mine up, and then we'll go on to yours.'

They blew fine streams of smoke into the still air.

'I can blow rings. Look.'

She screwed her mouth up, and he kissed it. 'Idiot!' she said, choking.

'Why did we light these? I don't know, do you?'

'No.'

'I don't want to smoke. Let's throw them away.'

'Wasteful.'

'Shame on you, miser. I was paid yesterday.'

'Careful, Roly, stub it out properly or we'll start a bush fire.'

'In this damp, stupid? All right, if it pleases you.' He lay back, drawing up his knees. She rested her head on his shoulder.

'Look at that fat bird, darling, sitting right up there. He's been overfed. He'll burst.'

'Not he. They can eat their own weight.'

Presently he passed his hand over her face. She bit his finger as it touched her mouth.

'Savage!'

She bit harder.

'Let go, you animal!' He sat up. 'Now, look what you've done. I'm scarred for life. See all those teethmarks? They're yours.'

'I don't mind.'

'Well, you ought to. Kiss the place. Go on.'

'I shan't.'

'You will. Quickly now, or I'll punish you.'

'How?'

'Do you know what mother did to me once, when, as a little boy, I took a good chew at her hand? Well, she bit me back, really hard. That's what I'm going to do to you.'

He took a stranglehold of her throat. 'Now will you kiss it well?'

'No, no, no.'

'All right. Your doom is sealed.' He took her little finger and lifted it to his mouth, grinding his teeth ferociously as he did so. 'Now for a crunching of bones.'

'Please! Let me go.'

'Not on your life.'

He put it to his lips. Forcing another finger inside his mouth, she pulled at his tongue. 'Now who's top dog?'

He grunted, and she let him go.

'For that,' he said, calmly, 'you get spanked.' He dragged her across his knee and gave her several slaps. She lay still, her head hanging down, her hair brushing the grass.

'Dead? Surely not.'

'Yes,' she answered, 'I am, and I hope you're sorry.' He pulled her up again. She rested limply in his arms as if she were a rag doll. Stretching her on the ground, he gazed silently down upon her. She opened one eye.

'Would you care?'

'For what?'

'If I were?'

'Were what?'

'Dead.'

'Oh, but you are,' he said firmly, crossing her arms on her breast, 'and I'm going to bury you.' He sprinkled a handful of leaves lightly on her face.

'You beast!' She sat up, and they wrestled for a while, wordlessly, shaken with laughter. Then he pinned her arms with his own, and kissed her, while the trees spun round above them.

'Elsie, sweet.'

'I love you.'

'Is it nice to be dead?'

'Lovely. Like Heaven.'

'It would be, of course.' They rolled on to their backs, breathless.

'Sleeping?' he said.

'Almost. I'm exhausted.'

'Let's go to sleep.'

'Suppose we don't wake up again until it's dark, and all the stars are out?'

'Then we'll find our way home by matchlight. Shut eyes.'

They lay still for several minutes. Stealing a surreptitious glance at him, she saw that he was staring at her.

'Darling,' he said, putting his arms around her. The day stood on tiptoe. The faint halloos from the hills quietened. A bird cried as it swept the surface of the distant pond.

Slipping his hands under the ribbing at the waist of her sweater, he felt for her breasts.

'Sweet.'

'Roly, darling, darling. Kiss me.'

Her mouth was as fresh as the grass. She locked her lip over his. They lay together on the ground, lost in their love and want. At last she drew his hands away.

'Why?'

'No.'

'But why? Don't we love each other?'

'Just because.'

There was anger in his lips and in his fingers. Shutting her eyes, she felt his breath on her face. She looked up, to find that he was above her.

'Roly, no.'

He pressed her, his cheeks red, hot with his need of her. She forced him away with such sudden strength that he rolled down a slight slope into a hollow place. There he lay, turned away from her.

'Roly.'

'Where's that fag end?' He searched for it with his open hand, his face still averted. Finding it, he tore away the stub that was draggled with the grass, and relit it.

Wisely, she did not speak.

After a while, he said, 'Really, I don't see what's the use of us going on.'

'Why?' she asked, her voice trembling with fear.

'Well, you don't seem to care about me as I care for you.'

'Oh, you know, you know!'

'How can I know? You push me away.'

'I must,' she whispered, trying to force explanation into her voice, 'I must. Do you suppose I like to?'

'Seems like it.'

'Roly, look at me.'

'What for?'

'Just look.'

He sat up. His face terrified her. The eyes, red-rimmed, were stranger's eyes.

'Now, what do you want?'

'Roly, don't. You scare me.'

For answer, he held her down, leaning hardly on her shoulders. Earth and sky rushed to meet each other, shutting her out from reason.

Just as suddenly, he drew away.

'I'm sorry, Elsie. I'll never be like that again, never.'

She was so relieved that she started to cry.

'Please, darling, don't do that. I couldn't help it. I promise you it shall never happen again. I wouldn't hurt you for all the world. Oh, you do know that, don't you? Say you do.'

Seeing tears in his own eyes, she was ashamed. She kissed him gently. 'Let's forget it.'

The afternoon drew down into the evening. The sweeping of tree against cloud increased; the children went home.

'We'll be married as soon after my birthday as you like. I can't go on as we are.'

'Nor can I.'

'Elsie, I wrote you a letter last night, just before I went to bed. Was it silly of me? Just to tell you I did truly love you.'

'Silly? Oh, my dear, show me.'

'I can't.'

'Please.'

'Promise you won't laugh?'

He took out his pocket book. 'Here it is, darling. I'm an idiot, I know, but I do care, so very much.'

But she was staring at something else. 'Roly, I want to see that letter.'

He flushed. 'It's nothing.'

'Let me see it. It's from that girl.'

'Don't be so silly.'

'It is. I can see the signature.'

He made a quick decision. 'Elsie, my darling. Let me explain first, and then you shall read it. It's a very old letter.'

She snatched it from him. 'I want to see now. It's dated last week. She says "after what you've done." Tell me quickly, please. I can bear it.'

'I wanted to, dear. You see, when we had that row and you went away for your change at Brighton, I was terribly miserable. She asked me to go out with her again, and I did, once or twice. Do understand, she's not like you. She wanted me to – you know, and I was a fool and did.'

'Where.'

'Here. We came out one evening.'

'Go on.'

'Elsie, please try to forgive me. I wasn't her first, or anything like that. She just went with every man she met. I've told her it's all over now, and there's nothing doing, so I know she won't bother me again. Sweetheart, men do these things, you know. I couldn't help it. I was so wretched without you.'

'Don't dare to talk to me,' she said, 'It was here. Out here, where you've been loving me, you did that, that filthy, beastly thing, with her. Oh, God, what am I going to do?'

'Elsie, for Christ's sake, don't be like that. You do believe it's over, don't you?'

'Oh, I don't know what I believe. It's that you could, you could, after all you said to me, and then you bring me here. You dirty animal.'

'It's only what you and I, one day—'

'Don't mention you and me in the same breath with her! Damn you! Damn you!'

'Elsie.'

'I'm going. By myself. Don't try to follow. If you do, I'll hit you.'

The threat did not strike him as ludicrous.

'Please stay, and let's talk it over. I know I've been a fool, but try to see why. For all I knew, when I did it, there wasn't any you, nor would be, ever again.'

She ran away from him, ripping her way through the bushes, mad with anger and grief. The evening was sick and tawdry around her. I must get away from this horrible place.

Her flight so took him by surprise that it was several seconds before he followed her. He did not catch her up until she was on the hill beyond the lake.

'Elsie.'

'Go away. Can't you see I want to be alone? Take your hands off me.'

'No. No, I shan't. Listen to me. We're grown man and woman, aren't we? Well, we've got to face things. I've done wrong and I've hurt you. I'd rather have died than done it, if I'd only known, but it's over now, and there are years and years ahead in which I can make up for it. Darling, I'm not asking you to forgive me, but can't you just forget it? Listen. When I was a kid I thought I was a hell of a one with the girls. I used to run around with all the bits on the common, kiss them, and all that, and of course when I grew older it got more serious. It had to. Now that's all over; I love you, and only you, and you

213

say you don't want me. Darling, I was going out with her even when I knew you in the early days, because I thought I was so bloody clever to have two girls at the same time. Would I tell you all that if I were going on the same way? Please look at me.'

He was so pitiful in his unwonted humility that she stopped, to draw her hands over his eyes and his mouth, for she could not see his face in the growing dark.

'Roly, is it really all right now?'

'Really.'

'I believe you. We won't talk about it again.'

He shouted, with such joy that she was half-resentful, 'Oh, my love!'

'But if I do really forget it—'

'Sweetheart, you shall walk on my chest for ever more.'

'You can kiss me, if you like.'

'If I like! Oh, Elsie!'

They walked on, their arms about each other once more.

'Happy now?'

'Yes,' she said, but she was not. It would be a long time before she was really happy again, and before her trust returned to her.

They had tea at a café by the bus stop. The fact of walking suddenly into bright light, into the noise of talking and the rattling of cups and saucers, restored her a little.

He said: 'Look here, we'll ask your mother, when we get home, if she won't let us be engaged, and then I'll ask Aunt Rose, though I don't see how she can stop me, damn her.'

'We really will?'

'Really. And then you can be quite sure of me, for ever and ever.'

They found Mrs Cotton utterly unprepared for shocks. She was sitting in the window seat, darning stockings, with the sash right down that she might smell the air of spring. 'Hullo, you two.'

Elsie kissed her.

'What's all this? What have you been doing wrong, dearie?'

'Nothing. Tell her, Roly.'

'Then it is something.' She put down a stocking, and braced herself.

'Mrs Cotton, there's something I want to ask you, and I may as well do it now.'

She smiled at him fondly. Roly, the renegade, the prodigal, was nevertheless dear to her. Also, he would be well in some day. Elsie slipped her hand into her lover's, to give him strength.

'I want to marry Elsie when I'm twenty-one, and I'd like to be engaged to her now. May I?'

Mrs Cotton dropped her scissors. She had not anticipated that this question would arise so soon.

'I love him,' Elsie said defiantly, 'and we're not too young. That's what you were going to say, weren't you?'

'I don't quite know what I was going to say, as a matter of fact. Whatever shall I do with you two? You can't be sure of yourselves yet. Roly's only twenty, and you're sixteen.'

'Seventeen this summer.'

'It's too young, dearie.'

'There you go.'

'We don't want to get married at once,' said Roly.

'That's splendid.' Mrs Cotton was a little ironic. 'What's your Aunt Rose going to say?'

'That's just it,' Elsie put in eagerly, 'we thought you'd talk to her.'

'No. No you don't. She'd put me out with a flea in my ear.'

'I'll get her to see you,' said Roly, 'and you can talk it over between you. I shall be able to keep Elsie, you know,' he added, feeling that this fact had to be mentioned. 'I only get a small salary at present, of course, three pounds a week, but next year I shall have full control of what he left me. Rose reckons that there ought to be about five hundred a year coming into me from investments.'

Mrs Cotton tried to check a spontaneous display of enthusiasm. 'Well, that's all very nice, but you can see for yourselves what a difficult position I'm placed in.'

'An engagement couldn't hurt, could it? I mean, if we did change our minds, we could break it off; it isn't binding,' said Elsie, craftily.

'We do want to be all official,' Roly pleaded, 'and I'm not still a boy.'

'That's for others to judge.'

'Elsie.' He stood up, stern in his new dignity. 'Would you leave me with your mother? There are several things I should like to speak to her about.'

'No. I'm going to stay with you.'

'Darling, I'd much rather you went.'

She left them, her eyes shining with admiration.

Roly sat down by Mrs Cotton.

'May I smoke?'

'Of course. You always have, haven't you?'

This was not encouraging. He crossed and recrossed his legs several times. Then he said, boldly, 'Mrs Cotton, I do want you to understand that I am really fond of Elsie.'

'So I gathered. So you ought to be.' She stared at him, a mother hen with her hackles up.

'When I said I wasn't still a boy, it was true. I've had more experience than most men of my age. There were two women before I met Elsie.'

'Then you ought to be ashamed of yourself,' was all the appreciation he received.

'It will never happen again. I wouldn't have mentioned it to you, and I know you'll never speak of it to her, but I didn't want you to suppose I was thinking of marriage lightly. This isn't calf love.'

216

'I think Elsie ought to know.'

'She has some idea, but you won't tell her more, will you? It's between you and me.'

He was a little alarmed. He had meant to mention one woman only, but on an impulse had found the truth more impressive.

'What you say in confidence, Roly, I shall naturally respect.'

His spirits rose. How easily they were talking together, knowledgable man to knowledgable woman.

'Well, may I?'

She weakened. 'You must ask your Aunt Rose first. I wish I had Elsie's father to help me. This is such a business for me to decide alone, you know, dear. Personally, I do believe you two could get along all right, but I think you're young, as I said.'

'As you said,' he answered, 'but you don't really believe it? May I call Elsie in and tell her it's all right with you?'

She knuckled her forehead anxiously. 'Oh, go on, then.'

Elsie, seeing light in her lover's face and defeat in her mother's, did not ask the news.

'Oh, Roly!' she kissed him.

'Here, here, here,' said Mrs Cotton, 'steady on.'

They celebrated the engagement with a drink of the medicine brandy. Roly left at eight o'clock to talk Aunt Rose around.

'Shall I go with you?' Elsie clung to him.

'No, dear.' He pressed her arm. 'I think I'd better tackle her alone, and if it's all right, you can come to tea tomorrow. I'll be over first thing in the morning with the news, and on Monday we can start collecting things for the home.'

'Don't count your chickens before they're hatched,' Mrs Cotton said, 'you've got your aunt's consent to get.' She was sorely troubled. 'There's going to be a lot of gossip about this.' Inwardly she cursed herself for a weak, silly mother.

When Roly had gone, Elsie flung herself ecstatically on to the sofa.

'I'm so happy.'

'Ah.'

'Mother, it will be better when we're married.' The muffled lamplight in the room gave her courage. 'You see, I want him so badly, just as you must have wanted Daddy. I want to sleep with him.'

'Look here,' said Mrs Cotton, irrationally, passing a fretted hand through her hair, 'if you're going to talk like that, we'll call the whole thing off.'

Aunt Rose, younger than Mrs Cotton, and wise with the wisdom of one who remembered more than she had forgotten, was more of a problem. Roly explained the situation to her.

'No,' she said.

'But, Rose, people in Society get engaged early, nearly always. You've only got to read the papers.'

'You're not Society.'

'Why be an old crab?' He tickled her knee affectionately. She had not seen him behave like this since, as a little boy, he had wanted something very badly. 'She's awfully sweet, Rose. You'd like her.'

'I never like young girls. I always have the feeling that they're laughing at me when my back's turned.'

'Elsie's not like that. She's rather like mother to look at.'

'Roly, I am not, nor ever was, a sentimentalist.'

Walking away from her, he began to play simple tunes on the piano, with one finger.

'Stop that. The people next door will hear you. These walls are as thin as paper.'

'I don't care.' He came back to her. 'Rose, I've made up my mind. I'm going to announce my engagement, and if you like

218

to make us both look silly by trotting round saying it isn't true, that's your lookout.'

'It wouldn't worry me in the least, I assure you.'

Aunt Rose had a small castle of flesh on the end of her nose, almost an extra nose, in fact, and this wobbled when she became excited, a state that was rare in her.

'I don't know,' she went on, 'what the mother can be about.'

'Oh, she wouldn't say anything definite before she heard what your opinion was.'

'I should hope not.'

'See her, please.'

'No.'

'Well, *ask* Elsie over to tea tomorrow.'

'Roly, it's ridiculous, the whole idea.'

He lit a cigarette. 'You're a tough old nut to crack, aren't you?'

'I don't mind abuse, either.'

He played his last card. 'Rose, weren't you engaged when you were seventeen?'

She frowned. 'No, that's not fair. That's another appeal to my sentiment, which, I assure you, is non-existent. Yes, I was, and I broke it off without a qualm because it was a mistake of youth. I've never had another chance to marry, but I've never once regretted the fact that I gave my first and only lover the go-by. The main cross the unmarried woman has to bear is not that she has no husband, but that she is unnecessarily pitied by the women who have. Do I look like a soured old virgin to you? Because that's what your mother once called me in a moment of anger, when she imagined I was out.'

He was so embarrassed that he could have cried. 'No, of course not. She couldn't have been speaking of you.'

'Oh yes, she was. But I didn't resent it, because we all say things about perfectly pleasant people that we are fond of, who would have died of rage could they have heard us.'

219

'Rose, may I please be engaged to Elsie? I'm asking your consent as a formality only.'

Sensing the aggressive manhood in him, she answered, sharply, 'You'll do as I say. I'm your legal guardian for a year.'

'And you'd take advantage of that! It's less than a year, anyhow. Rose, it's a mean trick.'

'Roly, will you stop babbling, and go and get me some aspirin? You've given me a headache.'

'Not till you say yes, and let me ask Elsie over tomorrow.'

'Don't be ridiculous. When I say a thing I mean it.'

She put her legs apart, setting her strong hands on her knees. He thought her almost grotesque, with her twitching nose, her too-heavy bun of red hair.

'Go on. Do as I tell you. I can hardly see out of my eyes.'

'I want an answer.'

'You've had it. No.'

'Rose, I love Elsie and she loves me. Isn't that enough for you?' He went back to strum on the piano, playing the bass notes so hardly that a photograph on top of the case fell down.

'Will you please get me those aspirins? I'd go myself, but I feel my head would split apart if I moved a step. Haven't you a grain of sympathy?'

'It's a sudden headache,' he intoned, accompanying himself by a shower of discords.

But Rose was seeking for an excuse to yield. 'Roly, please . . .'

'Say I can be engaged to Elsie, then.'

So she cried, at last, 'Roly, you can be engaged to everyone in the British Isles, if you'll only do as I tell you.'

He could not wait until the morrow. After seeing that Aunt Rose was safely in bed, he left the house and ran as fast as he could go to Stanley Street. Seeing that all the lights in Mrs Cotton's home were out, he dared not knock her up. Fortunately, by standing on the drawing room sill, he could just reach high enough to tap on Elsie's window with a twig he had broken from the privet hedge.

She flung up the sash, and looked down at him,

'What on earth are you doing here?'

'I couldn't wait till tomorrow. I had to tell you the news.'

'Sh-h! Don't make such a noise. If a policeman notices you, he'll think you're a burglar, or something.'

'Damn the whole police force. Darling, I've talked old Rose over. We're engaged! You're coming to my place to tea tomorrow and on Monday we'll tell the whole neighbourhood!'

'Oh, my dear!'

'I love you. Love me?'

'Of course, but do go away. I can't realise I'm not asleep.'

'I'll call for you tomorrow. Elsie, darling, I suppose if you leaned a long way out of the window, with your stomach on the sill, you couldn't kiss me without breaking your neck?'

'No, I couldn't.'

'And to think of what some women have risked for a man! Goodnight, nasty.'

'Goodnight. Happy?'

'I should say, yes.'

'And no regrets?'

'Not a smell of one.'

He climbed down. Shutting the window, she went back to bed, wondering, suddenly, if she had done the right thing. Suppose I find I don't love him? Please, God, make me love him and let him love me always.

When she awoke in the very early morning, her mind was bleak with fear, all happiness forgotten. The thought of the afternoon's shock was so agonising that she had to get up and walk round the room to drive it away.

She did not love him at all. He was horrible, and his touch made her sick. Lying between the sheets again, she shivered as though she would never get warm.

When Mrs Cotton called her at nine o'clock, she awoke with a feeling that she had just escaped something terrible. What this something was, or why it was, she could not recall.

'Happy now?' said her mother gloomily. She had had a very bad night.

Elsie tried to comprehend the reality of the morning. 'Yes.'

'I hope I'm not going to regret this engagement. You ought to have had your fun with other men before you rushed into anything serious.'

'There was one man.' Elsie's voice held the softness of regret for a colourful past.

'A bit of seaside nonsense.'

'Well, Mother, don't start worrying me before I've had my breakfast. I can always worry better afterwards.'

'You'd better wear your new dress if you're going to see that aunt of Roly's. You haven't had her consent yet.'

'Yes, I have.'

'How do you know, Miss Clever?'

'Roly knocked on my window last night. She's said "Yes." I very nearly came into your room to tell you, but I thought you'd be angry.'

'I wish you had. I lay awake half last night wondering what sort of a fool the woman would think I was. I suppose she'll want to meet me. Thank heavens I shall have some sort of support.'

They were both invited to Lister Gardens for tea that afternoon.

'What do you think about our children?' babbled poor Mrs Cotton, trying to overcome her nervousness of a formidable Aunt Rose.

222

'I think it's perfect nonsense, myself, but I suppose they may as well have their heads – or lose them – now, as later.'

Mrs Cotton, overawed by the comparative splendour of Roly's home, spilt her tea.

'Don't worry. The girl will mop it up. It's only gone in the fender.'

Mrs Cotton wished that she, too, were in the fender, shrunken to an insignificant cinder among a heap of cinders.

'I shall let him have some of his money to buy Elsie a tasteful little ring,' said Aunt Rose.

'What would you like?' Roly asked, determined to have some voice in the matter.

'I don't mind,' Elsie answered, wondering, should she say sapphires, whether Aunt Rose would think them too expensive.

'We'll go and choose something tomorrow, dear.'

'But not before I've been to the bank,' Rose said. For two hours they talked of everything in the world but the engagement. 'You'll stay to supper?'

'No, thank you,' Mrs Cotton answered, scared out of her wits. 'We must get back, really. I expect you'll be seeing a good deal of Elsie. If you don't mind, that is.'

'She must come here as often as she likes.' Rose smiled widely. 'After all, they're our children now, aren't they, both of them?'

She saw them to the door. To Mrs Cotton's great surprise she kissed Elsie, who shied visibly. Oh, what great teeth you have, grandmamma. All the better to eat you with, my dear.

'I think you're a very nice little girl,' the wolf said, unexpectedly, 'Roly is a luckier boy than he deserves to be.'

'She seems nice,' remarked Mrs Cotton, doubtfully, once they were safely outside. 'Rather hard to get to know. Plain, isn't she? She appeared to like you, and so she ought. I've always said, and I always shall say, you're a great sight too good for him.'

Elsie, tired with the cataclysmic happenings of the last two days, said: 'I shall have an early bed tonight.'

'I'll see you do. What ring would you like?'

'A sapphire, I think, with a small diamond either side. Do you suppose he can afford that?'

'Of course he can, if that aunt of his opens up her purse strings sufficiently. Why didn't you tell her what you'd like?'

'I didn't dare. Anyway, I thought that was something for Roly and me to discuss on our own.'

'I agree,' said Mrs Cotton truculently. 'You don't want any interference at this stage, or any other stage. Blue's lucky for you, isn't it?'

'I think so. I hope so. Don't you think we'd have pretty children? Suppose I had a girl, with my colour hair and Roly's wave in it, my eyes, and Roly's nose and chin!'

'You can't order your babies by post card, and I hope that even if you do get married as early as next year, which Heaven forbid, that you won't rush into that all at once.'

'Well, suppose they just come? How can I prevent it?'

'Never mind about that.'

'But didn't you?'

'We didn't seem to have to prevent anything in my young days. We just had children when we wanted them, as far as I can remember. It's this modern civilisation,' she added, gravely. She went on: 'You want to enjoy your married life for a bit before you really settle down to the ties of children. Anyway, you'll be very, very young, and not properly developed.' The conversation was embarrassing her very much indeed.

'Would you like to be a grandmother?'

'Don't rush ahead like that. Now look here, I'm going to give you some cocoa when we get home to make you sleep properly, or you'll be babbling about babies all night.'

But Elsie found that the new visions she might now summon out of her twilit brain were too exciting to let her rest. At last they failed, leaving her wakeful, with the germ of fear in her mind.

Anything but that. Not like last night. Gentle Jesus meek and mild. Now, suppose I start counting. Over go the sheep; there's a black one, struggling over the gate. I've seen men on the pictures pushing them into pools to rid them of vermin or something. I'll have a ring with two sapphires and one diamond, or all diamonds. One day I shall say to Roly, 'This is your son.' My head is full of rings, going round and round like the ropes the cowboys twirl in the Westerns. Send me to sleep. One, two, three, four. That lamb doesn't want to go into the water. What can I see in the farmyard? Sheep, and pigs, and cows, and chickens; a hen, a black cat. One, two, three, four. Let me think of as many things beginning with A as I can. Apples, asters, agony. If there hadn't been that girl. He must have loved her at the time, forgetting me. She can't love him. Oh, God, if she ever worries him again. Antlers, Arthur, Ada Mary. Alfalfa grass. There's the plain, stretching up to the sky, with mountains in the distance. I'll walk over it for miles until I reach the foot of the range, where we will be married. How dark the clouds are. There is no path, so I shall follow the tracks of the cattle.

She went towards the mountains.

If I open my eyes they will vanish, and I'll be awake again. I wonder how it will feel to see him lying beside me in the morning? Suppose I hate him? Now I must go on. A hundred miles before the morning, and even when I come to the hills I may have to climb them. There's a cold wind blowing.

I suppose the window is too far down, but I can't bother to get out of bed and shut it.

She walked on towards the mountains.

225

Moritura

Roland, returning home with Elsie after the purchase of a ten pound engagement ring, a sum which Aunt Rose thought good and sufficient, caught sight of Mrs Maginnis walking along the road some fifty yards in front of them. He stopped.

'I want you to meet a friend of mine. Will you? That's Mrs Maginnis. Do you know her at all?'

Elsie was surprised. 'Oh, but she's a dreadful woman, isn't she?'

'I don't think so. I often have a chat with her when we meet, and I think she's rather wonderful.'

'But isn't she – isn't she a street-walker?'

'I don't think she'd like to be called that. Come on, dear, I've told her all about you. Let's run.'

But she hung back, a fearful doubt in her mind. 'Roly, surely you've never—?'

He looked at her straightly, almost persuaded that he was about to tell her the truth. 'Would I ask you to meet her if I had?'

She was satisfied. 'No, darling.'

'Come on, then.' They ran helter-skelter down the street towards the retreating form of Mrs Maginnis. She turned round as she heard their running feet, throwing up her hands in amazement.

'Well, fancy it being you!'

'I want you to meet Elsie Cotton. We're engaged.'

'What news! How do you do, Elsie. I've known you for a long time, though that might seem queer to you. When you were a little thing about so high, I used to see you staggering off to school with a great satchel, and think to myself, What a lot for a mite like that to have to learn! Congratulations, both of you. I think you're very lucky to get each other. How did you talk your people over, and when is it to be?'

'Our people were reasonable, you know. They had to be. We made them. We're not getting married till next year, but you'll come, won't you?'

'It's a very long time to next year. I may be in Australia by then. Show me your ring, Elsie, I'm all excited. Oh, what a pretty one! It's like the one Bert gave me, only mine wasn't so nice.' She turned it round on Elsie's hand, so that the stone lay on the inside of her palm. 'That's what it will look like next year. Aren't you all up in the air?'

'I am. I don't know how to wait.'

'Well, you'll be married a long while. I suppose I mustn't ask you and your young lady to come and have a drink with me to celebrate?'

Roly looked at Elsie. 'No, I don't think we'd better stop, thank you. I just thought we'd tell you our news.'

'I'll bet hundreds of people know it already, don't they?'

'Of course we told the office, and Mother told Mr Parsons when she was at the stalls this morning. Then I met a friend and told her.'

'It's lucky for you I didn't see Parsons today,' Mrs Maginnis laughed, 'or you wouldn't have been able to spring the big surprise on me. Well, I must be getting along. I just took a turn round the shops before I went to keep my usual *rendez-vous*, as they say in France, but I must hurry now, or I'll keep all the boys and girls waiting.' She admired Elsie openly. 'Isn't she pretty, Roly? You ought to have your behind kicked for taking her away from all the other fellows. He's all right, too,

Elsie. I knew him when he wore a school cap, and a funny little fellow he was. Careful of her eyes, Roly; they're so big you might fall inside them and get lost.' She put her hand to her forehead, clicking her heels sharply together. 'Here's to the bride and bridegroom. I'll have a drink for both of you if you won't have one with me. All the best.'

Waving to them gaily, she went off, the lamplight shining down upon her like the sun on a handsome galley.

'She's not so bad, is she?' Roly demanded.

'She's rather nice, I think. Of course, she did talk about behinds, and she doesn't really know me properly.'

'She's always like that. She doesn't care a damn for what people think. She enjoys life more than anyone I know.'

'Does she drink much?'

'Not such a terrible amount. At one time she was awfully worried about a growth she had; I suppose it was a growth, or do you call it a tumour? I think that made her drink rather heavily for a while, but she's all right again now. By the way, you'd better not tell your mother we spoke to her. She mightn't understand. She's rather behind the times in some respects, isn't she? A bit naughty nineties.'

'No worse than your Aunt Rose.' They wrangled for a time, until the glory of their new status overcame them.

Mrs Maginnis banged into The Admiral, waving her hat like a flag. 'Hullo, all!'

'Hullo, Patty!'

'Blow 'em all dead,' said Teep, slumped against the wall, his eyes glowering over the coat collar which he had pulled up to his nose.

'And so you shall!' Mrs Maginnis uprooted him by main force, making him waltz a few steps with her. 'So we will. We'll tie big bombs under their tails, like a sort of Guy Fawkes night, and then we'll send 'em all sky high, so they'll come down in little pieces. After that, we'll collect the bits and put them into sandwiches under those glass bell things, in place of Maisie's stale sausage rolls.'

'My rolls aren't stale!'

Mrs Maginnis threw little Teep back into the sea. 'Of course they're not, dearie, and I'll eat one to prove it. I haven't had my supper. Didn't feel like it.'

She ate two sausage rolls in swift succession, singing snatches of *Il Bacio* between bites.

'You're jolly tonight,' said Parsons appreciatively. 'Come into money?'

'No, but I've got some news. Young Roly Dexter is engaged.'

'I knew that this morning.'

'So you did, so you did. I forgot. Isn't it fine, though? Marriage, that's what I believe in. Don't you, Ma? You love your old man, don't you?'

'Never you mind,' said Ma Ditch. 'You ask 'im. I threw a plate at 'im the other night, for spoiling trade – came up to my stall, 'e did, just when we was doing a good business, and shouted out, so as everyone could 'ear 'im, "What a stink! What a stink! Your meats 'ave all gone bad. You'll poison the cats." 'E was drunk, mind you, at twelve o'clock in the morning. Where 'e gets it from, I don't know, and I've 'unted all over the 'ouse. Well, I stood on my dignity with 'im until I got 'im 'ome, and then I told 'im a thing or two. Now 'e'll be buying me a new pair of earrings, just to make up. I know 'im.'

Willy Sample struck up the Wedding March.

'Here, let's celebrate the coming event,' Mrs Maginnis cried, 'I'm the bride.' She ravished the vase of daffodils that stood on the bar, and stuck some of them in her hair, carrying the remainder as a bouquet. 'Mr Parsons, you're the

229

groom. Come on, Ma, you can be bridesmaid. Off we go. Mr Teep's the parson. We all know the words he'll address to the happy couple, but we'll pretend they're the proper ones.'

Clutching the embarrassed Parsons, Mrs Maginnis circled the room, to the accompaniment of great laughter. Ma Ditch, the histrionic, caught up the back of the bride's dress as if it were a train. 'Careful,' said Mrs Maginnis, 'you'll show my knickers, and that won't do in church.'

Once more they marched round the floor. Willy banged away with the loud pedal hard down.

'Joke over!' Mrs Maginnis cried, at last. 'Drinks all round on me.' They crowded to the bar. 'Go on, don't be shy. Have anything you want. You mustn't drink beer on my wedding day. What's your old woman going to say about this, Mr Parsons?'

'What the eye don't see,' said Mr Parsons.

'You have one too, Maisie, and Mr W. My God, doesn't your husband look whoopsy tonight? How can you keep his high spirits down?'

'He couldn't keep them down last night,', Maisie whispered cloudily, 'that's why he's so yellowish today. Furious with him, I was. Found him stretched out like a stinking fish on the bathroom floor. It isn't as if he was really a heavy drinker, either. He told me this morning that he'd been betting again, and got tight so as to give himself enough pluck to tell me.'

'Well, don't be cross with him now. Life's too short to be angry. Just cut his throat next time he bets, and tell him what you intend doing beforehand. That ought to fix him. Ah, music!'

A cornetist had thrust his head around the door, bending himself into an S-shape, in the curious manner of public house musicians. 'Poor old chap!' she exclaimed, 'look at him, with his head all warm in here and his bottom all cold outside!'

'He's not cold,' Wilkinson grumbled, 'it's like summer.'

'Never mind, let's have him in. Come on, you, give us a nice tune and you shall have one on me.'

He flapped inside, swinging his head nervously, one eye slanted towards the bar. 'Tune first, drink afterwards,' she said. He quavered into *Loch Lomond*. Mrs Maginnis knowing how to entertain her friends, performed a slow polka, holding her skirts very daintily.

'I 'ate that noise,' Teep said, suddenly and loudly. She stopped. 'All right, we'll shut him up. Everyone's going to be happy tonight. This is my birthday, or rather, I'm keeping my birthday today. A double scotch for the band, Maisie, and meanwhile we'll take a little collection.'

She snatched the cornetist's cap from his head and set it on her hair, holding her own hat out to all comers.

'Step up, step up now; don't be mean. Thank you, Mr Parsons. Come on, Ma, haven't you got threepence?'

'A penny and two 'apennies,' said Ma Ditch, 'and that will 'ave to do. I'm nearly in the gutter myself, what with that old swine letting down trade.'

'Now then, Willy, don't you hide behind the piano. Sixpence from you. Divvy up. Quick.'

She tipped the money from her hat into the cap and restored it to the man, who had finished his drink quickly that he might disappear before the dream faded.

'Thank you, mum. God bless you.'

'God never has, but I'll give Him another chance. Goodnight, Cholmondeley, and the same to you.' She turned back to the company. 'Now what? Can't let the party down. Shall I recite to you, *It was Christmas Day in the Workhouse?*'

'Here, what's up with her?' Wilkinson murmured to Maisie. 'Is she drunk?'

'She can't be; she's hardly had anything.'

Happily, Mrs Maginnis decided not to continue her recitation, but she played several merry tricks on the company, snatching the piano stool from under Willy just as he was about to sit down, pulling out strands of her hair to drop them into Parsons's beer. She stood everybody another drink, and yet another round, until Ma Ditch, quite pale with curiosity, demanded: 'You come into a little nest egg?'

Mrs Maginnis laughed as if she would never stop. 'Well, I have got a little nest egg, if you want to know, a hard white one which is more trouble than it's worth; but never you mind about that.'

'What are you talking about?' Wilkinson fixed her with a cold eye.

'Don't listen to me. I'm just trying to get you all guessing. Now what shall we do? Shall we have community singing?' She took a forgotten daffodil from her hair. 'I'll stand on Willy's stool – off you go, my man – and conduct.'

'No, you don't.' Wilkinson was firm. 'We'll have the police in.'

'We'll just hum,' Mrs Maginnis pleaded.

' 'Ere, I wash; I do!' shouted Ma Ditch, who was full of jokes that night.

'No humming, either. Come on, Mrs Maginnis, you simmer down.'

She climbed from the stool. 'All right, Spoilsport. Oh look, Maisie, we've only ten minutes to go!'

Mr Teep went out to be sick.

'Well, it seems that all we can do is to have one for the road. Come on, one for my birthday, with me.'

This round went sour on the palate. Her friends, reckoning that she must have spent something like five pounds that evening, were too puzzled to enjoy it very much.

'Now,' she cried, 'Three cheers for me!'

'We can't have cheering,' Wilkinson announced, ungratefully.

'Oh yes, we can, if they're quiet ones. Come on. Three cheers for Patty, though I say it myself as shouldn't. Hip, hip, hooray!'

232

They were given, politely, nervously. At the conclusion, Mrs Maginnis leaned over the bar, kissed Maisie, hit Wilkinson on the chest, and walked out abruptly without saying goodnight to anyone.

Nobody made any comment after she had gone. The Admiral was dead.

Mrs Maginnis, as she walked to Lincoln Street, ran her fingers along the railings. That was a night. There's never been such a time in the old Admiral before, and no-one's going to forget it in a hurry.

She let herself in. As she rose up through the still, dark waters of the house, she thought of Ada Mary. 'Hullo,' she said aloud, 'you here? Well, we'll have a talk later, maybe.' No point in lighting the gas on the stairs.

She undressed herself in the bedroom, and had a tepid bath. She made up her face very carefully, smoothing the rouge towards the nose to make her cheeks look less round, and she picked out each separate eyelash with mascara.

Then the pain ran through her so suddenly and so violently that her hand, jerking downwards, smeared a brushful of dark grease over her cheeks. Very carefully, she removed it with cold cream. Now I'll have to start all over again. Half a mo'; before I forget, a bob for the meter. Drawing her new silk kimono around her, she fumbled in her purse for the coin, and, going out on to the landing, she put it in the slot. She returned to the dressing table, admiring, in the glass, the folds of silk about her hanging breasts. You look lovely in pink, my girl, especially in this light. She turned out the gas. I can do my hair by the candles.

Lovingly she combed it out, strand by strand, drawing a lock forward to see if she could detect any grey, but it was still as bright as a new sovereign. She pinned it carefully into place, pulling it low over her forehead and well round her ears, to conceal the lines about her jawbone. You've never looked better. A kid. That's what you are still, if you did but know it. A mere kid, in the dark with the light behind you.

Her toilet preparations complete, she took down two photographs from the mantelpiece, one of her husband and one of her lost lover. Then she blew out the candles and went into the kitchen. Here she lit the small oil lamp, setting the pictures on the plate rack above the gas stove. She stepped back to admire the effect, stepped forward again to slant one of them that the light should fall upon it. She quickly tidied the room, pushing a pile of dirty plates behind the check curtain that hung beneath the dresser.

'Now,' she said, and looked round instantly, as if she dreaded an echo. Returning to the bedroom, she collected an eiderdown, a blanket and a pillow. She went into the kitchen, and, kneeling on the floor, rolled the blanket into the eiderdown to form a soft bed to lie on. Pushing the end of it so that it lay just on the iron of the stove, she touched it with her foot to make sure that it would not slip. That's nice. Now for the pillow. She took it up, draping across it a square of blue silk she had used as a table centre, then laid it inside the oven.

All set, aren't we? Carrying her handbag to the lamp, she touched her face with powder and washed her hands in the sink, lest any particle of grease from the stove should adhere to them. She shut the door and the window to make sure that her journey should be uninterrupted.

For a short while she lingered, thinking of this and that. I wonder what he'll think? I don't suppose he'll mind. But The Admiral will mind, for they liked me there. They won't forget me, either: whenever they think of me, they'll say: 'How kind Patty was; she was so jolly.' Putting her hand inside the folds of her kimono, she rolled the silver nutmeg between finger and thumb. Nuts to you, my lad. I'll show you where you get off. Wait till I know you better? Not me. Not Patty. Poor Ada Mary. Water makes you ugly, you swell, you go blue. I shall

234

not look ugly at all. 'The mysterious princess is here, Oh, isn't she a pretty dear?' A soft bed to lie on. There, I knew I'd forgotten something. She left the room once more to fetch a bolster.

I'll hold you in my arms whether you like it or not, and you shan't escape again. Yes, I've got a cigarette. Here's fourpence. Buy yourself ten small ones and don't make such a fuss: when your ship comes home I'll have it off you, my lad, you'll see.

She closed her eyes for a moment that she might visualise, somewhere in her head, the bar of The Admiral, where the lights revolved and swung, where the skittle ball, clicking and flying, won a beer for Parsons. She kissed Maisie goodnight, she hit Wilkinson on the chest.

Smiling to herself, Mrs Maginnis crossed the room. She gave a final touch to her bright hair. Then, turning on the gas, she lay down to sleep.

235

'Change is the Nursery . . .'

The neighbourhood fell with the fall of the year. At the end of August a whole block of houses in Lincoln Street, including Number Twenty-four, was bought and demolished, and out of this ruined Pompeii arose a large picture palace, with one thousand seats for seven pence, and a noble façade, moulded with stags and Greek notabilities. They were building a new bridge across the river, almost facing the end of Belvedere Row, that the danger of buses and lorries falling, at any moment, through the crumbling stonework of the old one into the stream, might be avoided. Along the Parade, where the lovers walked by night, the Borough Council had set up twice the number of lamps that had been there previously, for it had come to the Council's ears that the lovers had abused their privileges for some time past. The school, where Elsie, for eight years, had worked so hard to avoid work, was torn down, and a new building set up over the far side of the common.

Maisie, seeing all these changes, and realising that the march of progress was inevitable, had the outside of The Admiral repainted, and the bar and the back parlour knocked into one: For few of the old people come in, she thought, since Patty went, and the new ones like a bit of smartness. So she bought some palms in Wedgwood pots, a few glass-topped tables, and some tub chairs.

All this, of course, had its disadvantage. Parsons, finding that the new magnificence disturbed him, upsetting his luck with the skittles, transferred his patronage to The Antlers. Ma Ditch made several rude remarks in a loud voice about Maisie's decorations, and immediately took her custom to 'somewhere homey'.

Roly continued to visit The Admiral three or four times in the week. He had even persuaded Elsie to come with him on two occasions, extracting from her a promise that Mrs Cotton under no circumstances should be told about it.

Wilkinson, wearing a dinner jacket, roved miserably through the jungle of palms. 'Smart, aren't we?' he said to Roly, pleading with his eyes for a favourable answer. 'Twice the business now.'

Elsie answered him. 'I think it all looks lovely, but then, I never saw it before.'

'Mrs Maginnis used to make it pretty lively,' Wilkinson said, moving away to fetch their drinks.

'Aren't we lively now?' cried Maisie, across the bar. It was early in the evening and few people were there. 'Haven't we got a radiogram? We never have a dull moment. Willy plays until eight, and then we have the wireless. We've got a singer coming down the week after next, too. You must drop in and hear him. Lovely deep voice, and he does all the old songs, you know, that people really like.'

Roly went to speak to her. 'Piling it up, aren't you?'

'We're not out of the wood yet,' said Wilkinson, cautiously.

'But things are bucking up all round,' Willy put in, turning himself on the piano stool, 'and everyone feels the benefit. Look at the neighbourhood, new bridge, super cinema, and all that.'

'Seems a pity all the same,' observed Teep, who didn't care a pin where he went each night, provided that he might rehearse his theories of elementary anarchy undisturbed.

'Everything's changing everywhere. Look at the country; nothing but petrol stations and hostels for rambling clubs,'

Roly said, gazing into his beer as if it were a crystal wherein the future was made plain.

'But do you like our decorations?' asked Maisie.

'Oh, fine.' He whispered in her ear: 'I never could get Elsie here in the old days, you know, but now she says she doesn't mind a bit. She says: "I never thought it was so respectable!"'

'Indeed!' Maisie bridled. 'And what were we before? I never allowed any nonsense in this house.' She pulled at his sleeve. 'Don't turn round this minute, but when you get a chance, take a look at who's coming in. Our new-marrieds. You remember the girl who used to be at the public library? Patty said you knew her once, I believe. Go on, they're not looking our way. They're sitting in the corner, under the window. He's not a local man, or anything, but they've come round here to live. They got hitched up last July. Case of had to, if you ask me.'

Cautiously, Roly turned his head. There was the girl, dull-faced, conspicuously pregnant, scowling at the fat young man by her side.

'What is it today?' Maisie murmured, 'Let me see. October the tenth. July, I said they got married, didn't I, and look at her! A good seven months gone. Nerve, hasn't she?'

'I wonder why women who are going to have babies always wear silk mackintoshes with belts drawn tightly round the middle?'

'Oh, you do see everything, don't you?' Maisie giggled. 'When my ma was a young girl, they used to wear things called golf capes. Of course, directly you saw the woman next door swishing along in one of those, you knew what was up all right. Look, your girl wants you. She'll be getting jealous.'

Roland went back to Elsie. 'Sorry. Maisie will gas on and on. Would you like another drink, or shall we go? I think perhaps we'd better be getting along.' Without waiting for an answer he hurried her out, his head averted from the table under the window.

'Well,' he said, 'now what? Home?' She nodded.

'I want you to see some things I've bought for us. I wish I didn't have to go to work because it means that I have to do my shopping in such a rush. Still, I've got two lovely check tablecloths, awfully artistic, for one-and-six each – pure linen, it says on the label.'

'Have you?'

'And a dozen dusters.'

'Good God, are we going to be as dirty as all that?'

'Not if I know anything about it, but it's best to be on the safe side.'

Mrs Cotton was out. 'The house to ourselves!' Elsie pressed his arm. 'I'm so glad she doesn't mind us being alone now.'

'Why should she?'

'Oh, you know.'

'Old people are dirty-minded.'

'Well,' said Elsie, trying to be fair, 'she says it's only natural for engaged couples to be hot headed.'

'She says a damn lot too much. Bung up to the neck with theories, she is.' They went in.

'Roly, why don't you like my mother?'

'I do, you fool. Don't talk nonsense.'

'I don't like the way you speak of her, sometimes.'

'And I don't like the way she discusses us. It isn't her business.'

'I'm her business, aren't I? Isn't it natural that she should be interested in me?'

'Filthy minded.'

'Roly, if you're going to talk like that you can go home.'

'You know that if I did you'd be crying to her about what a brute I am.'

'You're jealous of her.'

'Filthy minded.'

'Look here, darling, I love you and mother more than anyone else in the world, and it does make me so wretched to think you don't like each other.'

'You talk a lot of rot, sometimes, don't you?'

'So do you.'

'Your mother this and your mother that. Who are you going to marry, her or me?'

'What's the good of answering you when you're like this?' Then she put her arms round his neck, rubbing her nose up and down his cheek. 'Darling, why do we always quarrel?'

'You start it nine times out of ten.'

'We've been snarking at each other all the time we've been engaged.'

'Don't I know it?'

'Once it was lovely to quarrel, or rather, it used to be so lovely afterwards, but now we never really come together again after rows. We just leave them in the air, and love each other a little less each time.'

He kicked at the coal scuttle. 'I don't enjoy it any more than you do.'

'Roly, when we're married, do you think we shall be happy?'

'It will be different then.' He held her at arm's length. 'Don't you see what's wrong? I love you, you love me, and we can't do anything about it.'

'But we will soon. Next June. That's not so long, is it?'

'Long enough for me. You don't feel the same. You can't. You're not built like a man.'

'Lucky for you I'm not.'

'Oh, for Christ's sake, don't try to be funny. You know what I mean well enough. It's the whole social system that's at fault.'

'Yes,' said Elsie.

'When a man loves a woman, he ought to be able to sleep with her right away, and then there would be no repressions or inhibitions or anything. It's only that we all lack the courage to take what we want,' he continued.

'Sometimes you sound so terribly old that I'm afraid of you.'

'My dear, I'm older than you, after all.'

'Not so much.'

'Oh, blast you, don't quibble. Elsie, why can't we have courage? I want you. It would be all right.'

'I might have a baby.'

'The chances are that you wouldn't. Anyway, there are ways and means.'

'I know all about that, but it makes it so sordid and beastly. Roly, what's the use? We've been all over this time and time again. You know we only talk about it because it makes us feel big and progressive, but we won't do it.'

'You won't; you're scared.'

'Yes, I am! So would you be if you were me. Anyway, there's mother to consider. It would break her heart.'

'Let it. She's got to realise that we're no longer children.'

Children, Elsie thought with one of the flashes of penetration that came to her so frequently now, of course we're children. I know it, so why doesn't he? 'Oh, don't touch me, Roly.'

'Now what's up?'

'Nothing. I'm just—' She laid her head on his shoulder. 'I'm so unhappy.'

'You always damn well are. And what about me?'

'I love you.'

'Never mind about that. What about me, I said?'

'If you don't mind about "that," as you call it, why don't you leave me? I'll release you, if that's what you want.'

'Don't be dramatic. You know damn well I don't want to leave you.'

'Then why—?' Seeing the strain in her eyes, he answered: 'It'll be better next year. Not so long now, dear. I'm sorry I'm being such a swine.'

The door slammed.

'There's your damned mother.' And so they were angry with each other for the rest of the evening.

'I'm so tired that I know I shall drop off the moment my head touches the pillow.' Maisie stretched her arms above her head, gripping her fingers around the bedrail. Wilkinson, gazing upon the swelling cords in her armpits, at the swelling sweetness of her body beneath the eiderdown, was unmoved. 'Put your hands down, Maisie, it's bad for the heart.'

'Get on with you. Mine's as strong as a bell. Come here and give me a kiss. As poor Patty Maginnis would have said, "What are you looking so happy about, Mr W.?" He obeyed her.

'I wish you'd grow a moustache, Harry. You're so tall, you'd look like a guardsman.'

'Too much trouble. I tell you' – he pointed an angry finger at her, 'it takes me all my time struggling out of these damn clothes. I've no time to bother about growing more hair on my face.'

'You wouldn't have to shave.'

'Oh, yes I should. And what is more, I'd have to remember where not to. Don't be silly.'

She drew the sheets up to her chin, flashing her merry eyes at him. 'Maisie silly girl?'

He glowered.

'Oh, Harry, do be more tidy! There's your suspenders on the floor. I hate muddle.'

'And I hate fuss. I'm tired.'

Wisely, she said no more about it. 'It was a good night tonight.'

He grunted.

'I like that man, Mr Sanderson, who comes in with his girl, don't you? He's funny, I think. You know, not that coarse, music hall kind of humour, but real wit.'

'I hate wit.'

'There isn't much you don't hate but dogs, is there?'

She had not meant to mention dogs until the morrow, when both of them were in finer shape for battle.

Standing in his pyjama coat, he leaned over the rail at the foot of the bed.

'Still on about that? Little trustful, you are.'

'I know, you can't deceive me, Harry, so why do you keep on trying?'

Wilkinson never asked how she knew these things. He just accepted her statement that she did.

'Always on, on, on. What harm do I do? I made a quid last week and I lost twenty-two bob this. What's the odds?'

'Two bob, and one day it'll be a damn sight more. Ask me something harder, and put your trousers on.'

He did not like her. She made him feel ridiculous, and she denied him his heart's desire. Rather, she attempted to deny it him, and by so doing, soured its fulfilment. She was ugly. Her hair should be grey, and it was not. Her eyes should be dull, and they were not. She was active while he was passive, alive for him and to him, forever sharp to his clumsiness, and she made him wear a dinner jacket.

He turned out the light. 'Move over,' he said.

Ma Ditch sat in her parlour. With her were Parsons and Mrs Parsons. It was, for no reason, a festival night, a

243

festival for those who had died and for those who were about to die.

Ma Ditch cried into her gin. Of late she had taken to gin. 'It warms you,' she would say, 'and people of my age need warmth.'

Her parlour was a pleasant place, so tightly packed with furniture, so closely hung with photographs, that there was no room in it for thinking. Mr Ditch, who was a legendary character in the neighbourhood, bore out his reputation by being absent. He had retired to bed early, before the guests arrived, for he was not a sociable man.

'None of the old ones left,' wept Ma Ditch. 'New faces everywhere. Remember when Patty did the sword dance?'

Reverently, Parsons remembered. Mrs Parsons smiled. She had heard about it.

'Remember when you and Patty pretended you was being married?'

Parsons remembered. Mrs Parsons did not smile. She had heard about it.

'The days that will never come again,' said Ma Ditch, happily maudlin. 'I always get a lump in my throat at *Auld Lang Syne*, though I never know what it's there for.'

'Growing pains,' said Parsons.

They sat in silence over their drinks. Below them, the fire dropped to a cinder. Above them, Ma Ditch's relatives smiled down at them, sympathetic yet uncomprehending.

'Even the young ones growing up,' Mrs Parsons murmured, 'getting married, and starting on life proper.'

'Patty always knew what was coming to her.'

'But she didn't sit and wait for it.'

Parsons drank to the dead. 'No sitting around waiting for trouble. 'Ow many of us would 'ave dared to do what she did?'

Again they were silent. Then Mrs Parsons said, tremulously, 'Aren't we a gloomy party?'

They stared at her. No bellowing in the world of silence could have been as terrible as her thin voice at that moment.

Mrs Cotton poured out the tea. With her were Roly, Elsie, and Aunt Rose. On the days when Rose paid a visit there was ceremony; the cake stand appeared, cups and saucers were balanced on the knee.

'I don't see,' said Aunt Rose, 'why they shouldn't live in the old house. Elsie can redecorate to her own taste, of course, but it does seem a pity for Roly to have all the trouble of selling. It isn't as if there were a great market for these old fashioned houses, anyway. What do you think, Mrs Cotton?'

Mrs Cotton looked at Elsie. She never dared to think alone. Elsie looked at Roly. 'Would you like that?' she said.

'I wouldn't mind.'

'Of course,' Aunt Rose went on, 'Elsie could have a maid, either daily or living-in, and a charwoman, so there wouldn't be much work for her.'

'I hope not. She's not too strong, and she'll be very young indeed to take over all the cares and responsibilities of housework.'

'We all come to it sooner or later.' Aunt Rose rippled her muscles. 'Anyhow, as I say, there will be precious little for her to do.'

Mrs Cotton, fearing that her daughter was being sadly overruled, dared to say: 'Didn't you talk about wanting a nice little flat, darling?'

Elsie was tired of the whole subject. Oh, anything. I don't care, so long as we get married soon. 'Yes, I did, but it seems a shame not to live in Roly's house when it's all ready for us.'

'Well, you are a funny girl.'

'Not at all,' said Aunt Rose, 'Good horse sense. Elsie takes the long view.'

'I'd like to alter the dining room,' murmured Elsie, 'I think it would look better with blue curtains and yellow walls.'

Aunt Rose looked at her. 'Oh, my dear, what's wrong with those plush hangings that are there already? There's nothing the matter with them, you know.'

'Elsie's got to live there.' This was from Roly. 'She'd better have things her own way.'

'All right. Don't get so excited. I was only trying to help. You know how I detest interference of any kind. Let the young fight it out for themselves, I always say.'

'Elsie leaves the office next week,' Mrs Cotton put in. 'I can afford quite well to keep her until the wedding, and I don't see why she should work right up to the last moment.'

'I don't call eight months the last moment.'

'Well, she's not keen, and she shall do as she pleases. I may be spoiling her, but she's all I've got to spoil. Try the ginger cake, Rose.'

'Gives me indigestion. I'm sure it's very nice, though. Who are you having for your bridesmaids, dear?'

'I'm not having any. We're going to be married as quietly as possible, with only you and Mother, two aunts of mine, and one uncle to give me away. And, of course, the best man.'

'This is all news to me!' Mrs Cotton looked sharply at Elsie. 'When did you decide it all?'

'Last night. You see, Roly thinks – don't you, darling? – that marriage is purely a matter of form.'

'Legalising a spiritual pact between two parties. Do you mind my pipe?'

'And so,' Elsie went on, 'we thought at first that we'd just go to a registry office, but I knew Mother would hate that, so we decided that we'd have the quietest church ceremony possible. Anyway, if I had a bridesmaid, it would have to be Joan, and she'd look awful. Well, we thought out something else, too; that we wouldn't go on a honeymoon at all, but return to our own house afterwards and have a proper holiday later in the year.'

'Well, I think it's nonsense,' said Mrs Cotton, whose romantic dream had fallen into the dust. 'I always thought of you being married in white, with a lot of flowers and a choral service.'

'Pagan,' said Roly.

'He's so progressive,' added Elsie, apologetically.

'They're right.' Aunt Rose, gave unexpected support. 'Not, mind you, that I can get used to these new ideas all of a sudden, but I do think they ought to be allowed to do as they like in a matter like this.'

Mrs Cotton pursed her lips to mark her antagonism. 'That's where we agree to differ, then, Rose. You see, a mother has certain plans, or rather, hopes for her daughter, and it isn't nice to see them disappear all of a sudden. After all, Elsie's wedding is all I've got to look forward to.'

'Nonsense. I'm only going to live a short walk away. You'll see me every day, I expect.'

'It isn't the same, dear.'

'What difference does my wedding make, anyhow? The whole ceremony is pagan.' Roly knocked his pipe out on the fender. 'It should be a civil contract between two parties. Bad taste, I call it, all this show and dressing-up, to mark the fact that two people are about to perform the intensely personal business of consummating a union.'

This sort of thing made Mrs Cotton fidgety. 'Roly, dear.'

'There's no harm in speaking the truth. What do you think about it, Rose?'

'Think about what? Calling a spade a certain shovel, or the whole idea?'

'The whole idea?'

'I've told you. I think you should both do exactly as you please.'

'We shall.' Elsie sat on the arm of her lover's chair. 'You'll get used to it, Mother.'

'In another minute,' Aunt Rose announced, 'Roly is going to say something about not losing a daughter but gaining a son. I'm saying it first just to stop him.'

'I don't produce clichés like that.'

'You can talk now, my dear, but I could see the remark coming. I must be going. Will you and Elsie come to tea with me on Tuesday?'

'Thank you,' said Mrs Cotton, who would have liked to refuse.

'Are you going, Roly?'

'I must, darling. I had to take a lot of work home with me from the office, and I must get it done.'

When Aunt Rose had departed with Roly, Mrs Cotton started to cry. 'I'm so disappointed, dearie. What's changed you so?'

Elsie was impatient. 'Nothing in particular. Only, you see, I want to marry Roly so badly that I don't care how I do it. I can hardly wait. The time seems so terribly long.'

'Some people have to wait much longer. I was engaged to your father for over a year before I married him.'

'And did you still want him when you'd got him?'

'Elsie, dear.'

'Well, did you? Was he still exciting to you?'

'I don't think we thought very much about being excited in those days. He was a good man, and very kind, so I considered myself a lucky woman to have him.'

'It sounds beastly dull to me. Mother, what can I wear at the wedding?'

'You know my views.'

'No, not white; Roly doesn't want it, and I would rather do as he pleases. How do you fancy me in green crêpe-de-chine?'

'Unlucky.' Mrs Cotton was interested despite herself.

'I'm not superstitious. I think I'll try to buy it readymade, too. A dressmaker might make a mess of it.'

'Censure is all I shall get from this affair, censure and blame. People will say you're too young, and then they'll wonder why a young girl has to be married in that hole-in-the-corner way. What could be prettier than a young thing all in white, with lilies and orange blossom?'

Elsie took no notice.

'I don't know whether to say "obey" or not. It seems so stupid, somehow, to go to a lot of trouble arranging not to; as though I intend to start quarrelling with Roly the moment we get home. On the other hand, I shan't always obey him, of course. Why should I?'

'Don't you think you could wear a white hat and frock, anyway?'

'No, I don't. I don't and I won't.'

'I may as well go to the pictures as sit and talk to you. You're growing farther away from me every day.'

Elsie rubbed her chin with the back of her hand. 'I'm not, Mother, only you don't understand. I want Roly so badly that it's making me nervy and bad tempered.'

'What you young people need is more self control. I've no patience with you.'

Elsie looked out on to the darkening road. 'Mother, didn't you ever feel, with Daddy, that if you didn't get him, you'd die? Didn't you ever get that maddening, prickling feeling?'

'No, I didn't, and even if your father did, we didn't talk about it. This new freedom of speech business is responsible for more trouble than anything else. You can laugh at modesty between engaged couples if you like, but when I was young they didn't get themselves into nervy states because they had to wait for the wedding, and they didn't prickle.'

'If you never talked about it, how do you know?'

'Well, I didn't, at any rate.'

'Perhaps you've forgotten.'

Mrs Cotton wondered if she had. Of her own love affair she remembered little, save that she had been proud of her good-looking husband, proud in her acquiescence to his desires. She took Elsie's hand. 'I don't like my little girl talking like this. It isn't right.'

'It's natural and right.'

'Men still admire modest women.'

'Well, I'm not modest.'

'Then, I'm sorry to hear it.'

'You know what I mean. Mother, try to understand. I'm miserable.'

'Darling, what are you crying about? You ought to be the happiest girl in the world, marrying the man you love at an age when lots of girls are still at school. You do love him, don't you?'

'I don't know. That's why I'm miserable and scared. I've wanted him so long, that now I don't know.'

Mrs Cotton, searching in the recesses of her mind for some sort of comfort, could find none. Smoothing Elsie's hair, she only said: 'Your blood's out of order, dear.'

'Blast my blood.'

'No, darling, don't say that. I'm afraid Roly's coarsening you.'

Out of the dark, a thought so dreadful occurred to Mrs Cotton that her stomach seemed to drop through a thousand years.

'Elsie. Tell me this, my dearie, and don't be afraid, because mother isn't going to scold you. She'll understand. You haven't done anything you're ashamed of, have you? I mean, that isn't why you and Roly are in such a hurry to get married?'

Elsie looked at her. Then she started to laugh as if her heart would break. 'Oh no, stupid, no, no, no. It's what I want to do, not what I've done!'

Mrs Cotton, dizzy with relief, understood less than ever.

'Thank God for that.'

'I wouldn't do anything that would hurt you, Mother, you know that. But try, try to understand me. I want him, but I don't know if I want him,'

'You're growing past me, dearie. You're too old.'

'And I'm too young. It's so terrible to be both.'

'Quiet, darling.'

'Yes, yes, I will be quiet. Let's go to the pictures, shall we?'

'It's past six. We'll have to pay two and four.'

'Well, let's pay two and four, but for God's sake, let's get out of here.'

As the neighbourhood fell with the falling year, so it mounted with the springtime.

'We don't know ourselves,' said Parsons, eyeing, from his barrow, a new and ostentatious fruitshop that had opened on the corner of the street.

'No competition in the cats' meat trade,' Ma Ditch called, waving a bunch of lights at him. 'They don't put up super pussy butcher's, thank God.'

'We're going to 'ave a new town 'all,' said Mrs Parsons, 'all designed modern by a famous architect.'

'They'll make us the capital of England, soon,' Parsons observed. 'What about 'Aig Crescent, now they've broadened it? Looks like Regent Street. Wonder what Ma Godshill would think if she saw it? Never 'eard any more about them, did we?'

'Even the people seem different, some'ow.' Ma Ditch sniffed contemptuously. 'Young tart in a fur coat was down 'ere yesterday with 'er dog. "Oh, what lovely liver!" says she, all posh, "Little Bobbykins, thank the lady nicely!" Makes me sick.'

'We don't change, worse luck,' sighed Mrs Parsons, 'I still get me colds and they say Mr Wilkinson is still dog mad.'

'Old "Blow-'em-all-dead" 'as changed,' said Ma Ditch, 'all them new shops 'e's bought. Mean bastard. Smelling with money, 'e is, and wouldn't give you the price of a Guinness. "Them capitalists," 'e says; what is 'e but a bloody capitalist?'

'Maisie don't change, except she dresses nicer.' Mrs Parsons smiled.

'Oh, yes, she 'as. She's not nearly so bright as she used to be. 'E plays 'er up, Minnie, only she don't tell.' Parsons draped several bunches of black grapes over his lemons. 'Pretty, eh? Well, no more gossiping now. Business is business, and my customers aren't going over to that done up stink 'ole while I'm 'ere to stop them. Lemons, lovely – lovely! Three for two, keep away the flu!'

Elsie stopped at his stall. 'Good morning, Mr Parsons. I want a pound of really nice tomatoes. Why, here's Mrs Parsons, too! How's your hay fever?'

'Bad, ducks. It'll take me off one of these days.'

'Oh, surely it can never be as bad as that!'

'Getting married soon, ain't you, Elsie?' said Parsons, taking her tomatoes from the less impressive pile at the back of the stall.

'Next month. I'm getting quite thrilled. We're going to live in Lister Gardens, you know. Mr Dexter thinks it a pity to sell the house, and I agree with him.'

Sidey little runt, thought Parsons. He took her money and she passed on.

'They grow up, them bits, don't they? Make you and me feel 'ags, don't they, Mrs Ditch?'

'Oh, I don't know, Mrs P. I shan't feel old till I drop dead. Like me new blouse? Mr Ditch bought it for me. 'E knows an 'olesale 'ouse.'

'Minnie's careful never to wear 'er new things at work,' Parsons said, fiercely, 'Got an 'ole trunk of 'em at 'ome, she 'as, but I always say she must save 'em for best.'

Mrs Parsons, who loved her husband, did not contradict him.

So the month went by, with the great transition of the year as May passed into June. With the darkening of the sap in the leaves, so Elsie's heart darkened. Day by day, her fear mounted in her. Sometimes, seeking his aid, she would tell him of this. 'It's natural,' he said, speaking from his tower, 'It's natural for you to feel like that. Soon it will be different.'

Perfect love casteth out fear, she thought, as she walked through the little hills to sit alone by the pond. When we have loved each other for the first time, everything will change and I shall be able to feel myself alive again.

The surface of the pond bloomed with coming summer. Anyhow, I'm not going away from all this. It will be here, near me, all the time. I am going to Roland, whom I love, whom I must love, and not to a stranger. I am not going into a strange house. We will lie together as we lay under the trees last year, only we shall not lie as we lay then.

Oh God, I don't want to get married.

He will kiss me, and I shall want him. Then we shall have years and years together, without fear.

Oh God, I don't want to get married.

I shall be Mrs Roland Dexter. All the other girls will be terribly jealous. I shall have a home of my own, where I can ask people to tea and to dinner. We shall have quite a lot of money. I will say to Mother, 'You can't call me your little girl any more. We're both married women together.' I shall have a child in a year or two's time, and we will call him Anthony. People will come to see me when I'm in bed, giving him milk, and they will think I look like the Virgin Mary. I shall be so happy that every day will be too short, and the years will fly by until I have grown old. Anthony's children will come to me, and they will be surprised that I understand them so well.

Elsie. You love Roland? Of course you do. You want him, don't you? Yes. It has been terrible, all this waiting, having him touch you and never having him completely? Yes, it has been terrible. Oh God, I don't want to get married. She looked fearfully around her. There were people on the paths, on the jetty, people walking between the trees, and not one of them could help her.

None of them know my heart. Not Mother, not Roly. I am quite alone. It's terrible to live. To be given a body is too great a responsibility, as if someone came to you and said: 'Here is a great factory; run it until you die. Keep it clean inside and out. None of the engines must get rusty.'

She touched her face, her hand, her breast. I am quite alone, but though no-one can help me, it is beautiful to be alone. I am strong. Perfect love casteth out fear. Everything is ready for me, and I am ready. It is three days from tomorrow.

Oh God, I don't want to get married.

The Bitter Paradox

The morning, drawing within itself, moved in sun and shadow over the common and through the pond, till it came to settle in dust over the room where Elsie had lain wakeful all the night through.

To her heavy eyes, everything had already changed. The house, the room where she slept, these had commenced their recession into the past. Even as she gazed at the brightening walls they drew away from her, leaving her naked.

Mrs Cotton, gloom in her heart, dragged upstairs with the breakfast tray. Elsie, hearing the rattling of cups, pretended to be asleep.

Her mother drew the clothes away from her face and kissed her.

'Wake up, my dearie.'

Why not? Elsie thought, Why not? I have been asleep too long. She opened her eyes. 'Mother.'

'Did you sleep well? I hope so, because you've a great day ahead of you.'

'Fairly.'

'Overexcited, that's what you were. I know I've hardly had half an hour's rest all night.' She sat down by Elsie's side.

'My darling.'

'What's the time?'

'Well, I was going to let you sleep late, but I couldn't, somehow. It may have been selfish of me, but I wanted you

255

just a little while longer to myself. Anyway, there's a great deal to do. It's half-past eight.'

'Will you pour me out a cup of tea? I'm so thirsty.'

'Yes, of course, but you must eat something as well. It will be hours before you get anything else.'

My last meal as I am. How shall I be feeling in, let me see – half-past eight, nine, half-past two – seven hours?

'Are you happy?'

'Of course.'

'Not frightened are you, dearie? I don't approve of make-up at weddings, but I think you'll have to put just a little colour on today. You're very pale.'

'I was silly to go to bed so early last night. It didn't make me sleep.'

'Your last night here. How does it feel, to be getting married and leaving home?'

How does it feel. When I was confirmed she asked me the same question. How could I tell anybody?

'Oh, funny, naturally.'

'Never mind; in the course of a few days it will all be over. You'll be settled in, all important, and I shall be almost used to the loneliness.'

'But you won't be alone, really.'

'You won't be sleeping in the next room, though, and I shan't have you sitting with me at breakfast complaining because I make you eat your egg. I hope Roly takes good care of you. He'll hear about it from me if he doesn't.'

'You do like him?'

'What a question! I think you're a very lucky girl. There's one person only that's luckier, and that's him. Why, dearie, pull yourself together, or you'll make me very miserable! What a weepy thing you are, these days. You never cried when you were small, not even when your daddy spanked you, but now you're always at it. Sit up and eat a good meal, or Roly won't be proud of his bride.'

'I can't eat. I feel sick.'

'You must. Come on, just the bread and butter, then. Do you remember how I used to make you eat your cabbage? 'Here's pussy's bit. Surely you wouldn't steal from poor pussy? Here's mummy's bit. No little girl would take mummy's.' And down it went, just because you thought someone else wanted it.'

Elsie laughed.

'That's better. Aren't you longing to put all your new things on? I've washed those silly thin stockings you insisted on buying, because it makes them wear better, and I've laid all your clothes out on my bed. Your undies are fit for a princess.'

'I want to get up.'

'No, you stay where you are for a while. Look, I've got everything quite ready. Fancy if we'd had your little reception at Roly's, as Rose suggested! People would have hung about, and hung about, and you'd both have been tired, with the place reeking of smoke and all messy with the left-overs from the party. Far better for you to have it here, although it does mean a lot of work for me.'

'It isn't much of a party, is it? Just the nine of us. Roly wasn't going to have any of his relations at all but Rose, only she said he'd better ask his Uncle Robert, as he's the one with the money, and Roly may get it one day.'

'Well, you would keep it small. Sure you're not sorry you did?'

'No.'

Elsie lay back, staring up at the ceiling.

'It's a lovely day, dearie. Happy the bride the sun shines on.'

'Oh, I'll be happy.'

'Of course you will.'

'I feel as if I'd left already. The house is strange. You're strange.'

'Don't say that, darling, please!'

'I'm frightened.'

'What of?'

257

'You know.'

'There's no need to be. You know how kind Roly is.'

'Yes, he'll be kind, I'm sure of that. Mother, please let me get up. I want my bath now. I'm all hot and sticky.'

'You'll have to wait. It's very bad to have a bath immediately after eating, but you can come downstairs in your dressing-gown and help me put the finishing touches. The flowers have come. I said 'early,' and they were early all right. Eight o'clock, the boy called. I want you to think out how we can arrange them. The ones you're carrying are beautiful. Mrs Wills brought my clothes in after you'd gone to bed, and she's really made them quite professionally. Now, I think violet is a becoming colour for the bride's mother to wear at a wedding, don't you? Rose is getting herself up in an awful shade of green. I shan't let her go very near you in it, either, if I can help it, or she'll kill your pretty dress stone dead. And I hope she won't be around too much after you're married. She's a bit too chock-a-block with advice for my liking.'

Elsie went downstairs. 'You have been working hard!'

Mrs Cotton smiled. 'I'm glad you're pleased.'

The house was grim with preparation. The partition had been taken down between the drawing room and the sitting room; the table, with two extra leaves in it, was placed down the centre. The food was covered with napkins, as if the plates of sandwiches and the bowls of trifle were the faces of the dead. Everywhere there were vases, ready to be filled with flowers.

Elsie kissed her mother. 'It looks wonderful, but you've bought far too much for nine people, haven't you?'

'I can eat up what they don't, or perhaps you and Roly might be glad to take some of it tomorrow. You could send Annie round.'

'I wish I could see him now. I hate convention. If only he'd call round, I shouldn't feel so bad.'

'I never heard of such a thing! If he did call, I wouldn't let you appear. Will you do the flowers, or will it tire you?'

'I'll see to them. You turn my bath on. Mother, will you come and sit with me while I'm having it?'

'Why?'

'I don't want to be alone.'

For if I am by myself, I shall look at my body and know that it is mine no longer. I wonder if he will watch me undress, or whether he'll come upstairs later. Oh, God, I don't want to get married.

But she felt happier as she dressed herself in all her new clothes, for she knew that she looked beautiful.

'Don't put your hat on yet; it's hours before we need go, and it will give you a headache.'

'I must be quite ready. I'll feel better if I am. Do I look all right?'

Mrs Cotton, herself half dressed, her stays unlaced, took the girl to her breast and wept.

Elsie went into her own room, to sit in quietness for a few moments. She placed a chair before the mirror, that the sight of her unaccustomed self should reassure her.

What is it right to think about on a wedding morning? I might pray, but God is out of reach. I might think of my childhood, but that is so long ago. I might practise what I am going to say in church, but that would make me nervous.

So she sat between the two walls of her life, as if they pressed her so closely that she could scarcely breathe.

'Come and fasten me up,' Mrs Cotton called out. 'What are you doing in there?'

'Thinking.'

'Well, come in here. A little attention to the old lady, if you please. How do I look?'

'I shall be proud of you.'

'I suppose your uncle will be round early. I wish your father were alive. He would have enjoyed giving you away.'

259

'Which wouldn't have been very nice of him, would it?'

'If you make me laugh, I shall start grizzelling again. Aren't we a couple? Anyone would think you were going to be taken out and shot.'

'I almost wish I were.'

'None of that nonsense, now. You run downstairs and read a book till it's time to go.'

Uncle Ernest, jolly and nervous, arrived very early indeed.

'Well, well, well,' he said to Elsie, whom he had not seen for three years. 'Well, well, well.'

'Isn't she a big girl?' Mrs Cotton eyed her with watery pride. 'You don't think she's too young to marry, do you, Ernest?'

'Certainly I do!' He winked at Mrs Cotton to let her know that this was all in fun. 'She ought to be playing with dolls at her age.'

Elsie left the room.

'Don't joke with her. She's scared to death. Surely it's time we started out?'

'Half an hour to spare yet.'

They talked of little things, of the health of aunts and cousins, of the criminal price of flowers, of the traffic problem. At last it was time to go. The church was only one hundred yards down the road, so there was no need for a car.

'Buck up, dearie,' whispered Mrs Cotton, as they neared the porch, 'It will soon be over.' She peered in at the door. 'There's quite a lot of people there. I can see some of your old school-friends sitting up front. There's that Joan, in a new hat. I'll bet she's jealous. Well, I must go along in, and you can follow in a minute. Of course, it's not really done for me to arrive with you like this, but I don't care. Kiss me, my little girl.'

Blowing her nose, she left them. Elsie looked at Uncle Ernest and began to giggle.

'Here, here, here!' he said.

'I can't stop. Don't let's go in for a minute.' She shook with laughter.

'You're squeezing your flowers to death. Careful. Come along, now, or your mother will wonder what on earth's happened.'

'Am I on the right side of you?'

'Thank Heavens you thought of that. No, you're not. Change over.'

'Just like musical chairs,' she whispered.

They went in. Elsie could remember very little of the ceremony afterwards. She only knew that Roly looked everywhere but at herself, and that he had a small, suppurating boil on his neck. He must be upset about that. He's scared, too. But he wants me and I want him. Oh, God, don't let me cry.

And then it was all over. Elsie, trembling with the reaction of it, was in the vestry, being kissed by what seemed to her a thousand relations. It was such a muddle that she was certain she kissed some of them three times and others not at all. She hated kissing the best man, because he was short and ugly, and she did not know him very well.

'How does it feel to be Mrs Dexter?' said Aunt Rose, loudly. Elsie was grateful to her, because here was a thought to which she might cling.

'So unconventional,' said Roly's Uncle Robert to Mrs Cotton, 'all of us walking back to the house together. I think it is most charming. So simple.'

'I'm glad you think so. It was the children's idea.' Mrs Cotton's eyes strayed to Elsie and Roland, who were walking a little ahead, their faces averted from each other.

On reaching home, the guests tactfully left them alone together for a few minutes. 'Well?' said Roly.

'Didn't the church smell damp? I was cold, weren't you?'

'A bit. I was so scared, you know. Perhaps it was that.'

'I was too. Awfully.'

'Not sorry we're married?'

'Why should I be? I can't believe it, though.'

He kissed her. 'Isn't it wonderful? Very few people have our luck – getting married at our age, I mean.'

They looked at each other, and, finding no words to say, laughed a little. Then he held her to him. 'I love you. My wife.'

'I love you.'

'Go on.'

'My husband.' Now I feel silly, Elsie thought, just as silly as I did when I quoted the poem to Leda. Roly and I don't know each other at all. We're strangers.

Mrs Cotton knocked on the door. 'May we come in?' she called, her voice weirdly merry.

In they all came, and the kissing began once more. At last they sat down to the breakfast.

The best man, whose name was Tweedie, said to Elsie, 'I say, this is all grand, you know. So original. Roly says I haven't got to make a speech, or anything awful like that. I've scarcely had anything to do at all.' She smiled at him. Her lover touched her hand. 'You're very quiet. I feel like the man who had a dumb wife.'

'I wish we were out of this,' she mumbled.

'So do I, but we've got to make the best of it.'

'If Uncle Ernest says anything about troubles being little ones, I shall go mad.'

'He wouldn't dare.'

'Wouldn't he. You don't know Uncle Ernest.'

The breakfast lasted a long time, for everyone was aware of the dreadful hiatus that must follow it. Despite Roly's orders, several speeches were made, for there was, of course, no stopping Uncle Ernest, and no-one was very comfortable.

'Do try to smile,' Mrs Cotton said to Elsie, under cover of conversation. 'People will think it so odd.'

'Damn people.'

The wedding presents were inspected and admired, and this, happily, occupied another twenty minutes.

Now what shall we do? Elsie thought. Roly and I can't possibly move for another two hours, and if we do we shall feel awful all by ourselves in Lister Gardens for the rest of the afternoon and evening.

Oh, mother, mother, I want to die. I want to hide in the cupboard, as I used to do when there was a thunderstorm. No, I mustn't think of that. Perfect love casteth out fear.

'You looked lovely as you came up the aisle,' said Roly, knowing there was something he had forgotten.

Perfect love casteth out fear. There was cold between them, and fear.

'I think we might have a little music,' Mrs Cotton suggested, 'Shall I turn on the radio?'

'Let's make our own music!' said one of Elsie's aunts. 'We can have the wireless any day, and it's so seldom we're all together. You know, I haven't heard Ernest sing for years, and I seem to remember that he had a fine voice.'

Mrs Cotton looked at her hands. Uncle Ernest sang very dreadfully.

'Out of practice,' he murmured, 'and I'm not so young as I used to be. You pick on someone else. Anyway, I haven't got my music.' But his eye roved to the piano, on the top of which lay a volume of *Songs of All Nations*, and sing he did.

'Let's make a move now,' Roly whispered, as Uncle Ernest, with thick and embarrassing dialect, was singing an Irish ballad.

'We can't.'

'Yes, we can. I'll speak to your mother.'

He crept across the room to where Mrs Cotton sat, poor Mrs Cotton, who wished that she were dead.

> *'Oh, the days of the Kerry dancing,*
> *Oh, the ring of the piper's tune!'*

roared Uncle Ernest, with double volume. He was trying to express by the tone of his voice that he did not like people walking about while he was singing.

Mrs Cotton, understanding by the movements of Roly's lips what he wanted, did her best to make an annnoucement, but her brother sang two more songs in succession before she could get a word in. Then she gave it up, for she saw that Uncle Robert intended to recite.

When at last it was realised that Roland and Elsie were leaving, the interest in them revived. The guests followed them out into the street, calling their good wishes. Mr Tweedie had performed one good office. He had taken a bag of confetti away from Uncle Ernest.

When the lovers were out of sight and the temperature of the party fell to zero, Mrs Cotton was led upstairs by Aunt Rose, who gave her a stiff whisky. 'This is a festive occasion, not a funeral,' she said firmly, as if to drive her words into the unreceptive mind by hypnotic force. But Mrs Cotton mourned and would not be comforted.

Elsie and Roland were admitted to the house in Lister Gardens by Annie, whom they had retained as a resident maid. Carefully schooled by Aunt Rose, she gasped: 'Congratulations, Mr and Mrs Dexter,' running, on completion of this remark, into the kitchen and slamming the door.

The lovers went into the dining room. Dinner was laid for them, and the air was heavy with flowers.

'How nice of her,' Elsie said, 'But do you think you'll ever be able to eat again?'

'Not for hours, anyway.'

'I'd better go upstairs and take my things off.'

264

She went into the newly decorated bedroom. Sitting down at the dressing table, she laid her head on the glass top of it. Closing her eyes – I love him, of course I do. But it has all been so exciting that I can't think. Mrs Roland Dexter, very young to be married. She turned the ring on her finger If this were a magic ring, I could wish myself back home, but there's no more magic left in the world. You can see and touch everything, now.

When she rejoined him, he was reading the newspaper. He rose and kissed her.

'Isn't it wonderful, darling?' He fingered her breasts, but they did not move him.

Annie butted her head round the door. 'Will you 'ave your dinner now, Mum?' She looked at Elsie, and giggled. 'It's all cold stuff.'

'No, thank you. Later, please. We're not hungry.'

Again they were alone.

'It's strange, isn't it?'

'Of course. It will be different tomorrow. I mean – we shall get used to having the house to ourselves. Rose was sorry to leave, I think. She liked it here.'

'Poor Rose.' Elsie turned on the wireless.

'See if you can find some dance music.'

After listening for a while, they rolled back the carpet to dance, moving together through the singing space.

Roly thought of Mrs Maginnis. I am old to Elsie. There were two women before her, and to each of them I gave ten years of my youth. The first was fattish and her skin was old, but she had bright hair. How can I touch Elsie, who is so young?

He smiled at her with pity from his tower.

Elsie thought of the man she had met on holiday. There was one besides Roland. Two men have kissed me, but now I must stay with one for ever and ever.

Suddenly entering into service, she kissed his shoulder to tell him that she would be faithful.

The hours were slow before them. They ate a little food and drank a little wine. Annie cleared away and went to bed.

'It's only ten to nine,' Roly said. 'Are you very tired? It's been a long day.'

'Not a bit.'

'Nor am I.'

They sat looking at each other, one on either side of the fireplace. Elsie dared not sit by his side, lest he should touch her.

Oh, mother, mother!

She thought of the house in Stanley Street, where Mrs Cotton roved comfortless.

'Do you suppose they've all gone home, or is Uncle Ernest still singing?'

'I expect they'll keep it up late. He's got a terrible voice, hasn't he, darling? Come here.'

She came.

'We're awfully shy of each other, aren't we?' Roly said.

'Well, it's so new and strange. We'd be funny people if we weren't.'

'That's it, of course.' They both laughed with relief. They sat in silence for a while. Then they talked about the wedding, how Mrs Cotton had looked, how cold the church was, how drearily Uncle Robert recited. A cinder from the small fire which they had asked Annie to light for their comfort, although the night was warm, clicked into the grate. The flowers over the mantelshelf curled in the heat.

They danced for another half an hour, until neither of them could bear the sound of music any longer.

'It will be fun seeing Mother tomorrow,' Elsie said, 'and feeling both she and I are married women.'

He looked at her, saying nothing.

Later, he dared to draw her close to him. 'I love you.' He

smoothed the hair right away from her brow and ears, so that her face was strange to him. 'Skinned rabbit.'

She put up her hands, cupping them to hide his own hair. 'You don't look very handsome, either.'

'That's your bad taste.'

'Do you think I'm pretty? I don't believe you've ever told me so.'

'Of course I have, silly, but I'll tell you again.' He gazed at her critically. 'Good eyes, pretty good hair, nose a little too small, and no chin. I suppose we might say that you're average.'

'I think you're beastly. My chin's very nice. I hate huge lantern jaws.'

That was that. Now what can I say? she thought. Time is passing, and I'm afraid.

'Are you frightened?' he asked her, boldly.

She looked away. 'Awfully.'

'You needn't be. You know that, don't you?'

'Yes.'

A wave of joy took him. Standing up, he lifted her in his arms and ran round the room with her. 'Over the sticks!' he cried, jumping laboriously across the sofa, for her height made her no lightweight. 'Gee up, Neddy! Darling, isn't it wonderful? We're married! I'm almost beginning to realise it. You and I, for ever and ever!'

'Roly, put me down. I'm giddy.' He laid her on the rug, setting his foot lightly on her throat. 'Now you can't get up. St. George and the Dragon. Love me?'

'Yes.'

'Be more enthusiastic about it, then, or you shall stay there all night.'

'I do. Please, darling.'

He allowed her to rise. They sat soberly side by side on the couch. He picked up the paper. 'There's another Welsh

267

colliery disaster. Isn't it terrible? Makes one feel one has no right to be even a little happy.'

She looked over his arm at the picture page. 'Poor people,' she said, 'standing about in the rain, waiting for news. It seems worse in the rain, somehow.'

'I don't know. It would be worse to stand about for hours on a blazing summer day, with everything looking bright and alive, waiting to hear that your husband or brother was one of the casualties. It makes me feel sick to think about it.'

Her eyes were wet with admiration for his pity.

'I couldn't bear to lose you.'

'You won't. I shall hang on and on till you're aching to get rid of me, and then I'll hang on some more.'

'Give me a cigarette.'

'It's late. Do you know the time? Ten to eleven.'

How quickly time flies, she thought, when it is flying slowly.

'I don't care. I'm not tired.'

'Nor am I.' So they talked of small things.

It was twenty-past one before he said, very gently and nervously, 'I think we'd better be getting some rest, darling.'

'All right.'

'Would you like to go along up? I'll follow.'

She was so tired that she could not plead with him. Silently she arose and went upstairs.

Annie had laid her new nightgown on the bed, the special satin one that Mrs Cotton had made. Elsie started to undress. Her fingers were so cold that she could hardly unhook her suspender belt. Going into the bathroom, which was next door, she had a sketchy wash, splashing the water over her shoulders that she might be freshened. Returning to the bedroom, she turned off all the lights save a reading lamp, for she did not wish him to see her face too clearly.

She was shivering violently, and her stomach was sick. The room was monstrous with hooded shadows, towering like giants about her head. Turning her eyes to one side, she could just see the shape of her own face on the wall. The clock on the table ticked so loudly that she got out of bed to stop it.

Oh, Mother, Mother, I'm afraid. If only I could have loved him when I wanted to. Leda, you are so beautiful. I love you, Leda, and there's nothing horrible about that, nothing to hide. If only I were my own again! I should never get married. I'd have a career, and become very clever. One, two, buckle my shoe. Three four, open the door. When he comes, I will say to him: 'Darling, I'm so terribly tired. I want to sleep' She laid her head on the pillow, but there was no quiet there. She sat up. Now he's folding the paper. He's putting out his cigarette. Soon he will come upstairs.

I remember that day last spring, when the leaves were silver, and we were so happy until he frightened me, until he told me about the girl. I said: 'You dirty animal.' Please, God, don't let me think of that. Let me love him and let him love me for ever and ever, Amen. Leda first taught me how to love. I wish she never had. Now I'm in prison and I can't get out. I've just got to wait and wait and wait. Oh, Mother, I'm afraid! If only you were so afraid for me, feeling my fear coming to you over the streets and through the walls, that you hurried round to save me! If only you did.

Now he's put out the hall light. That's true. I could hear that. He's coming up the stairs.

Her hands were soaking wet. The nightgown clung beneath her armpits.

He came in, his head turned away from her. 'Comfortable, darling? You're not too hot in here? Let me open a window.'

'No, I'm all right.'

He leaned across her to get his pyjamas. 'I'm just going into the bathroom. I won't be long.' He kissed her cheek. 'You look so sweet, Elsie.'

She thought: Everything is wrong. I thought that this was the end of my life, the last settling down, but it's the beginning.

I have nearly eighteen years to unlearn. Nearly. It's as though I were just born. It is the end and the beginning, the end of my love and the beginning of my love. That's bitter, and I'm afraid. There's no happiness in this, no joy. Why do people want it? I wish I had my life to live again. I should know, then, that when I gain what I want I lose it all, and to lose is bitter.

All this she thought, unknowing of her thoughts. She only knew that she could hear him moving about, hear the running of the water taps. That was the fall of his shoes.

Roly, as he slapped a cold flannel over his body, did not think at all, for he knew that a single thought would liberate his fear.

Mrs Cotton, in the house in Stanley Street, wandered from room to room, up and down the stairways and along the passages. The door of the room that had been Elsie's was ajar. Mrs Cotton tried to fancy that if she listened very hard she would hear the girl's breathing. But why should I listen hard? For I know she is there.

Still she walked up and down, her dressing gown flying open, her hair, plaited for the night, swinging across her shoulders. Up and down the city wall, in and out the Eagle.

She's asleep now, said Mrs Cotton to herself, and it's all over. Tomorrow, life will go on again, just where it stopped. She tried to imagine that, if she spoke aloud, Elsie's voice would cry: 'Is that you, Mother? Why are you walking about, up and down, up and down, all night?'

The back door, which she had left unlatched, creaked to and fro. Perhaps burglars are trying to break in. I wish they would. It would be someone for me to talk to. I'll call on Elsie tomorrow, whether he likes it or not. She'll be glad to see me, unless it's all him now.

You're a wicked woman. She's too young, years and years too young.

Never mind. It's all over now. They are lying together like little children in each other's arms, her head on his breast, his

270

face in her pretty hair. When they wake in the morning, they will say: 'How beautiful it is to be in love!'

Oh, if Elsie would only cry out: 'Is that you, Mother? Why are you walking about, up and down, up and down, all night?'

Mrs Maginnis's lost lover, lying in a commercial hotel some fifty miles away, had that day heard strange news through an unexpected quarter.

So Patty's dead, he thought. Poor old Patty, with her head stuck in a gas oven, all her bouncing ended. Fancy her doing that. The only time she ever went to bed without a man. This made him laugh. I hope she didn't do it because of me. But then, she knew our bit of fun couldn't last. Wonder if she left anything, if she had anything to leave. Fourpences, she used to give me, for cigarettes. Never close, she was, never mean. What she had she gave, and when the end came she let me go without a fuss. Poor old Patty's dead, he thought, poor Patty with her head in the gas oven. The only time she ever went to bed without a man.

Mrs Godshill, kneeling on the floor of her bedroom in a North London lodging house, wrestled with the Lord. She was convinced that if she wrestled with Him long enough, she would throw Him. Over the candle lighted walls moved the shapes of sin, crawling like bugs up and down the paper. She squeezed her dead breast as if she were forcing the soul back within it. In the next room Arthur lay awake. Through the matchboard partition she could hear his coughing.

She knew that soon there must be victory. Either she must conquer the Lord, or He must conquer her. There was no room in the world for both of them. The sins, clinging to the pendulum of the clock, slid up and down the hours.

All my life I have fought, and mine enemies have overtaken me.

It would be two hours until the dawn, and Mrs Godshill must fight on. When the battle was won, she would stoop to the Defeated, lifting Him again to her bosom. Then they would go out on the roads once more, He, and she and Arthur, setting up the rostrum in windy places, on the broad commons and on the corners of the city streets, where Sin, trousered like man, walked on two legs. She would forgive God for all He had done to her; only now and then, when there were mockers at her feet, would she turn, to sling her *Eli* in His face.

Drawing a shawl over her dead breast, her eyes tight shut against the sins that crawled up the wall and down the pendulum of the clock, Mrs Godshill wrestled with the Lord.

So now he was coming. Elsie shut the door of her mind. There was nothing more to remember, save the memory of what was to be. The room was as tall as heaven, the bed a white plain with no shelter anywhere at all. Sitting up very stiffly, her back parallel with the head of the bed, she waited. She was all alone, her heart tightly locked within her. She could no longer cry for help, nor did she desire it. There was no fear in her, nor love, only a great loneliness. She moved her legs beneath the clothes to sense the power that stirred her. She had sufficient strength to conquer the whole world; she was a woman colossus, with her head in the moon, ruling alone over the earth that she was too tall to see. The lamplight was small in the dark.

And now his hand was at the door. There was nothing more in all the world but this, no more weeping to be done, no more thinking. Alone she waited, her back parallel with the head of the bed.

For companionship, she put out a hand to touch her own shadow on the wall.

I made up my mind that I would not see Iris Allbright again,
not after so many years. I do not like looking back down the
chasm of the past and seeing, in a moment of vertigo, some
terror that looks like a joy, some joy crouched like a terror.
It is better to keep one's eyes on the rock-face of the present,
for that is real; what is under your nose is actual, but the
past is full of lies, and the only accurate memories are those
we refuse to admit to our consciousness. I did not want to
see Iris; we had grown out of each other twenty years ago
and could have nothing more to say. It might be interesting
to see if she had kept her looks, if she had worn as well as I
had; but not so interesting that I was prepared to endure an
afternoon of reminiscence for the possible satisfaction of a
vanity.

Also, she had had only one brief moment of real impor-
tance in my life, which was now shrivelled by memory almost
to silliness. I doubted whether she herself would remember it
at all. I would not see her; I had made up my mind.

But it was not so easy. Iris was determined that I should
visit her, now she had returned to Clapham, and to this end
kept up a campaign of letters and telephone calls. Didn't I
want to talk over old times? If not, why not? She was longing
to tell me all about her life in South America, all about her
marriage, her children, her widowhood – didn't I *want* to
hear? She was longing to hear all about me. ('How you've got
on! Little Christie!') I couldn't be so busy as to be unable to
spare just half an hour. Why not this Wednesday? Or

Wednesday week? Or any day the following week? She was always at home.

I began to feel like the unfortunate solicitor badgered with tea invitations by Armstrong, the poisoner of Hay. Knowing that if he accepted he would be murdered with a meat-paste sandwich, in constant touch with the police who had warned him what his fate was likely to be, he was nevertheless tortured by his social sense into feeling that if Armstrong were not soon arrested he would have to go to tea, to accept the sand-wich, and to die. It was a hideous position for a man naturally polite and of good feeling.

My own position was in a sense more difficult, for no one was likely to arrest Iris Allbright, and I felt the time approach-ing when I must either bitterly offend her or go to Clapham.

In the end I went to Clapham.

In a London precariously balanced between two wars, how is a young woman supposed to make her way in the world? This is the question which Christine faces. Dissatisfied with her life spent working in a bank and living in the shadow of her more beautiful and beguil-ing best friend, Iris, Christine is quick to fall under the smooth, heady charm of Ned, an older man who seems to hold the key to the future she wants.

But appearances are fickle, and soon, Christine finds herself isolated inside an increasingly sinister marriage. As time begins to tick, Christine must find her way out, at the risk of becoming trapped forever. . .

An Impossible Marriage | 9781473679801 | £8.99 | Hodder

Pamela Hansford Johnson

Pamela Hansford Johnson was born in Clapham in 1912 to an actress and a colonial civil servant, who died when she was 11, leaving the family in debt. Pamela excelled in school, particularly in English and Drama, and became Dylan Thomas' first love after writing to him when they had poems in the same magazine. She went on to write her daring first novel, *This Bed Thy Centre*, aged 23, marking the beginning of a prolific literary career which would span her lifetime.

In 1936 she married journalist Neil Stewart, who left her for another woman; in 1950, she married novelist C.P. Snow, and for thirty years they formed an ambitious and infamous couple.

Johnson remained a productive and acclaimed writer her whole life, and was the recipient of several honorary degrees as well as a CBE in 1975. She was also made a Fellow of the Royal Society of Literature. By her death in 1981, she was one of Britain's best-known and best-selling authors, having written twenty-seven novels, alongside several plays, critical studies of writers such as Thomas Wolfe and Marcel Proust, poetry, translation and a memoir.

Praise for Pamela Hansford Johnson

'Very funny' *Independent*

'Witty, satirical and deftly malicious' Anthony Burgess

'Sharply observed, artfully constructed and always enlivened by the freshness of an imagery that derives from [Johnson's] poetic beginnings' *TLS*

'Miss Johnson is one of the most accomplished of the English women writers' *Kirkus*